SEX, MURD

Lock Down Presents

SEX, MURDER AND GOD
STREET GOSPEL

Written By
LO-LIFE

SEX, MURDER AND GOD | LO-LIFE

Copyright © 2024 LO-LIFE
Sex, Murder and God

All rights reserved. No part of this book may be reproduced in any form or by electronic or mechanical means, including information storage and retrieval systems without permission in writing from the publisher, except by a reviewer who may quote brief passages in review.

First Edition 2024

Printed in the United States of America

This is a work of fiction. Names, characters, places, and incidents either are products of the author's imagination or are used fictitiously. Any similarity to actual events or locales or persons, living or dead, is entirely coincidental.

Lock Down Publications
P.O. Box 944
Stockbridge, GA 30281
www.lockdownpublications.com

Like our page on Facebook: Lock Down Publications
www.facebook.com/lockdownpublications.ldp

Stay Connected with Us!

Text **LOCKDOWN** to 22828 to stay up-to-date with new releases, sneak peaks, contests and more…

Like our page on Facebook:
Lock Down Publications

Join Lock Down Publications/The New Era Reading Group

Visit our website:
www.lockdownpublications.com

Follow us on Instagram:
Lock Down Publications

Email Us: We want to hear from you!

Dedication

First, I would like to thank the most High. Without the gift you've bestowed upon me, none of this would have been possible. To the twins, Lucy and Luciana (Tita), I've always considered myself fortunate for having two mothers growing up. Each of you contributed to the man you see today. To my sister, Tina Rene, aka Boss Lady, thank you for taking the time to sit in front of the computer night after night. Your opinion and insight means the world to me. Thank you to my lil brother, Junior, for all those late night trips to the store and hitting that highway for your big bro, even though that isn't your lane. Thank you so much. To my kids, JaKoreyon, Lo'Honeyana, and DJ, I know I haven't been the best dad in the world, but I'm trying. Thank y'all for giving me a reason to. To my missing son, Marcus, when your momma feels it's time, she'll introduce us. Just know, I wanted to be there. To my cousin, Niya, you give me a reason to watch women's basketball again. I'm waiting to see you play under the big lights. To my niece and nephew, Allanah and Aiden (Nah Nah and Geeta), Thank y'all for giving my lil sis someone to love. She's not as angry all the time. Lord knows we needed that. Lol. To my old man, Milo, we spent twenty years not speaking to each other. That was one of the greatest mistakes I've ever made. To the greatest family and support system a person can ask for, thank you.

Thanks goes out to all my niggas fighting for their lives. I've met some of the realest, most genuine people, while going through this journey. I hope I complimented your lives, as you've done mine. Joshua Lamb aka Damn Fool aka Da Champ, say bro, if we knew then, what we know now, huh. It's all good, though. We gone rise up out the ashes, better than before. To my nigga A-1 (Antoine), I couldn't believe when they got you. You were the last one to stand strong. Hold your head, my nigga. It'll be over soon. To "The Guys" Khamp (Marlo), Lucky 400, Cleveland, Boobie, East up! (Always made sure a nigga kept his weight up.) To my niggas Money Black (Ricky), KG (Kyle Green), Paccy (OG Wacco), East up! J Bang, East up! Paco, we made a way for niggas to eat, even if they forgot. Smoke and Slug, your grandpa would be proud of the young men you've become. My lil bro, Allen G, keep doing what you doing, you're almost home. If I forgot you this go round, I got you on book 2.

To the down ass woman in my corner, Aia Miller, from day one you've been in a nigga corner. You inspired me to do greater things by your actions. You know I had to buy "The Diary of a Side Chick!" Brittany Riley, I watched you grow and transform. You don't know how much your visits, phone calls, and trips you take help me. Thirty-two countries and counting. World Wide Boss shit. Ebone Gordon, you hell! I know the love is still there. I'm just waiting to see you exhibit it. Keep your head up. To Lakiesha Freeman, no one can say you ain't do your part. I appreciate the support and love. Tell Rodger I said wassup and East Up! Jeanette Collins, your son will be a playa, his momma's one of the best to do it. Cierra Brinker, Stomp down Hustla Sarah Mann, thank you for being a lifelong friend. To Krystina Simmons, the original MHB, we could have been great together. I guess love conquers everything but jail time. Still, much love. You sacrificed a lot for a P. To my loving and beautiful wife, Tracie Lajoy Lamb, it's been a long, long journey. When everyone else turned their back, you stepped up. That's why you'll forever be #1. Thank you my love. Two Souls One Heart. No Lies, just Loyalty!

To all those fuck niggas and bitches. I used to care what y'all thought about a nigga. Now I know what y'all think doesn't mean shit. I would say names, but y'all aren't worth that. Still, God Bless you fuck niggas.

If I forgot you, I promise I'll get you on the next joint. This is the first of many to come. Stay tuned. To my Eastside niggas, East Up till my feet up. Bombs over Baghdad!

Chapter 1
Sunday

Lucus Jr.
"Today is about accountability, taking responsibility for your actions..." Yeah right. I couldn't help but giggle on the inside as I listened to my father, Reverend Lucas Johnson Sr., deliver one of his illustrious sermons. Taking accountability for your actions, huh? Someone should have told him to follow his own script.

My dad has been the pastor at Last Hope Missionary Baptist Church for the last six years. I remember when he first became pastor. I was sixteen years old at the time, and had just made the Varsity basketball team. I remember coming home from practice and catching my parents celebrating like we had won the lottery or something. When they had finally told me what they were celebrating, I looked at them like they had lost their minds. Little did I know, even though we didn't win the lotto, we were about to come into a surplus of cash.

We went from a two bedroom duplex, into a two story, five bedroom home in a gated community. We upgraded the old Explorer for a Cadillac Escalade and my mom got her a new Nissan Altima. I never understood where the extra money was coming from, until I overheard my dad and his best friend, Deacon Copper, talking about it one day.

"Say, Lucas, you have to start easing up on the coffers man. Deacon Carter is starting to ask questions about where all the money is going."

"Man, fuck that nigga. I don't give a fuck what his bitch ass is talking bout. At the end of the day, his ass can't prove a thing. He needs to worry bout his ex wife and whose cock she has stuffed down her throat."

I knew then that my pops was up to no good. At the same time, I was getting a thousand dollars a month just to keep my grades up and play ball. *Fuck it!*

"What's on your mind, baby?" My girlfriend Amber whispered in my ear. I almost forgot that she was sitting next to me. Amber had been my girlfriend since my sophomore year in high school. Her family had a little money, so she grew up in the suburbs, but you could tell she had an infatuation with the streets.

She was what you called slim thick. 5'4", 128 lbs, with a fat ass. Her skin was as smooth as Hershey chocolate and her pussy was just as sweet. Amber had the type of pussy that would cream all over your dick, right before she milked you for all you're worth.

The first time we fucked, I didn't know what I had gotten myself into. Two minutes after I slid between her velvet folds, my dick was spitting up baby batter. You know a nigga couldn't go out like that. After I got my second wind, I got back on the horse, so to speak, and by the end of the night she had came six times and that pussy was officially mine.

Just thinking about it got my dick straining to buss out of my Versace slacks. I lean over and whisper in her ear. "I was thinking about your lips wrapped around my dick, while I slow feed you this cock, until my nut splashes the back of your throat."

Amber gave my hand a lil squeeze. "Don't worry, baby, I'ma eat that dick all the way home. And I'm a swallow every drop, until your balls are empty and my belly is full."

Damn, I love when she turns her freak up. I remember I damn near had to beg her to suck a nigga's dick. Then, when she finally did, I had to grab her head and hold her down in order for her to swallow the nut. Boy, once she tasted that sweet dick milk for the first time, she couldn't get enough of it. Next thing I knew, she was trying to eat a nigga's dick every chance she got. I remember one time, I had snuck over to her house while her mom was in one of her drunken stupors and her dad was out doing him.

"Damn, babe, you sure your moms not going to wake up and catch us?" I asked as she sucked gently on the head of my dick. I felt the tip of her tongue slide in my piss hole and my balls started to ache. With a mouth full of cock, she was mumbling but it sounded as if she said, "Naw, we good, she'll be out cold til morning."

That was all the reassurance I needed. I laid back and watched Amber go to work. First, she made sure my dick was saturated with spit. Sloppy, just the way I like it. Her mouth felt like an oven mitt as she slurped and sucked my cock. Both her hands gripped, twisted and rotated around my shaft. I couldn't help but to moan. "Shhhiitttt. Damn, girl. Eat that dick up." That seemed to activate a switch. She pushed her head into my lap until damn near all eight and a half inches were lodged into her throat.

She grabbed a hold of my nuts and massaged them while humming around my cock. That did it. Before I could utter another word, my nuts snapped, crackled and popped. What seemed like quarts of cum, shot from my dick and sprayed the back of her throat.

"Ohh shit. Awww fuck," I howled as my legs shot straight out and my toes curled.

Once my vision returned, I looked down at Amber. She still had my dick twitching between her lips, while she lightly massaged my balls, getting the last couple drops. I have to admit, I love a greedy bitch. Her lips were greasy from the spit and cum, but I didn't hesitate to give her a kiss and tell her that was the best head ever...

Now I'm stuck in church, listening to my dad talk about a bunch of shit that he doesn't even follow himself. With a hard dick and aching nuts, I was ready to go but I know if I leave now, I wouldn't hear the end of it.

I wonder how many of these poor suckers are actually paying attention. I scan the congregation. I spot some of my mom's friends. Some of them were fine as hell and I can't help but to wonder if they sucked dick as good as Amber. Probably not.

Then I saw him. DC aka Derrick Cooper. DC had just been released from prison about a month ago. He had done five years for pistol whipping a dude behind some money that was owed to him. I remember when I was just a kid, DC used to come over our house with his dad all the time. His dad and my dad were best friends, but DC was six years older than me, so he and I never really built any type of bond.

When he approached me with an offer to make money, I agreed simply to impress him. My dad gave me an allowance, so I really didn't need the money, but I felt like I needed DC's acceptance. I took the pack with the intention of flipping it once, bringing him his money, and then telling him I was good after that.

As soon as I grabbed the work from him, I drove to the school gym for practice. When I came back out, my car had been broken into and the pack was gone. I tried to call DC and let him know what had happened, but the nigga wasn't trying to hear that shit.

"Say, nigga, I ain't trying to hear any excuses. You need to get my bread together and that's *that*."

"But I don't have the... Hello? Hello?" The nigga hung up in my face.

I already knew that crazy ass nigga didn't play about his bread, but where the hell was I going to get five thousand dollars from. It wasn't like I'd been saving up. Shit, I had one of the sickest wardrobes at school. Your boy was putting that shit on. Plus, I was pushing a SRT Charger on 22's. All I had to my name was a hundred fifty dollars and I wouldn't get my allowance until the following week.

DC must have felt me looking his way because he turned his head on a swivel and smirked. My palms started sweating. I didn't know how the fuck I was supposed to pay the nigga back. What I did know was, if I didn't, then shit would get ugly real fast.

***

First Lady Charllessa Johnson
Look at this motherfucka up there ranting about taking responsibility for your actions. Negro please! I'd been married to this sorry son of bitch for fifteen years and I couldn't tell you one time he had taken responsibility for his actions. Don't get me wrong, when we first started seeing each other, Lucas was all that and some. He was a stand out football player and I was the head cheerleader, so of course it was only logical that we started dating. The sex was fantastic. Lucas definitely knew his way around a snatch. With a nice 8 inch cock that was as thick as my wrist, that man had my coochie, mouth, and yes, booty hole, screaming his name. There was nothing I wouldn't do to please him.

Imagine how I felt, when I found out he was dipping his pole in other women's ponds. The first time it happened, I had come home early one day and caught our then neighbor, Jackie, chewing on his nuts like a piece of bubblegum. I sat back and watched for a few minutes as he slid his dick between her lips and stretched her jaw to capacity. To be honest, I was curious. I wanted to know if this bitch could suck this negroe's dick better than me. Maybe then I could understand why he felt the need to cheat.

So I stood there and watched him tap the back of her throat with like 4 inches of dick still showing. *This chick has to be a rookie,* I thought as she struggled to maintain. He began to wind his hips, fucking her mouth like a tight coochie. I stood there and watched this bitch damn near throw up on herself as Lucas grabbed her head with both hands, (the way I like it) and pushed all eight glorious inches down her gullet. I could damn near see the imprint of his dick head in her throat like a snake when it's digesting its prey.

I should have put a stop to it but something told me to keep quiet. I backed out of the house, hopped in my car and drove to my sister's house. Of course, I didn't tell her messy ass what was going on because I didn't need her in my mix. I just sat there in her living room, drinking Long Island Iced Teas until it was 6pm. I drove home like I had just gotten off of work.

When I pulled up, the bitch Jackie was outside sitting on her porch with a huge smile on her face. "Heyyy Charley," she called out. I debated on cussing her trifling ass out, but I elected to keep it civil.

"Hey girl," I mustered.

"You just getting off work?"

Bitch you know what time I get off work. "Yeah girl, I'm just getting home." I looked at her chin and noticed specs of dried nut. This bitch ain't even have the decency to properly clean herself up. "Well..Let me get in this house so I can cook Lucas his dinner before I have to hear his mouth." I excused myself, hoping she didn't say anything else.

"Yeah, girl, I hear you. I just had a very big meal myself," the bitch had the nerve to say. I stopped dead in my tracks. It took every ounce of civility in me not to give her a piece of my mind.

Instead, I calmly replied, "Yeah. I noticed the food stains on your chin." With that, I entered my apartment.

I found Lucas on the couch, drinking a glass of Hennessy in nothing but his boxers. He looked up at me and smiled. "Hey, baby. How was work?"

"Oh, work was... Well, work." I looked at the kitchen. "Have you ate yet?" Just as I said it, thoughts of him feasting on Jackie's snatch invaded my mind.

"Naw, babe, I haven't. What you plan on cooking?"

"What you feel like eating?"

He tilted his head while he thought about it. "How bout some steak?" I knew he loved eating steak after a good round of sex. My stomach clenched just thinking bout it.

"Steak it is," I said as a thought crept into my head. I went into the bedroom and stripped naked. I rubbed my fingers across my sex lips and took a whiff of myself. I wasn't as fresh as I could be, but shit, a girl was just on her feet for 9 hours, so her cat should have a little taint to it.

I walked back into the living room. Lucas was busy watching the game. I stood in front of him and placed one foot on the coffee table. My coochie was literally inches away from his face. "First, you need to snack on this appetizer." I spread my lips apart, so he could see the wetness around my clit. With two fingers, I slid into my cunt, making sure he heard how disgustingly wet I was. Without hesitation, he grabbed my ass and pulled my crotch into his face.

My legs buckled as his tongue tapped against my special button. My juices cascaded down my inner thigh. "Shit. Eat that coochie, baby. Eat momma's musty ass coochie." It seemed as if that turned him on even more. Lucas attacked my twat like the rabid dog he was. He trapped my clit between his lips, and with his tongue, he swiped back and forth, like a black MasterCard.

I grabbed his head, forcing him to suck and slurp up every drop of honey dew. "Slurp. Slurp. Slurp," was all I heard as he drank his fill. I felt him slide two fingers inside and massage my g spot. I shattered on impact.

"Oh my Jesus. I'm bout to cum. I'm bout to cum. I'm cummmiiinng, Lucas," I screamed as I squirted my cum all over his lips, until it dripped down the sides of his chin. He licked my crevices until my orgasm subsided.

I was so light headed, I had to lay down. "Damn. That was some of the best head I've ever had," I panted as my coochie throbbed. Lucas got up and tried to kiss me. I dodged his kiss, mumbling something about having to get dinner ready.

"Damn, it's like that, baby? You don't want to taste your own nut all of a sudden?"

I looked over my shoulder as I was walking off. "Not until I take a shower first," I remarked, leaving him sitting on the couch with a stiff dick and a look of bewilderment.

I learned something about myself that day. I could overlook Lucas's indiscretions, but I'd be damned if I sat around the house and waited on him to give me a piece of what was rightfully mine.

Not long after I caught Lucas with the neighbor, I had my legs behind my head as my young coworker, Charles, designated my coochie for remodeling.

I knew he had been eyeing me. At first, I thought it was just a simple crush between a younger man and an older woman. Every now and then, I would catch him staring at my DD's or my 38 inch hips and ass. I could tell that he had a nice sized dick by the lump that was always in front of his khakis. Due to the fact I was always faithful, I never pursued or acted on it.

Two days after I caught Lucas in the act, I went to work with it on my mind. My coochie was throbbing as I thought about what this twenty-one year old stud could do to it.

"Heyy, Charles," I purred as I crept up behind him.

"Oh hey, Mrs. Johnson. How are you doing today?"

"First off, let's drop the Mrs. Johnson. Just call me Charllessa, or just plain ole Charley. Unless, you'd prefer to call me momma."

He looked up at me confused. I licked my lips and reached for his dick. I felt that bad boy grow from my touch, and my cat began to leak down my thighs. With no panties on, I knew I needed to get my pants off quickly, before I soaked and ruined the crotch area. While squeezing and holding on to his dick, I went in for the kill.

"How about we take our lunch break together and you could feed me this big ole sausage of yours," I asked, while staring a hole into his soul. I felt his cock twitch and I knew I had my answer.

A couple hours later, we were at the nearest motel. I tried my best to turn that young man out. First, I gave him some of this seasoned A-1 head, making sure to devote enough attention to each of his balls, while I slowly jacked him off. I even pushed his legs all the way back and grazed my tongue against his puckered asshole, to let him know that he could get it however he wanted, and I was a stone cold freak, nasty as they come.

After I swallowed the first load, I assumed the position, face down, ass up. When I felt that boy's dick head penetrate my opening, I damn near fainted. He slowly fed me inch by inch, until I felt his balls slapping against my clit. "Ohhh shit, Charles. I neeeeddd you to fuck momma good. You hear me? Beat that coochie up."

He slid out and left just the tip in. He rotated his hips and without warning, he slammed it home. "Smack."

"Ohh fuck," I screamed, as Charles beat my cat into submission.

We only had an hour for break, but I swear that boy beat my box up for forty minutes straight. I came all over his cock three times, and it would have been a fourth, if we would have had more time.

Ever since that day, I'd been hooked on young meat, but not too young, mind you. If they are old enough to drink, then they are old enough to get a double shot of this twat.

As for my husband, hey, I know he's around here fucking anything with a skirt. To be honest, I couldn't care less. Nowadays, when I'm feeling extra nasty, I'll let him eat my coochie with another man's cum marinating in it. Take responsibility for your own actions, huh? Yeah, what a joke.

***

Derrick Cooper aka DC

What time is it? Man, I'm ready to get the fuck up out of here. If it wasn't for all the money to be made up in this bitch, I never would come to church. Well, that, and plus all the wet ass pussy these church freaks be throwing at a nigga. *Oohh Weee!*

Look at this shit. All these motherfuckas up in here screaming bout how they sanctified and holy. Half them gone be hitting my cell up right after church, looking for some coke, crack, or just some good ole weed. *Fuck it.* They like it, I love it.

Aww shit, check lil Jr. out. That nigga looks scared as shit. Hmm. Then again, he should be. That weeny motherfucka better have my five bands, I know that. I don't care what his excuse is. Fuck around and break both his legs. His ass won't be able to jump two inches, much less two feet. I hope he don't think, just cause his pops and my pops are cool, that I'ma let him make it. *Yeah right.* Ain't no stupid shit going on.

I'm not gone lie, though. That lil bitch he got on his arm is definitely my speed. It was a chick working on the unit I was on that looks just like her. She used to stand in front of my cell and let me jack that dick.

"Let me see that big motherfucka spit," she would whisper, right before my dick would throw up all over the bars.

Yeah, Amber reminded me so much of her. Just thinking about it, got a nigga dick twitching. I know that soft ass nigga ain't beating that pussy up right. She need a certified gangsta to get up in them guts.

Damn. I feel someone watching me. I knew it! Soon as I turn my head back to the front, I see my stepmom, Yolanda, staring me down. To keep it all the way G, lil momma fine as fuck; pretty face, slim waist, thick thighs, and big ole ghetto booty. She had married my old man when I was in the joint. When he shot me pictures of the bitch, I couldn't believe it. She looked like one of those Instagram models. I used to pass her pics around, so nigga's could get their rocks off for a couple soups. Now that I'm home, though, I can't lie, baby look ten times better in person. I can tell she wants this dick, too.

The other day, I was taking my first morning piss, when all of a sudden, the bathroom door swung open.

"Oh. I'm sorry. I didn't know anyone was in here," she stammered.

I just looked back at her, shook the extra drops of piss off my dick and said, "don't worry 'bout it. All this shit yours." The comment was laced with double meaning. Just in case she felt offended, it sounded like I said everything in this house is yours, but what I meant was, everything bout this dick is yours.

When you're in the pen, you have to learn to be careful with your words. Saying the wrong thing, to the wrong guard, at the wrong time, can get you a major case, and even though a nigga ain't sweating no case, that shit is still a hassle. But yeah, last night? Now that was a trip.

I had my homie named Blade drop me off at my pops crib because that's where I had paroled to. I noticed my old mans' SUV was gone, so I figured him and the missus went out for the night. As I came in, I went straight to the kitchen to fix me something to eat. After about five minutes, Yolanda comes out in a see-through joint, smelling like cocoa butter lotion. Man, it took every ounce of me, not to pull my dick out and beat my shit right in front of her. Shorty pussy lips were poking through the lace panties, and that ass was looking fat as hell from the front.

"Oops, I'm sorry, honey. I didn't think anyone was here," she claimed as she slid in front of me to get to the fridge. My dick was so hard it was hurting, tryna buss out my 501's. I took a second to readjust myself. The smirk on Yolanda's face let me know she was pleased with the effect she was having on me. She opened the fridge, bent down to get some grapes at the bottom, and all I seen was pussy lips poking out the edges of her panty lines.

I turned my head, before she could catch me looking, and said, "Yeah, I just pulled up, but I'm bout to be in my room," as I made a beeline to the bedroom I was sleeping in.

Damn. I was trying to keep it a stack with my old man, but it's only so much a nigga can take. Plus, I'm fresh home. If I so much as smell some pussy, my dick will brick up. Soon as I shut the door, I got my cock in my hand. With a few drops of lotion, I went to work, doing the same thing I'd been doing for the last five years.

Before I realized it, my nut was working it's way up the pipeline. "Agghh shit. Fuck," I growled as white milk shot forth and drizzled over my hand. As I stared at the cum all over my fist, I wondered if Yolanda liked to swallow nut. I laid there out of breath as I tried to get myself together.

After I cleaned myself up, I must have dozed off for a second because my eyes were shut but I swore I heard soft moaning. *Pops must have come home horny as hell and now he's giving her the bidness.* My stomach started growling. I realized I never got to finish my meal because Yolanda had interrupted me with that see-through negligée on.

I jumped out of bed and debated putting on shorts over my boxers, but said fuck it. As I entered the kitchen, I noticed my dad's bedroom door looked like it was cracked open. The sounds of sex were getting louder. To be honest with you, as much as I didn't want to see my dad slanging dick, a part of me was yearning to see Yolanda throwing that ass back, putting in work.

I crept towards their bedroom door, pushed it further in and took a look. What I saw caught me off guard. There, in the middle of the bed, was Yolanda with her legs spread wide open. Pussy lips puffy and glistening as she fucked herself with a nine-inch black dildo. Even from that distance, I could tell that her pussy was extra tight by the way it gripped the sides of the dildo as she dug in her cunt hole with purpose. Her snatch was so wet, I could hear it talking to me from clear across the room. "Squish. Squish. Squish." Her clit was poking from underneath the hood. I don't know if I was tripping, but it seemed like we made eye contact for a brief moment. Then just as suddenly, the moment had passed.

I reached into my boxers and fished out my rod. With three short strokes, my shit was at full strength, nine and a half inches of grade A Texas beef. I rubbed the tip of my dick head and felt the pre cum oozing from it. I watched as she used her left hand to spread her lips apart, while her right gripped the dildo, plunging it deep within her depths. I could see the cream begin to lather around the toy dick.

I gripped my shit tight and timed my strokes to match hers. What she did next fucked me up. I watched her grip the nine-inch dildo with both hands and begin to power fuck her cunt long, deep and hard. Her moans turned into screams as her asshole became drenched from the tears her pussy hole emitted. The black dildo turned white with froth as cum continued to squeeze out her crevices, splashing onto the comforter. My legs shook and my knees buckled as my own orgasm took hold of me. #

"Ughh. Fuck." I gritted my teeth, and for the second time in less than an hour, I came all over my hand. I made my mind up right then and there, I had to get some of that pussy. Pops would have to understand. Before I could go with my move, I heard the garage door open up. Shit. That nigga was back. I ran into my room, dick slanging drops of cum everywhere. I hopped in the shower and started scheming on how I could get a taste of that pretty pink pussy. Now we were in church and the bitch couldn't keep her eyes off a nigga. I acted as if I didn't see her, but I nonchalantly licked my lips, letting her know I'm 'bout whatever she's 'bout. Yeah, pops gone have to understand.

***

Chelsea Johnson

Man, I hate Sundays. Everybody dresses up and parades in front of each other like they aren't drunk, adulterous, drug addicts. Sex addicts. Only thing worse than a Sunday is a Monday, back to work and back to school. If my dad wasn't the pastor for this black church for the boujie, I wouldn't even be in attendance. Matter fact, at this very second, I should've had a nice, fat dick stuffed down my throat, with another one bussin' my pussy wide open. Then, when I'm done draining those two, I might call up my boyfriend, Bobby, and drain his balls dry.

Damn. Just thinking about all that dick had my pussy dripping something fierce. I don't care who's judging me because I enjoy sex so much, I can't eat or sleep unless I buss a nut. Or maybe it's the fact that I'm not ashamed to tell you to your face that if you leave your man around me, not only will I fuck him but I will suck his dick so good, that when you come home the locks will be changed.

Nymphomaniac? Naw, I just like to think of myself as a free spirited, liberated woman. I don't discriminate. In my short eighteen years, I've tried out many shapes, sizes, and colors. I've had threesomes, group sex, and orgies. I've tried out brothers, cousins, and even uncles and nephews. Don't just think I love dick. I'll fuck a nigga on Tuesday, then suck the cum out of his bitch's pussy on Wednesday.

Yeah, I would love to be doing any one of these things, but instead, I'm stuck in church, listening to my dad talk about a bunch of bullshit he doesn't even live by. Hey, it pays the bills, right?

I wasn't always like this, and before you even ask— no, I wasn't molested as a child. My household was a typical two parent household in the hood. Both my parents worked, but my dad ended up losing his warehouse job, so moms held it down until daddy got this preaching gig. Up to now, I still don't know how he got it. Who does the hiring for these churches?

Anyway, I was in middle school when it happened, so I didn't really understand. My best friend, Tammy, used to always tell me that things would change for us. I didn't believe it but now we stay in a two story, five bedroom home. I went from going to Robert E. Lee High School, which is mostly black and Hispanic, to going to Champion Forest High, a miniature mall.

No shit, we have a Micky D's and a Taco Bell in our school. Everybody pulls up in either sports cars or SUV's. Yet and still, you know what they say, you can take the hoe out the hood, but can't take the hood out the hoe.

I learned to suck dick in middle school, watching Tammy gobble up her boyfriends, who were almost always in high school. They would always bring their homeboys, who were hoping they would be the first to break me in. The crazy thing is, when I finally did lose my V card, it was to one of Tammy's boyfriends at the time named Scott.

Scott was from our old neighborhood. He was already smoking weed, drinking liquor and hustling. He was rocking gold chains and grills with diamonds in it, at a young age.

One day, I was spending the night at Tammy's house. Her mom had died some years before. They say it was a random drive by. Tammy's dad was cool as shit. He let us get away with murder. He would invite different women over, and once he went into his room with them, he would be in there all night, trying to rearrange a bitch's walls. Tammy and I would spend many nights listening to her dad lay the pipe down. We used to put our ears to the door and hear bitches screaming, begging to be fucked in the ass, pleading to swallow his cum, and even crying as he long dicked them down, nice and slow.

This particular night, Tammy's dad had our sixth grade English teacher, Mrs. Reynolds, face down with her ass full of Jimmy Dean sausage. Tammy decided to invite her boyfriend, Scott, over. I can't even lie, Scott was a sexy ass chocolate motherfucka. Six feet tall, medium build, with a dick that had to be close to nine inches, with a slight curve.

I used to cream in my panties watching Tammy handle that bad boy like a professional hooker. I sat on the edge of the bed as she rode him so good his toes popped and curled in his Jordan socks. I wet my lips, watching his balls swing up and down as her cum saturated his nut sack. Up until that point, I had never been penetrated orally, vaginally or anally—a true virgin.

I had on some pink satin boy shorts but watching those two had my coochie begging for air. I slipped them off and rubbed my clit with the tip of my middle finger. I was soaked. I instantly started to moan. Scott must have heard my cries and wanted to get a closer look. He told Tammy to get on all fours with her face in the mattress. My pussy was on full display and Scott couldn't keep his eyes off my fat ass sex lips or my gumdrop clit.

With one hand on the back of Tammy's head, he slid balls deep in her wet cunt.

"Ohhh shit. Gawd, that dick is soooo fucking deep," Tammy blurted out as Scott began to stroke. "Clap. Clap. Clap," Was all you heard as Tammy's bubble but crashed against his abs.

While staring me down, Scott bit his bottom lip, while stuffing his thumb in Tammy's ass down to the second joint. This was too much for her.

"Ohh shit, damn it. I'm bout to cum on that dick baby. Shit, I'm bout to cum on it. Agh. Agh. Here it cummmsss," she screamed as her pussy exploded. Nut squirted everywhere. It sounded as if she was pissing all over him. Scott pulled out, leaned over and started to lap up her cum.

That was it, and off I went. I couldn't contain myself. "Awgh. Awgh. Awgh. Ohhh shitttt!" My body trembled as I continued to skeet everywhere. I wanted so bad to feel what Tammy was feeling, to know how it felt to have your pussy slayed by a big dick, pussy eating specialist.

He hadn't busted his nut yet, so I left the two of them to handle their bidness and went to hop in the shower. When I got out, I noticed Scott was gone. I can't lie, I was a little disappointed. I walked in the room. It still smelled like hot sweaty sex.

Tammy was laid out on the bed, spread eagle, with her sex lips swollen and red. Her slit was still wet and dripping. She heard me come into the room and found enough strength to lift her head.

"Where's Scott at?" I asked.

She was groggy from the exhaustion, but still replied, "He left to go pick some shit up. He should be back in about ten minutes." With that, she forced herself to get up and go wash her ass.

Twenty minutes later, Scott returned with some food, a bag of weed, and a bottle of pills. Until then, I hadn't done anything but smoke a lil weed, but Tammy was already on four bars. She loved taking them but could never handle the drug.

Scott pulled out the pill bottle and dumped the contents into his hand. He looked at Tammy. "A'ight, babe, I went to holla at Baby D. He said he only had three bars left, so I went ahead and grabbed all three of them for you. I'ma pop a molly. Tammy seemed satisfied and she hurriedly scooped up the three white pills. With a glass of orange juice, she downed all three of them at once.

Scott offered me a molly. "Here, Chelsea. Do you want to try one of these with me?" Even though I had no desire to do the drug itself, the fact that he said *with me* was all it took for me to take that leap of faith.

"Sure, why not?" I eagerly replied.

Now look, before you judge me, I don't know exactly how it happened, but while my best friend lay knocked out from a drug induced coma, I had her boyfriends' dick stretching my virgin pussy to its limits. I don't know if it was the drugs or the dick, or it could have been both. I was deliriously out of my mind with pleasure.

First, Scott had me lay back, while he kissed my inner thigh. My skin instantly caught goosebumps and my box began to drip honey. Even though I felt Tammy was down for the count, I still struggled to keep quiet as he trapped my clit between his lips and sucked hungrily. My back rose up off the floor and legs began to quake, as soon as I felt two of his fattest fingers slide deep into my snatch.

"Damn...This pussy tastes so good Chelsea," he whispered, smacking his lips as he licked between my folds. I felt searing heat begin to form in my stomach, as I began to grind my pussy into his face.

"Ooohh, Scott. Suck this pussy. Please don't stop," I begged.

He talked to me as he fed on my flesh. "Slurp. You want... Slurp... To come... Slurp... In my mouth? Hmm?"

I grabbed the side of his face, while I rode him hard. "Ohh yeah, baby. I want to nut all in your mouth," I moaned, as I felt his fingers massage my g-spot. I lost control. "Oh my Gawd, I'm cumming, Scott." I grit my teeth and held on for dear life as I sprayed and sprayed. Every time his tongue touched my clit, I would jerk then squirt. I couldn't take it anymore. I had to beg him to stop. "Stop, baby, please. I can't take any more."

Scott eased up off me and slid his basketball ball shorts off. Out flopped his heavy ass dick. I'ma keep it a stack, a bitch was kind of scared. I had seen this nigga's work up close, and if a bitch ain't know how to handle him, he would fuck your insides up.

I looked over at Tammy. She was still knocked out, snoring peacefully. A part of me felt fucked up for what I was doing. Tammy and I had been friends our whole lives, since elementary, when they stayed next door to us, up until her mom, Jackie, had died. She ended up moving with her dad to the South, but was still coming to chill at our crib every chance she got.

All that didn't seem to matter now, as I opened up my legs and watched as her boyfriend slid the first two inches of his fat ass cock into my tiny little pussy. I had to grab his basketball shorts and stuff them in my mouth to muffle my screams, so I wouldn't wake the dead. It felt as if I was being split in half as he pushed through my barrier. *Fuck. This nigga bout to kill me.* I felt my juices run down the crack of my ass. I prayed it wasn't blood.

I looked down and saw he only had five inches in. Half his dick was still hanging out of my snatch. *How the hell was Tammy able to take all this dick?*

Scott looked down at me. "A'ight, Chelsea. I just bottomed out. So I'ma work slow until you open up all the way for me. A'ight?"

All I could do was nod my head and reply, "Ok. But please take it slow." I wanted to cry out when Scott began to hit me with slow, methodical strokes. My flower began to spread open for him and that shit started to feel like a slice of heaven. Next thing I knew, he was balls deep and my pussy was creaming all over them same pair of balls.

After I came for the third time, Scott made me get on my hands and knees. He rubbed his dick between the crack of my ass, then between my folds, before he slid it all the way home. I came again. With one hand pushing my face down, and his thumb fucking my back door, I came so hard, I blacked out.

When I came to, Scott was breathing heavily. "Ohh shit, ooh shit, Chelsea. Here it comes, girl. I want you to swallow it. Can you do that for daddy?"

I hopped smooth off the dick, letting it fall out my snatch. I turned around, got on my knees and opened wide. I had never sucked a dick, much less swallow cum, but I was about to drink down every ounce of this nigga's dick milk. I sat back and watched him jack himself at a fevered pace. His balls bounced to and fro. I instinctively knew what to do. I lifted one of his nuts and placed them into my mouth. I could taste the mixture of my cum and his sweat. The aroma had my pussy drenched.

"Yeah. Yeah, suck in them nuts, baby girl," he growled. "Uh. Uh. Shiittt. Here it comes. Awww fucckk."

I leaned back and caught a shot in my eye. Without warning, Scott grabbed the back of my head and shoved his spurting cock back into my mouth. I tasted hot nut, and fell in love with it, swallowing the first couple shots, and was disappointed when nothing else hit the back of my throat.

While jiggling his balls, I sucked on the head, praying I could coax at least one more shot of that delicious treat out from his dick. I felt it twitch, but nothing came forth, so I allowed it to fall from my mouth. Spit and cum covered my chin. I looked a mess, but the look that Scott gave me let me know that a man wants his woman to look like that after a round of sex.

"Damn, Chelsea. You got that gas, straight pressure. That was the best pussy I ever had," he admitted.

I giggled at his revelation. I couldn't help but glance at my best friend, still asleep, while her boyfriend praised my pussy, saying it was better than hers.

"Look, we will keep this between you and I for a lil while. Then, we could tell her if you want to, but for right now, I got to keep getting some of this right here," he told me.

I put my head down, cum still dripping from my chin.

He grabbed me by the face and tilted my head up until we locked eyes. "You do want some more of this dick, don't you?"

I nodded my head, like a child who was being punished.

"So, we good, right? This will be our lil secret?"

Once again, I nodded my head, and that became the beginning of an affair between my best friends' boyfriend and me.

For three straight months, Scott fucked me every which way till Sunday. I learned how to suck dick like a porn star and eat cum like I needed it to live. He introduced me to my first threesome. He and his brother took turns beating my pussy to shreds. They tag teamed me and had me cumming so hard, I forgot how to speak English. I learned how to take dick in all three holes, without flinching. By the time Scott went to jail and was sentenced to fifteen years for robbery, I was a full blown dick addict.

I never did get around to telling Tammy about me fucking her boyfriend, and once Scott went to jail and Tammy stopped messing with him, I honestly didn't see any reason to bring up old shit. Till this day, Tammy is none the wiser.

As I'm sitting here listening to my dad preach, I catch Deacon Cooper smiling at me and my mouth begins to water, remembering how less than twenty-four hours ago I had his thick black dick, clogging my windpipe.

My clit starts to pulsate. I reminisce on how he had pushed my head down and force fed me his deliciously creamy cum.

"Eat that nut up, baby girl. Yeah, that's it."

I sucked and slurped up every drop, until his balls were emptied and his dick was deflated. I waited until it became completely limp in my mouth, squeezed the head between my lips and pulled back, stretching his cock until he fell out my mouth with a small "pop." I had kissed his tip and Deacon Cooper had looked at me like I was from another planet.

"Girl. Where did you learn to suck dick like that?" He asked, clearly impressed.

"I had a great instructor," I answered. "But, I'm pretty sure you've had better," I added, hoping he would validate my skills.

He laughed. "Better? Little Miss Chelsea, that was by far the best head I *ever* got. You got me contemplating making this a permanent situation."

I knew that was something serious. I had known Deacon Cooper since I was born, and he and my dad had been friends since even before then, when they were in high school. For him to risk his reputation, his standing with the church, not to mention, his relationship with my dad, that meant the top I had just blessed him with was what he said it was—the best!

"Well, Deacon Cooper."

"Please, Chelsea, call me Dennis," he interrupted.

"Well, Dennis, I'm not tripping about us messing around on the low. After all, you do have a very delicious tasting cock, but I don't want to start no shit between our families."

"Oh, you don't have to worry about that, young lady. No one will know, I assure you of that. Plus, I will make it worth your while," he said.

"Worth my while?" Now he had me interested.

"Yes. Matter fact, here." He reached into his pocket and pulled out his wallet. After thumbing through the contents, he pulled out five crispy one hundred dollar bills. "Here, take this. It's just a little something for you. Every time you bless me, I will bless you."

I took the money and placed it in my bra. For some reason, getting paid for something I enjoyed doing had my pussy throbbing something fierce. After we discussed the rules of engagement, he dropped me off down the street from my parents' house.

While I showered that night, I couldn't help think about all the money I would make eating his cum and nutting on his dick. I played with my pussy until I came so hard I had to steady myself against the wall.

As I watched him watching me, I knew that he would be pulling up soon for a rerun. When he does, trust and believe, I will give him every bang for his buck.

***

Tammy Taylor

Look at this bitch. She really thinks she's all that because her daddy's the pastor of this wack ass church. She acts like she ain't from the ghetto, like she didn't have to sleep under the covers so the roaches couldn't crawl over her face at night.

Ever since her daddy came into that little money, this hoe be acting like she can't be touched. On top of that, she doesn't know that I know her backstabbing ass fucked my ex boyfriend, Scott. She was supposed to be my best friend. Yeah, you can make a case that it was partly my fault for allowing her to watch that big dick nigga fuck me down, night after night. Still. Where was the loyalty at?

The crazy thing is, I could have forgave her if she would have come clean, but she never did. I had to find out from his brother after he caught his robbery charge. And to think, I was actually thinking bout holding his trifling ass down while he was gone. Yeah right.

What he didn't know was, his lil brother, Byron, had been wanting to slide up in my guts for some time now. I peeped how he eyed me down every time I came over to their crib for a fuck session. I'll keep it eight more than ninety two though. I did watch the nigga jack his dick one time, while me and Scott was going at it, hot and heavy. Scott was too busy putting in work to notice his lil brother peeping through the door, stroking his fat ass cock. I guess big dicks run in their family.

Anyway, regardless of that, I never crossed the line. When Scott got his time, I went over to their spot to grab all his club pictures he had lying around. Plus, he wanted me to get his car, so I could get it to do things he needed me to do, like make sure I took my ass up there to visit at least twice a month.

When I got there, his brother, Byron, was in his boxers, playing Madden, but I didn't pay him any mind. "Do you know where Scott kept his club pictures?" I asked, trying not to stare at the thick ass dick print sitting in the front of his boxers.

Without looking in my direction, he said, "Probably in his room in one of the drawers."

"Thank you," I mumbled as I made my way to the back bedroom.

I entered Scott's room and instantly felt sorrow. There were many great memories made in that bed, on the dresser, on the floor, in the closet. Really, Scott and I fucked on every inch of space in his room. If the walls could talk. I looked and looked and looked but couldn't find the pictures. I went back in the living room to ask Byron if they could have been anywhere else and this nigga was sitting on the couch, butt ass naked, dick in his hand, stroking, while a Pinky flick was playing on the flat screen. "Byron. What the fuck you got going on? A bitch ain't trying to see all that shit, nigga. You tripping."

The nigga didn't even have the decency to put that shit up. He just looked up at me and kept on stroking. "Come on, Tammy. You act like you ain't never seen me jack my dick before. Keep it real, I know you wonder what this motherfucka tastes like."

I don't know why I licked my lips. Well I do know why, because he was right. I did wonder what his dick tasted like. So what? That didn't mean that I would suck him up. Then the fool hit me with a bombshell.

"Before you get all righteous on me, talking bout loyalty and all that faithful shit, how you gone be faithful to a nigga that's been fucking your best friend."

I felt like I had been kicked in the chest by a horse. "Say what? Look out, Byron, that's some lame ass shit to say, just to get some pussy, and if you think you had a chance before, you definitely don't have one now."

That nigga just kept on stroking with this cocky ass smirk on his face. "Oh. You think I'm gassing you up, huh? Well, what if I can show you the proof. Then what?"

I'm looking like, *this nigga has to be bluffing. Ain't no way he has proof.* Chelsea was my best friend. No, fuck that, she was like a sister to me.

"Ok. If you can show me proof, then I'll give you what you want."

"And what's that?" He answered, knowing damn well what I was getting at.

"Aghh. I'ma let you fuck me anyway you'd like and cum anywhere you'd like," I reluctantly submitted.

Byron's dick twitched as he emitted a moan. "Uhmm. I can't wait." With his left hand, he grabbed his cell phone and tossed it to me. "Here. Scroll through my videos. It's going to be under cum freak C."

My heart stopped. I took a deep breath to steady my nerves, and clicked play.

What I saw almost made me faint. There, live and in color, was not only my best friend fucking my then boyfriend, but Byron was also standing in front of her, feeding her dick like it was the last supper. My heart was shattered. I honestly wanted to cry. I hadn't felt pain like that since my momma died.

The video was twenty-three minutes and forty-nine seconds long, but I could only watch two minutes before I closed it out. The pain slowly turned into anger. How could they? I vowed right then and there. No one would ever be able to hurt me again, and I mean *no one*.

I wiped the tears that had fallen down my cheek and stared into the eyes of my liberator. Without so much of a word, I walked over to where Byron was sitting. I stood in front of him, dropped my handbag and my knees followed. I'm a woman of my word, so Byron fucked me exactly how he wanted to, with no mercy. Every hole I possessed became his playground. At first, what started as a way to exact revenge, became the source of my daily dose of vitamin D.I.C.K.

Sorry if you might want to turn your nose up at me. I didn't grow up with a silver spoon. I grew up in the slums; roaches, rats, snakes and snitches. My mom, Jackie Nicole Taylor, was once a badass bitch. I saw her fall from grace with my very own eyes.

Once my dad had caught her sucking her co-workers dick inside the men's restroom at her job, their marriage was over with. The fucked up thing was dad was up there to bring her lunch. He needed to take a piss and found out that she was already having all she could eat.

Once daddy was gone, momma began to rotate men quicker than NASCAR rotates tires. It had been more than a few times momma brought home someone, who felt it was okay to sneak into her daughter's room once they sexed her into a coma.

At first, I used to fight them off. Then, after a while, I used to just go with the flow. Due to that, my sex game was on point like a middle-aged porn star. Bitches my age were barely sucking dick. I was eating cum and eating ass. While they were thinking about having threesomes, I was running trains like a conductor. The only rule I had was, if I have a man, then I'm completely faithful. As long as I was in a committed relationship, I wouldn't cheat. Now, post Scott, a boyfriend to me is just a benefactor. The only man that I can honestly say I love is my dad.

I had been living with him ever since my mom died. One thing I can say about my old man, he's a big playa. Unlike momma, he was careful with who he brought to the house. When he did bring a woman to the house, he brought them straight to the room and kept them there. Most of the time, though, he was out and about. On those nights, I was left home alone. To say I turnt up would be an understatement.

I didn't give a fuck about a reputation. I was fucking like it was going out of style. I didn't give a damn who the man belonged to. I even fucked my cousin Trishas' husband. Look, he paid me two hundred dollars to eat my pussy. Once he got to sucking on that bad boy, I needed some hard dick and a good pounding. It only happened once, though. I think Trisha found out because I was never invited to their house again.

One of my dad's friends named Larry caught me coming home from school one day and offered me a ride. Next thing I know, we're at Choice Inn and this man got me on all fours, sticking his tongue up my asshole. Damn. That motherfucka knew his way around the booty for sure. Crazy thing is, that's all he wanted to do, suck on my pussy and lick out my ass.

One day I asked him why he didn't want to fuck. This retarded ass nigga had the nerve to say, "because you're too young." I looked at his goofy ass like he grew a second head. He didn't have anything to worry bout, though. I was young but I knew exactly what I was doing and who I was doing it with.

That's something that always confuses me. The state would say that I'm too young and not mature enough to choose who I want to sleep with, but let me shoot or rob somebody. They won't hesitate to say I'm mature enough to get sent away and do time. That shit is ass backwards, but anyway.

Yeah, I didn't have the best childhood, but neither did a lot of people coming from where I come from. Man, I can't stand that bitch Chelsea. One of these days, she'll pay for her betrayal. Right now, I'm rocking her stupid ass to sleep. She still considers herself my best friend, knowing what she did.

So that's the game she wants to play? A'ight, well we can play that, but best believe Tammy La'cole Taylor will not lose.

***

Yolanda Cooper

Jesus. Lord, help me. That motherfucka is beyond fine, and I can't take my eyes off my "step son," DC. I don't know if it's the tattoos, the thugged out persona that I grew up loving and now missed, or if it was that big bad black motherfucka he had dangling between his legs. When I walked in the bathroom that morning while he was pissing and caught a glance of that bad boy, I damn near fainted.

Now, I can't get the image out of my head. Even when I close my eyes, I see the elephant trunk flopping as he shook the piss from the tip. Call me what you want, but I would have loved to have him shake the piss off on my tongue. If I could have, I would have tasted that dick right there on the cold bathroom floor. I know I'm wrong for lusting after my husband's son; a husband who believed in me when no one else would; a husband who cared enough to take me out of the strip club and change me into a housewife.

When I met Dennis, a lot was going on in my life. I had a serious addiction to pain pills and molly. There was a pimp by the name of Saint Lucian. He had the type of game that every hoe wanted to be up under, *no nonsense finesse.* Being with him meant no drugs, except for liquor and weed, and he had me clocking fifteen hundred to two thousand dollars on a weeknight.

For the first time, I felt proud to be a bonafide hoe. Saint Lu got wrapped up in a state case involving an underage runaway. He was already being investigated for some murders, pimping and pandering, as well as a few other crimes. The case with the runaway took him down. He ended up getting sentenced to sixty-five years, and that broke all his bitches' hearts, especially mine because I was the one that brought the bitch home to him. We didn't know what to do.

I went back to renegading, back to popping Percs and drinking Molly. I went from charging six to eight hundred dollars a head to sixty to eighty dollars. I was even doing two for a hundred fifty dollars total. Shit was looking real bad for me, but then came Dennis.

He came into the club one Sunday night. Things were slow, as usual, so all of the dancers were doing their best to try and snatch him up. I just stood back on my hind legs and popped my forty-two inch ass. That's one thing Saint taught me, always do what others aren't, and what they are doing, you refrain from. Sure enough, Dennis made his way over.

"What's your name, precious?" His voice was silky smooth and my kitty began to moisten.

Like a shy school girl, I responded, "Everyone calls me Yummy."

He smiled at that and licked his lips. "Yummy, huh? Well, Yummy, I would like a few lap dances, if that's possible."

"Sure. Why not?" I told him as I turned around and began to pop my shit. I looked back at him. "I've never seen you in here before."

He laughed. "Well, I used to come here when you were probably still in elementary. I haven't set foot in this place in almost two years."

That's why I've never seen him, I thought. I had only been working there for like eighteen months.

Something about him felt different, and it turned me on He ended up getting six lap dances from me before he left. I thought that he would want to go to the Champagne room, but he just left with the promise that he would be back the next day, which he did. Then the next day, then the day after that. Each time he came, I thought he was going to finally want some pussy, or at least some head.

He told me, as long as I worked there, he didn't want to engage in anything sexual, but if I came to live with him, he would give me all the sex I could handle. Plus, I wouldn't want for anything.

Well, call me a fool but I left the club that night and moved in with him. He was staying by himself at the time. His wife had left him for the boss at her company, and his son had been sentenced to five years in prison, a few years prior.

Dennis and I played house. I kept his nuts empty and dry and kept my pussy tight and wet. For an older man, (I'm thirty-two and he's forty-eight), he knew how to have a girl speaking in tongues. His eigh- inch dick has a slight curve that would scrape my g spot something fierce.

After two months of living together, we got married. Sometimes I look back and ask myself did I move too fast? Dennis is a good man, but I missed that street shit. That wake a bitch up at 2:45am because he wants his dick sucked before he goes to sleep shit. That fuck you down while his homeboy's on the other couch because you was talking out the side of your neck shit. That pull out, nut on your face, then stick it back in your mouth so you can finish sucking his dick with a messy face shit. Just thinking about it gives me chills.

My heart craves for that thug love. My pussy craves for that thug dick. Even though DC's my step son, I know I won't stop until he's balls deep in his step mom's pussy. I squeeze my thighs together, hoping to quench the fire that's brewing between my legs. My clit is aching and I can feel my juices seeping out. I hope no one can smell my arousal. I know he wants this pussy just as bad as I want his dick. I caught him watching me double hand fuck myself with my all black dildo I named "The Black Mamba."

I still remember how his dick shot cum all over the floor. I would have licked his sperm off the tile if it was still there when I came out.

Yeah, I'm a Deacon's wife, but a nice long dick attached to a thug ass nigga will have me turned the fuck out. I wish

Dennis would allow me to fuck both of them. Now that would be a dream come true. *Best of both worlds.* I need to pray for strength and forgiveness because, if not, Yolanda, the Deacons' wife, will be gone, and coming to the stage will be Yummy, the step mommy.

***

Deacon Dennis Cooper

Yes, Lord. Yes, Lord. Another glorious Sunday. I stand in the back of the church, watching the congregation as my main man, Lucas, delivers the sermon. The only thing better than watching them young women in skirts and short dresses, switching their asses on the way to the restroom is passing the collection plate around.

Little do they know, Lucas and I have been pinching a little here and a little there. Shit, who am I kidding? We've been robbing them blind. This church has us both sitting on six figures. Well, I have six figures. Lucas has been doing a lot of gambling and a whole lot of losing. Just last week, he asked me to borrow ten thousand dollars. Who in the world asks someone to borrow ten thousand dollars? Shit, not black folk. If they do, it's on the other side of a gun.

That's my dawg, though. Lucas has been my ace since elementary school. He used to finesse the kids out their lunch money. Then, when we got to high school, he would finesse bitches out their drawers. I've always been good being his wingman. One thing about Lucas, if you mess with him long enough, you will either come up on some money or cum up in some pussy. That's why a lot of these women, especially the married ones, can't seem to get enough of him.

I told him he's playing a dangerous game, but Lucas didn't give a damn. To him, it ain't worth playing if it ain't dangerous. For example, right after service, Brother Paul will have to get to work because a pipeline has exploded and the water company needs all the extra workers they can find.

While he's laying pipe down, Lucas will be laying the pipe to his wife, Yvonne.

Yvonne's a thick, redbone, Cajun woman with a hell of an ass and a pair of hazel green eyes. Lucas told me that she likes for him to choke her out and spit in her face, while she's sucking his dick. According to him, Yvonne's got a nice deep pussy, a brother with some hang time could hang around in. I told him, one of these days, he should let me come through so we could flip her like the old days.

That's one thing we've never tripped about. Pussy. It's too much of it to go around. Only exception is the wives. Other than that, everyone else is up for grabs.

Yeah, Lucas loves married women. Me? I like mine young, soft and hungry for dick. Don't get me wrong, I love my wife, but it's something about a twenty something year old, cock crazed slut, that does something to me every time.

Speaking of cock crazed sluts. Young Miss Ashley is one of the best that's done it. Ashley is the 23 year old daughter of Sister Nicole and Brother Mikeal. Ashley is a stallion, smooth chocolate skin, five feet eight inches and one hundred sixty pounds of nothing but hips, tits, ass and thighs.

Ever since she came back from college in Atlanta, I've been having my eyes on her. Watching, waiting on the opportunity to present itself. I did a little research and found out that she was in a little bit of a financial crisis. She's staying at her parents' house until she has enough to get into her own spot. That's exactly what I needed to hear. I had no quarrels sponsoring women, especially one that is stacked like her. The only question was, should I approach? Then one day, at the church picnic, it was as if the Lord spoke to me.

Ashley was talking loudly on her cell phone, I guess to her boyfriend. Apparently, he had promised to give her some money to pay her car insurance and now he was reneging. With a little eavesdropping, I learned that her insurance was only two hundred fifty dollars. That's a mere drop in the bucket but I guess her boyfriend had misappropriated the funds somehow and Ashley was not too happy about it.

"You motherfucking lying ass nigga. You put it on your dead granny's grave that you would give me that money for my insurance, now you talking bout you had to let your momma borrow it. Nigga, let me find out you gave it to one of those dusty ass hoes that stay around the corner. What? Yeah whatever, nigga. What does that mean? Shit, you gone be extra spicy if I get me a sponsor since you wanna act like you can't keep your motherfucking word. A'ight, we'll see, nigga." She hung the phone up screaming in frustration.

I stalked her down like a panther. "Agh hum. Excuse me, Ms. Ashley. I couldn't help but overhear. You're having some financial difficulties?"

She looked at me with irritation, but softened her disposition after she realized that I could be the answer to her problems. She placed a strand of hair behind her ear and seductively bit her bottom lip. "Yeah. My boyfriend had promised me some money, so I could pay my car insurance, but once again, his sorry ah. My bad, Deacon, his sorry butt didn't come through."

I assured her that she didn't have to watch her language around me and said, "Well, you know, sometimes, when we're young, we tend to neglect the priorities that should come first for us. Or, maybe the young brother didn't have it to spare and instead of letting you down, he promised something he really didn't have."

She gave me a look as if she was thinking the same thing. "Well. If that's the case, I really wish he would have just told me instead of getting my hopes up."

"And I agree with you on that, Ms. Ashley, but umm. How much do you need, by the way?"

"My insurance is three hundred fifty dollars. I had gotten into a wreck a while back," she stated.

This lying ass bitch! She must have forgotten that I said I couldn't help but overhear. I distinctly heard her say her insurance was two hundred fifty dollars. No matter. Three hundred fifty dollars was a small price to pay for the fun I was going to have using her body as a cum dumpster.

"Well. Not to sound like I'm better than anyone else, but three hundred fifty dollars is definitely nothing for me to loan you." I had to make sure I used the word *loan* to get the understanding that this is a transaction and not a donation.

Her face sort of fell a little. "Deacon, I don't have a job, so I don't know if or when I could pay you back," she admitted.

"Ok. Well how about this. How about you allow an old man to take you out? When we get done, I'll give you the money, and we can call it even.

She couldn't hold back her smile, even if she wanted to. "Oh my God. Thank you so much, Deacon. For real, for real. You don't know how much this will help me out."

"You're perfectly welcome, young sister."

We exchanged numbers, with the promise to meet up later that night. We agreed that it wouldn't be wise for me to pick her up from her parents house, so I called her an Uber and paid for her to be delivered.

When we arrived at the restaurant, she was turning heads. With a cream colored sundress and some 4 inch heels, every time she took a step, that ass would jiggle and shake. She couldn't have had on any panties. That was the first thing I thought when I saw her.

We ordered our lobster and steak, and ate while we chatted it up. Towards the end of the night, it was perfectly clear what was expected from her for the insurance money.

On the way to the hotel, she sat in the front seat while I put some Keith Sweat on. With a few drinks in her system, I knew she was good and loose. I unbuckled and unzipped my pants, and fished my rod out. She didn't need any prodding. As soon as she saw that snake come out of hiding, she took her first dive of the night.

She grabbed my cock at the base, making sure to cuff my balls in her warm hands as she sucked on the tip until my dick was hard as steel. Her mouth was so hot and tight, I couldn't help but to moan when I felt her tongue wrap around my dick head.

"Aww shit. Suck that dick, young lady. Yeah, work for that money."

Ashley began to bob her head up and down. Spit drizzled down my shaft, saturating my balls. I reached over with my right hand and tapped her right thigh. She opened up her right leg, placing it against the back of the passenger seat, giving me the access I needed. I stuck my hands between her thighs and found what I had suspected. No panties. I dipped a finger into her box and put it to my nose. I sniffed. She smelled like French Vanilla. I sucked on my finger, enjoying her taste. Her sex lips were so fat and wet, my fingers slid right back in between her folds as I invaded her pussy crack.

I took the tip of my middle finger and started strumming her clit like I was Jimmy Hendrix playing the bass. She moaned around my cock, squeezing it even harder as she devoured my dick like a madwoman. Her juices poured over my fingers as I slid two digits into her snatch, finger fucking her like they were a dick.

Her body began to tremble as she screamed out, "Oh my gawd. I'm finna cum. I'm finna cum. I'm cummminngg." I felt her clit pulsate as her cum splashed against the palm of my hand. Knowing I had the young bitch in the palm of my hand, so to speak, had me ready to pop.

I grabbed the back of her head and slammed her skull into my dick. "Ugh. Ugh. Ugh. Ugh," was all you heard as my dick clogged her throat, stroke after stroke. She reached to grab my hand. I assume it was because she couldn't breathe, but fuck that. She was about to eat this dick, the way I want her to eat it. "Ugh. Ugh. Ugh. Ugh." She clawed at my hand just as my nut exploded into her mouth.

"Awww fucckk. You dirty little bitch. Eat that cum. And you better eat all that shit," I huffed and could hear her deep gulps as she obeyed my command. With my hand firmly in place, she couldn't lift her head until I allowed her to. I felt my dick still twitching. I whispered in her ear, "Did you swallow everything?"

She nodded, but I asked, "Are you sure you got every last drop from this cock?" She seemed to contemplate something. Then she squeezed the base of my dick with one hand while jiggling my balls with the other, hoping to pull the last remnants of cum to the surface. Once she felt confident I was sucked dry, she nodded once again.

I released my hold and she took a great big gulp of air. Her lips and around her mouth were slick and red. Her chest was heaving and I knew her clit and her heart were beating at the same rate.

We pulled up to the room just in time for the next round. When I tell you, this lil sexy motherfucka was a freak. Man. For the next hour and a half, I put this seasoned dick on her ass. The pussy was so good, I went ahead and gave her five hundred dollars instead of the three hundred fifty. I told her that I could move her out of her parents' house, but if I do that, then the pussy needs to be on standby, hot and ready when I call.

Of course, she agreed. Just three nights ago, I pulled up to her apartment. It was after 2:30am. I told my wife I was running to the store. I knocked on Ashley's door with my dick in my hand. As soon as she opened up, she dropped to her knees and gobbled my cock with expertise. Five minutes later, I was shooting my load down her throat. I pulled my pants up, zipped my fly, turned around and went home to my wife. I didn't even step foot inside. When you're paying for it, that's the type of shit you can get away with.

My newest pretty young thing might be a problem. Little Miss Chelsea. I'd been knowing that girl since she was in diapers and even though I should have looked at her as a daughter, the fact is I didn't. I noticed she started to look just like her momma, and Lord knows I wouldn't mind bussing Charllessa up, if she wasn't married to Lucas, of course. So. Maybe her daughter is the next best thing. Who knows?

Anyway, yesterday I went up to Circle A to grab me some blunt wraps and a pack of Newport shorts in a box. I was in the store, then suddenly my bladder got to tripping.

I head to the back of the store, but soon find out that the bathroom is in use. Some joker was obviously taking a shit. *Fuck it.* I didn't have to do nothing but piss, so I decided to go back behind the store. As I finish up and start to shake it off, I hear someone moaning. At first, I think I'm tripping, but then I hear the unmistakable sounds of someone receiving some A-1 head.

I decide to investigate and walk a little further behind the store. There, behind a dumpster, is none other than Chelsea, squatting down, skirt bunched around her waist, damp panties on display. Some dude, who looks closer to my age than hers, was standing in front of her with his jeans around his ankles and his dick inside her mouth. I couldn't believe what I was seeing. Dude grabbed a fistful of her hair with one hand, and with the other, grabbed the base of his dick.

I hear him tell her, "Open up your throat." Chelsea opened up her mouth wide and I watched as dude guided and slid his dick into her mouth and down the back of her throat. He bottomed out, nuts on her chin. Pre-cum stained the front of my slacks as my cock begged for release. The only things on my mind were: Where did she learn how to suck dick like that? And how could I get a sample?

I had an idea.

"Chelsea, is that you?" I questioned loud enough to be heard over their sex noises. I watched as they fumbled around, clearly embarrassed. Dude couldn't get his pants up quick enough. Chelsea saw it was me and her face fell. I knew she was wondering if I would tell her dad? Of course not. But she didn't know that.

Dude ran past me, clearly terrified. No doubt, he must have thought I was Lucas. I waited about ten seconds after dude left before I spoke.

"Look, young lady, I understand you're eighteen now, so in the eyes of the law, you're grown. But you have to understand that you represent, not only yourself and your family, but a whole community."

She took a second to lift her head up and acknowledge what I was saying. "I'm sorry, Deacon Cooper," she sighed.

"Girl, what are you sorry for? What? Because you were giving someone a blow job? You're a beautiful woman, and I hate to say it, but you'll be blowing plenty more dicks before you head into the afterlife. All I'm saying is damn, the lil nappy head nigga couldn't get you a room? He got you out here behind the store like a twenty dollar crack whore. If a man won't respect you, you still have to have respect for yourself."

She nodded her head in agreement, then asked the question that she had been wanting to know. "So. Are you going to tell my dad?"

"Well. That all depends," I counter. I can almost see the wheels spinning in her head as she tries to figure out exactly what I mean.

"It depends on what exactly?"

"Well, let's get you out of here and we can talk about it in the car, while I take you home. But first, I got to run to the church to grab some paperwork." I watched her collect her purse and pull her skirt back down. Damn! She got thick as hell. She reminded me of a young Nia Long. I watched her walk towards the car, ass twitching in her skirt. Images of her getting her face fucked invaded my thoughts. My cock began to rise.

While we drove, we talked about her college choices and what she planned to do for the summer. I asked her how she knew ole dude. She said they were just "sneaky links" and she would do anything for me not to tell her dad.

I pulled up to the church parking lot and turned the engine off. The parking lot was completely deserted. "Look, Chelsea. I've known you your whole life. I've known your father longer than that. Even though I know it's my duty to tell him, as friends, I also want you to know that you can trust me to keep a secret. I just want to know a few things."

"What's that?" She answered meekly.

"Where did you learn to suck dick like that? And how much would you need in your pocket to let a family friend sample those goods?"

At first she seemed shocked. Then shock turned into curiosity. Curiosity turned into eagerness. Ten minutes later, little Miss Chelsea had earned the crown as the best dick sucker alive. The things that lil girl can do with a dick are nothing short of breathtaking. I came so hard, I gripped the steering wheel until my knuckles turned white. With my dick deflated and my nuts depleted, I gladly gave her five hundred dollars and made sure we were on for a rerun.

Now I'm sitting here watching her move her lips to the song "This Little Light of Mine" and I can't wait until those same lips are wrapped around my cock again. Then I look toward my best friend, my main man, my road dawg on that podium preaching the gospel. I know it's dangerous as hell to be fucking his daughter, but like my friend would say, it ain't worth playing if it isn't dangerous.

***

Rev. Lucas Johnson

"You must take responsibility as not only a man or woman, but as a child of God. We have been bestowed the gift of free will. Therefore, we are burdened with accountability." As I deliver another riveting sermon, I look out over my flock. I still can't believe I'm able to stand up here, spit my shit, and get paid for it. Not to mention, all the freaky ass sex that's thrown my way from the women of my congregation. And when I say freaky, I do mean freaakkyyy. My eyes scan over the crowd and I spot the looks, the smiles, the eyes. More than a few of these women now sitting here like devoted housewives, next to their unsuspecting husbands, later tonight, while their husbands are asleep, getting ready for work in the morning, those same wives will be texting me, just so they can come meet up to get a quick drink from this cock straw.

My dick jumps as I lock eyes with Sister Denise. Uhm. Uhm. Uhm. Sister Denise. Now that's a stone cold, freaky ass motherfucka. Denise is a five foot three inch mixed breed, with brown eyes and wavy hair. She has a body like a young Rosie Perez, "White Men Can't Jump" Rosie. Her husband, Calvin, is a nigga I know from round the way.

Calvin worked at a furniture factory, and on his days off, he helped at his brothers' mechanic shop for a lil extra money. Calvin worked so much, Denise could probably have a nigga sleep over and not have to worry about her husband catching her. Not me. That's one thing I'm not about to do. I'll never fall asleep in another man's house, in another man's bed, with another man's wife.

The first time I ever dug up in Denise was about six months ago. We had gone on a church field trip to a seasonal water park. I saw Denise in that two piece bikini and knew right then and there, she would be sliding up and down my dick real soon.

Unfortunately, Calvin was also on the trip with us, so I had to figure out a way to get him out the way. I told my right hand man, Dennis "D-Rock" Cooper, to run a screen play. "Look, D, this what I need you to do for me. Take Calvin to a bar. Tell him you need some advice on marriage, and since he and Denise are going so strong, you figured he would be the best one to give you advice. Once y'all are in the bar, you pump him full of liquor and wait until he goes to take a piss. While he's in there, you unplug the battery so when it's time for y'all to go, the car won't start. You will spend thirty to forty-five minutes under the hood pretending to look for the problem. That should give me enough time to gut the bitch like a fish."

"Yeah, that's a bet Lucas. Matter of fact, I'll pretend that I lost my keys. That'll give you another fifteen to twenty minutes to do you," he offered.

"That's why I love you, dawg," I confessed. Ever since we were kids, Dennis had been my wing man. We been tossing and flipping bitches since we were doing back flips on the trampoline. We'd probably run the screen play so many times for each other, we should have gotten drafted by the NBA.

Once I had the play situated, I caught Denise coming out of her hotel room. "Say, Denise. Let me get a word with you real quick."

She stopped, smiled, and her eyes lit up. I knew I had her. "Yes, pastor?" She replied meekly.

"I wanted to know if it was possible for you and me to have a few drinks later on."

She looked unsure. "Umm. Pastor, I would, but Cal."

"Don't worry about Calvin tonight. Let's just say, he'll be taken care of," I interrupted. "So. How about it? Will you have a few drinks with your pastor tonight?"

She couldn't help but smile when she responded. "Sure. Why not?"

We parted ways. About three hours later, I received a text message from D, telling me he and Calvin were at a bar outside of town. At that same time, I was looking down at Denise as she gave me slow neck. It's something about seeing a married woman's wedding ring on the same hand that's gripping my cock that does something to me every time.

I moved her hair out the way so I could get a good look at my dick sliding in and out of her wet, greedy mouth. It's something about that slow neck. If a bitch knows what she's doing, she could make a nigga cum so hard, he'll see stars.

I grabbed a fist full of her long pretty hair and began to wind my hips, fucking her mouth with slow deep strokes. "Shhiiitttttt, baby. Eat that dick, you greedy bitch," I whispered as I felt the tip of my dick scrape the back of her throat. "Massage my balls with your right hand, but make sure you keep that left where I can see it," I commanded.

Of course, she obeyed. Denise wore bright red lipstick, which was now smeared. Rose colored spit candy coated my cock. I felt my balls draw up and I knew I was about to pop. I lightly smacked her on the cheek. She looked up.

"Back up," I said.

She leaned back, allowing my dick to fall free.

"Get on your hands and knees. I want to see that pussy hole bust open."

She got in position, face down, ass up.

"Spread that ass open for me," I told her as I slowly stroked myself. With both hands, she reached back and pulled her cheeks apart. I took my dick, rubbed it up and down her slit, wetting my tip in the process. I looked down at her hand and saw her wedding band. I grabbed her left hand and said, "Finger your asshole with your ring finger." As soon as I seen her digit disappear all the way down to her wedding ring, I slid in her balls deep.

"Oh my Jessusss," she screamed as I pushed deep into her cervix. Her pussy was hot as a furnace. "Ohh shit. Ohh shit. Fuck this pussy, pastor. Yes, Lawd. Fuck this pussy."

I grabbed a hold of them pretty round, golden brown cheeks and pounded her guts until I felt her squirt against my abs. She begged me to ease up, but I buckled down and gave her that dope dick. I wanted her to be strung out and full blown addicted. After about thirty minutes of hot intense sex, I gave her a break. Well technically, I was taking a break. She was giving my dick a tongue bath.

Her phone began to ring and she panicked. "Oh my God. Oh my God. Where's my phone at? That's Calvin. Please help me find my phone," she begged. I reached under my boxers, which were laying on the floor, and retrieved her phone.

She frantically punched her code in. "Hello? Oh, heyyy honey. You what?"

I got up, dick in hand, and walked over to where she sat on the bed, pussy splayed open.

"You what? Babe, I can't hear you. Go outside," she told him, while I took my semi erect cock and slid it across her lips.

She looked up with pleading eyes.

I mouthed the words, "open up."

She closed her eyes, shook her head, but still obeyed.

I slid in with care. With the phone in her right hand and my dick in her left, I slow fucked her mouth while her drunk husband explained that Deacon Cooper had somehow lost his keys and they were trying to find them. While he was letting her know that he loved her and didn't want her to worry, she had my nut sack in her mouth, sucking on each one as my dick was laying flat against the bridge of her nose. Now that my shit was back bricked, I wanted some ass.

I grabbed her hand and pushed her forward. With my hand against her lower back, I dipped down and licked her asshole before I stuck my tongue in it. She accidentally moaned in his ear, but he was too drunk to notice. I put the tip of my dick at her backdoor entrance. She looked back, and with pleading eyes, shook her head no.

I waved her off and pushed through her barrier.

"Awgghh. Fuckkk," she yelled into the pillow, as the first four inches of dick spread her open like a taco. I pulled back. Damn, her shit was so tight, I damn near came right then and there.

I began to rock slowly, back and forth, allowing her to try and finish her convo with her hubby. Each syllable she uttered was met with a stroke of the dick, until finally she had to hang up on his ass.

With her face buried into the mattress, I fucked her asshole until she shitted on herself. Now, most niggas would have been repulsed. To be honest, that wasn't the first time I made a woman shit on herself, and it wouldn't be the last.

Afterwards, we took a shower together. Then, she gave me head until Calvin called and said they were on the way back. Soon as she hung up, I pulled out and jacked my dick, while she sucked on my balls.

"Aghh shit. Cover your face with your hands," I ordered. She complied.

"Awww. Fuucckk. Dammnn." Spurts of white, hot cum splashed all over her hands, which were protecting her face. I aimed for her wedding ring, and spurts of cum dripped over her diamonds. "Let me see your face," I said breathlessly.

She removed her hands and I rubbed the tip against her lips, while squeezing what little cum I had left. I let my dick rest against her mouth as I caught my breath. She instinctively reached for it, licking my cock head clean. I knew she was just too freaky for me to let go. Before the trip was over, we hooked up one more time, but it was just some quick head, while her husband went to the store. That was six months ago, and the bitch is still freaky as ever.

As I'm standing here, she's sitting next to her husband, licking her lips and smiling. My dick begins to rise and I divert my eyes elsewhere. I see my son and his girlfriend. Damn, the boy is a spitting image of me. I have to be completely honest, though. He's too soft for my liking. He didn't have to get it out the trenches like I did. That's not a bad thing, though. I grind so my kids don't have to.

He's good enough to play pro ball, but he needs to be a lil more aggressive on the court. One thing I can say, he has my taste in women. That Amber is one fine piece of ass.

I keep scanning the room and see my wife side eyeing me. I love my wife, but fucking on married women gives me something she can't— a thrill that makes me feel alive. I look to the back of the church and spot him, Big Lou!.

Big Lou is a former lineman turned enforcer for Benny the Bookie. Ever since I went in debt sixty thousand dollars, Big Lou has been showing up to my services, pressing me afterwards for the money. I've been scheming from the church, trying to pay him off, but church folks only pay tithes once a week.

I take a look at the clock on the wall, 10:55am. I have five more minutes before I let the choir close out the service. I know my time is running out with Benny and can't help but wonder if today will be the day they do something to me about my debt.

I take one more look at my family. I kept them oblivious to what's been going on. Only one that does know something is Dennis. Damn, what have I got myself into?

***

After Service: 1 pm

Everyone had left the church. Well, not everyone, I didn't have to see him in the truck to know Big Lou was sitting behind the wheel of his all black F-350.

As I was leaving out of church, I watched my surroundings, hoping to see potential witnesses. Maybe Big Lou would think twice about killing me, if he felt like he would be compromised. Surprisingly, at 1 pm, there was no one outside anywhere around the church.

I tried to walk to my driver side door, but Big Lou's truck was parked directly next to mine, so I had to pass him to get to my vehicle. As I approached, his door opened up and I smelled the strong odor of marijuana, mixed with something else, most likely cocaine. I'd been around enough smokers to recognize a premo smoker when I saw one.

Big Lou stepped his six foot six inch, three hundred fifty pound frame out of the truck and I could clearly see the vehicle lift up from the relief of pressure. "What's up, Reverend?" He growled menacingly. "I saw you had a packed house in there this morning."

I knew where this was going but I answered anyway. "Yeah, we had a decent showing today."

Big Lou smiled at that, showing off his yellow stained teeth. "So. How much bread do you have for Benny? Since y'all were packed and everybody has to pay ten percent, you should have at least half of what you owe him."

That was the thing this big dummy didn't realize. Yeah, the Bible says you should pay ten percent of what you make, but honestly, who the hell would give up that much of their paycheck? Shit, that's a light bill or an insurance payment. For some people, that's a used car note. Then, only a small percentage of church folk pay meaningful tithes. Most church folk put in $3-$5 and call it a day.

The only good thing about our church was we produced some prominent sports and Hollywood figures. Alone, they would bring in tithes close to mid or high five figures every Sunday. Today was a mediocre day.

I pulled out a manilla envelope. "Here. That's sixty-five hundred dollars." Big Lou looked at my hand as if I had shit on it.

"Sixty-five hundred? Look, Rev., Benny already told you. If you don't have at least half, you don't have nothing. Sixty-five hundred is nothing but the interest he'll collect for another non-payment."

"Look, Lou, this a church, not a casino. I told Benny I got him. It's just going to take some time."

"Time? Time? Nigga, you had like three months," he bellowed. "Say, fuck all that. You have until next Sunday to come up with that bread or that's your ass, preacher man. And I hope *your* ass is saved." With that, he jumped in his truck and left me standing there with the money still in my hand.

Throughout my life, I'd done a lot of shady shit, but this was the first time I was actually scared of the consequences. My mind started to flash to my family, my wife and kids. I couldn't allow myself to be taken away from them. I had to think of a way to get out of this bullshit I had gotten myself in.

Chapter 2
Monday

Chelsea Johnson
I look at my Dior watch and notice it's already 12:45. My appointment is for 1 pm and I wasn't about to miss it for the world. Since I am a Senior with only a couple of weeks of school left, we had what they called half days. I don't know about others, but I use my half days wisely. If I'm not riding down on a fat ass dick, then I'm getting my hair and nails done.

Joy's Hair Palace was the only place on this side of town where a black woman can get her wig fixed. Plus, her shop was the only one that took appointments on Mondays. The rest of these so-called "salons" really only catered to whites or women with straight hair. My hairdresser Tracie was the only one I let in my shit. She had been my stylist since my family moved out here and she knew exactly how a bitch needed her wig done.

"Heyyy, girl," I acknowledged her as I stepped into her establishment. Her shop had just about everything you needed, with a hair supply store attached, just in case you needed a little extra.

"Hey, Chelsea girl. I know you happy as hell you bout to graduate soon," she stated as I sat down in her chair.

Tracie was a pretty brown skin woman with tattooed eyebrows and full luscious lips. She was in her mid thirties but you could easily mistake her for twenty-eight or twenty-nine.

"Girl, what? Am I? I just don't know if I want to go straight to college or sit out a year. I'm so tired of school. I just want some time to relax," I told her.

"Girl, I know that's right. Sooo. How your people doing?" By people, I knew she meant my brother. When I was younger, I didn't realize how much of a good looking family I had. Now that I'm older, women of all ages are either jocking my brother or my dad.

One time, my brother had to come pick me up from the salon because my car was in the shop. It wasn't lost on me, how he and Tracie flirted back and forth. Even though she is over ten years older than him, I couldn't blame her. When I get in my forties, I'ma want a young nigga's dick to play with, too.

"Yeah, my people doing a'ight. We was all in church yesterday. I had to listen to my dad do a bunch of capping."

Tracie buss out laughing. "Chelsea, you too much," she said before asking, "So what you want done this time?"

"You know what? I'ma keep it simple. Just hook me up with some box braids." I had plans to keep it casual this summer. Plus, when I get my pussy buss open, I don't like niggas fucking up my weave. With the braids, I can get loose and my shit will still look the same when I'm done.

Halfway through my hairdo, I hear a couple females entering the salon, laughing and giggling about something. "Ohh. Hey, Chelsea. We didn't know you came here, too," Lakiesha said.

Lakiehsa Foreman was a bitch I went to school with. We used to be in the same clique until she started hating on me because my people had come up. I wouldn't say she was a bad bitch, but she was cool to look at. At five feet five inches and a hundred twenty-something pounds, Lakiesha was top heavy, 44DD's, but she was flat backing, no ass. Yet and still, she was cute as hell in the face, so she got hers when it came to the guys.

"Oh. Hey, Kiesha," I responded. I don't know why bitches played that game like they were cool with a chick, knowing they couldn't stand her. If that's how she wanted to play it, fuck it.

"Hey, Chelsea," her best friend, NeNe, spoke up. She was your average looking hood chick, nothing special. I acknowledged her with a head nod and pulled out my phone. Brenda, the other stylist on duty, asked Lakiesha what she wanted done. She looked at me and replied that she wanted box braids. I flinched. *These hoes wanna ride a bitch wave.*

"So, girl," she began. "Have you found out what college you want to go to yet?"

I really didn't want to hold a conversation with her, but in the interest of keeping things civil, I indulged her. "Uhh, not yet. I'm thinking bout UT, but I might stay home and just go to U of H. How bout you?"

"Well, you know I'm looking into getting into the medical field, so I went ahead and registered at TSU," she proudly stated.

I decided to be petty. "What's up with Jacorey? Where is he going?" Lakiesha's face fell flat. For some odd reason, she thought her boyfriend, Jacorey, and I had fucked around. I knew my comment struck a nerve.

"He hasn't decided yet," she mumbled. At the same time, my phone chimed, notifying me of a text message. One of my jumpoffs was looking to link up. I let him know that I was at the salon getting my hair done, but we could link up afterwards. He told me he couldn't wait to eat my pussy. I told him I couldn't wait to suck his dick and swallow his babies.

While Lakiesha was yapping away about her and Jacorey getting married, he was all in my DM telling me he was going to let me ride his face until I buss a fat ass nut all over his lips and tongue. My clit throbbed as I imagined her kissing him with pussy juice staining his lips.

Yeah, I had been fucking her boyfriend for some months now. So what? The first time was at a house party the football team threw for making the playoffs. What was crazy was, she was at the same party, but she was too busy standing in a corner with those nothing ass hoes, talking 'bout what other bitches had on, to notice her man was MIA.

While the party was going on, Jacorey had me bent over the the A/C unit, stuffing me with his fat ass dick.

What turned me on even more, he had his homeboys posted up, watching out so no one could sneak up on us and tell his girlfriend. Even though they were supposed to be watching out, they were really just watching, dicks poking through their gym shorts, as Jacorey fucked me so good, my cum ran down my thighs. My panties were still on, just pushed to the side as he pounded away.

We couldn't really let loose that night, but we linked up the next night and I got to show him this million dollar mouthpiece until he begged me to let him go.

Now this dumb ass bitch is up in here talking bout marriage. Shit, that's cool with me. I might just let him slide up in it before he walks down the aisle. I was thanking God when Tracie had finally finished my braids. I was so ready to get up out of there. As soon as I hopped in the car, I called him up.

"Wassup?" He answered.

"Where you at right now?" I asked, eager to get myself tightened up.

"I'm at Jason's. We just over here smoking. What's good?"

"Y'all got some more smoke over there?" I inquired.

"Hell yeah. What, you bout to slide through?"

"Who all over there?" I asked like it mattered.

"Shit. Just me and Jason, right now."

"Well, yeah, I'm bout to slide through."

"Bet. Aye, pick us up some more wraps on your way."

"A'ight." With that, I put the car in drive and was on my way to get dicked down. As I was leaving out the parking lot, I looked into the shop window and could still see Kiesha yapping away. *Dumb bitch.*

***

Lucas Jr.

Damn. What am I going to do? It's been over a week and I still don't have any money to give DC for the pack he fronted me. It's just my luck, my car gets broken into the same day I grab the work. Now I owe this crazy ass nigga five bands. *Fuck.*

I pound on the steering wheel before I slide the keys in the ignition. On the way out the parking lot, I see a few of my jumpoffs trying to flag me down. More than likely, they want me to go to their dorm rooms for some quick fun. Not today.

My focus is on getting this money. I just don't know how yet. I head to the spot my girlfriend Amber and I share. It's not much, a one bedroom town house in the good part of town. I'm contemplating telling her, but I don't want her to worry.

As I pull up in the parking lot, I see a familiar truck. What looks like Deacon Cooper's burgundy Yukon Denali is parked two spots down from me. My heart starts to pound in my chest. I feel like I can barely breathe. I pray it wasn't who I think it was, but deep down I knew the truth.

I step out of my Charger. The Yukon door pops open. I didn't know whether to run to the crib or jump back in my whip and peel off. Neither one would have worked because my feet were glued.

All six feet four inches of DC stared me down as he stepped out the truck. "What's up, Jr.?" He hit his Newport once more, then flicked it out.

"Man, look, DC, I ain't got your money yet but."

"Let's step inside and talk about," he interrupted. I started to panic. Maybe he was going to kill me and Amber. I love my girl and didn't want her to get killed for something stupid I did. What was I supposed to do?

Reluctantly, I turned around and headed to the apartment, with DC in tow. I walked in and instantly smelled Amber's Chanel fragrance. Every time I came home to that smell, I knew she was feeling sexy and in the mood. I heard DC mumble, "Damn, someone sure smells good."

I was about to leave him in the living room and find Amber to let her know we had company, but before I could, she came out of the room rocking a pair of small red satin panties and a white wife beater with no bra. We keep the temperature at sixty-five degrees, so her nipples looked like a pair of Hershey kisses.

Her sex lips were so fat, her coochie was eating up the material from her small panties, which made her lips look even fatter.

"God damn," DC blurted out.

Amber saw DC and immediately got embarrassed.

"Oh damn, baby, why you ain't tell me we had company?" she shrieked as she retreated back to the bedroom. Her ass was shaking and jiggling while she ran. I started to go after her, but DC stopped me.

"Sit. We can talk while she's gone."

We both sat down on the couch.

He leaned back and said, "So what are we going to do about the money, Jr? It's been a week and you ain't shot a nigga one red nickel."

I looked away. "I know, DC, but you know I ain't got no job. My old man will shoot me a band soon. I can give that to you and work the rest off."

"Work the rest off? What you think this is? Lay-a-way or something?"

59

Just as I was about to respond, Amber came back out dressed in some white tights and a blue Old Navy tee. You could still see her camel toe, her snatch was so fat.

"I apologize for earlier. Um, DC, would you like something to drink?" She asked.

"Sure. What you got?"

"It depends. If you're looking for something strong, we got some Hennessy and we got some Ciroc."

DC thought about it, licked his lips and said, "I always go brown."

She then turned to me. "What you want, baby?"

Before I could answer, DC said, "Naw, he's good, Amber. Bring him some water."

Amber looked at me with question. I didn't respond, so she headed off to the kitchen to retrieve the drinks.

When she returned, she sat on the love seat, which was directly in front of DC and catacorner from me. "So. DC, how does it feel to finally be home?" she asked.

"Well, it feels good."

"Soooo, I have to ask. What's the one thing that you missed the most while you were gone?"

DC took a sip of his drink, paused, wet his lips and said, "Pussy. The taste of it. The smell of it. The feel of it wrapped around my ten-inch dick, while I'm dicking a bitch down so good, her pussy starts milking itself. The way the pussy grips my shaft, while I have her face down in the mattress and my finger in her asshole, fucking her so good, she can't even remember her name, much less her boyfriend's. I love sucking on pussy just as much as I love fucking it. I missed having a bitch cum all over my tongue, pussy juice coating my lips like lip gloss."

I was looking at this nigga DC like he done lost his mind, but I saw Amber's eyes light up and her thighs begin to open and close as DC described what he missed the most.

"Ugh. Umm," I interrupted. "Say, baby, can you shoot to the store to grab me some steak and shrimp for dinner tonight?"

Amber snapped out of her daze. "Uhhh. Yeah. Sure thing, babe." She got up and I can clearly see the crotch of her tights was soaked. She headed to the room and DC commented on how fat her pussy was. I was heated. I'm not a killer, but this nigga was surely pushing me.

After Amber left, DC said I had up until Sunday to pay him his bread. He alluded to the possibility of us working something out, but when I ask him how, he didn't say. He decided to finally leave, and I was left, sitting there in my living room, thinking about everything that had just transpired. I felt something significant had occurred in my living room, I just didn't know what.

***

Derrick Cooper aka DC

Damn. This ho's pussy is fat as hell. I'm watching her walk away and I can't help but to imagine her bent over, while I'm deep stroking her. So what Jr's in the room, he can watch if that's what gets him going. I know when I answered her question, her curiosity was piqued. That's all I needed. One thing I know about women is they want an Alpha male. Once they see the bitch in you, then it ain't nothing for a nigga like myself to come in and scoop them up.

I know that sucka Jr. won't be able to pay me my money, but looking at that fat ass pussy and that juicy bubble butt, I'm pretty sure we'll be able to work something out.

I leave his apartment and wait in the truck. I need a chance to talk to Amber one on one. I sit back and twist up some Sour Diesel. Even though this is my old man's truck, he smokes in it, *so fuck it.*

I'm halfway through my blunt when I spot her Camry pulling back up. She gets out the car and I immediately approach her.

"Wassup Amber?"

She sees me and becomes startled. I notice she quickly scans her eyes in search of her man.

"He's inside," I say, answering her mental query. She still seems uneasy. I need to say something that will bring her guards down. "Look, I just wanted to apologize if I offended you earlier. It's just when you're gone for a long time, a woman's touch is something you crave, almost as much as your freedom. A man is wired to appreciate everything about a woman. I guess I'm just not tactful when it comes to expressing myself."

"Oh no. You're good, DC. I asked and you were truthful. I can't be upset about that. Now that you're out, I know you're getting as much as you can handle," she added with a giggle.

"To be honest with you, I have had a couple of women since I've been home but it's hard to find one that can handle what I have to offer. I wasn't capping when I said I'm holding ten inches of dick." I watch as her eyes sparkle. Her curiosity is more than piqued. Her eyes instinctively travel down to my crotch and I close the gap between us.

I have her backed against the car door with my body pressed into hers. I whisper into her ear. "Go ahead and grab it. See for yourself."

Her body trembles. She responds, "I can't. I love Jr with all my..."

"This ain't about love. This is about need. You need to see if it's true. You need a real nigga to beat your back in. You need *this* nigga to fuck you until you're unconscious. Admit it." I reach into my sweats and pull out my dick. Even semi erect, it is impressive. I close the gap again. Due to my height, my dick is pressed against her sternum. My pre-cum stains her shirt. "Go ahead and touch it. Go ahead."

With trembling hands, she slowly reaches for it. Her touch is electrifying. Her small hand begins to stroke my dick until I'm at full attention. She gasps, as she witnesses the truth, ten and a half inches of prime cut beef.

She licks her lips and I think she's about to attempt to swallow me whole. We hear a car engine. Someone is pulling up to one of the empty parking spots. The trance is broken.

"Umm. I got to go, DC." She grabs her groceries and departs, leaving me standing there with my dick hanging out my sweats. I slowly slide my shit back in, hop in the truck and head home. Even though I didn't get to fill her mouth, I know it's only a matter of time before curiosity will let me kill that cat. I'll be waiting.

***

Deacon Dennis Cooper

"Welcome to Coops Coups, Sedans, Trucks and Vans. How may I help you?" April greets another one of our many customers. April is a twenty-two year old Puerto Rican I hired a couple months ago to help out at my detail shop.

Unlike Lucas, I took money I was scheming from the church and I invested in a few businesses, this detail shop being one of them. "That's going to be seventy-three dollars and sixty-eight cents for the deluxe package," she announces as she rings up the total.

I sit back and I watch April standing there in her tight fitting uniform. With an ass like J-Lo's little sister and some melon sized C-cup titties, April has my dick and balls blue from stress all day. In the two and a half months she has been with us, we have seen our customer rate triple. I made up my mind that I will give her a much needed raise pretty soon.

I decided to give her a break and relieve her from her duties at the register. One of my other employees takes over and April heads to the break room.

I retreat back to my office, but after ten minutes, I realize that I'm missing some important signatures on some paperwork. I sought out one of my most senior employees, Linda. As I pass up the break room, I happen to glance inside and catch April making out with her boyfriend Oscar, who was also one of my employees.

To be honest, I didn't want to hire him, but April begged me to. Apparently, he was on parole and needed a place of employment. Still I resisted, but April could be persuasive when she wants to be, so I gave him a shot.

Now I catch them getting their freak on, on company time, and I ain't going for that. "Excuse me," I snap. Startled, they break their embrace and immediately start apologizing.

"Oh, I'm sooo sorry, Mr. Cooper," April began.

Before she continued, I cut her off. "I don't want to hear any apologies, April. You know better than that. Matter fact, I need to see both of y'all in my office, right now. Wait for me until I get there." With that, I left in search of Linda, so I could get those signatures.

When I returned, both of them were standing outside my office whispering. When they saw me, they both became quiet. No doubt, waiting to hear my instructions.

I walked right by and said, "April, you first. Oscar, wait out here until she's done."

I hear a faint "yes sir" from him as his girlfriend follows me into my office.

I enter and without looking back, I order her to shut the door. She does as told. I look at the chair in front of my desk. She understands and sits down. "Now, April, I want to know something. Tell me why I shouldn't fire Oscar? The same one you begged me to give a chance. The same one you gave me your word and said he wouldn't disappoint me. I walk by the break room and catch his tongue down your throat and your breast out in the open, while he's groping it."

April pleads her case. "Yes, sir, I know, but it's all my fault. I called Oscar into the break room. If you're going to fire someone, fire me. If Oscar loses this job, he probably won't be able to get another, and his parole officer will violate him and send him back to jail!"

While standing directly in front of her, I look down and tell her, "Pick your head up." She slowly lifts her head. I can tell that her eyes are a bit misty. I stroke the side of her face and whisper. "Are you going to make this right?"

She nods her head yes.

"Do you know what you need to do to make this right?"

Once again, she nods her head yes.

I take a deep breath. "Well, April, I need you to make this right, ok? You need to fix this." With that, she reaches for my slacks, unbuckles and unzips them, and fishes my dick out of its confines.

With both hands gripping the base, April breathes in my scent before placing half of my limp cock in her mouth.

"Awww shit," I groan. "Eat that dick baby. Make it right for daddy."

April sucked me in deeper. Spit coated my shaft as she began to bob her head even faster.

"Suck that nut up out of there. If you love that nigga, baby girl, make this dick spit."

April grabs a hold of my ass cheeks and begins pulling me hard into her throat. My nut sack swings wildly, hitting her chin, as my dick disappears down her throat. April gobbles my cock with so much force, I thought her boyfriend would hear the wet sucking sounds, while standing outside the door. My legs shake and tremble.

"Oh shit. Oh shit, bitch, here it comes," I growl.

April grabs my balls and squeezes lightly as my dick jumps for joy.

"Awww shhhiittt. Eat it up. Eat all that nut up," I cry out as April does exactly what she's told. I feel my cum leave my piss hole and I can hear her swallow each load. I had to back up off of it when I saw she wasn't letting up.

"Damn, girl. You must really love that nigga," I say breathlessly. I used her shirt to dab up the spit that was on my dick.

With cum and saliva coating her lips, she looks up at me with a smile. "I do love him. A lot."

I slide my shit back into my slacks. "Well, don't worry about him losing his job. You made sure of that."

Her face lights up. "Thank you so much, Mr. Cooper."

"Don't thank me, you've earned it." She blushes. "Now clean yourself up before I open this door."

April takes the underside of her shirt and wipes her mouth clean. I unlock the door and watch as she steps out. She walks by Oscar with her head down, no doubt ashamed of cheating on him. Hey, sometimes, you gotta do what you got to do.

Oscar prepares to enter my office, but I stop him short. "You know what, Oscar, you're good. I had a long talk with April and she told me it was all her fault. She convinced me to give you another shot. Your girl has a really good *head* on her shoulders. You should track her down right now and give her a great big kiss for having your back."

The relief on Oscars' face was evident. "Oh thank you, Mr. Cooper. And I will." With that, he turns around and leaves to find his girlfriend.

I turn around and head back into my office. I pour a stiff shot of Hennessy. That was the third time April had blessed me with some top. It seems as if she gets better every time. Little did Oscar know, April's *head* on her shoulders is what got him the job in the first place. The things we do for love.

***

Lucus Jr.

What am I going to do? I just called pops to see if maybe he had some extra cash saved up, but no luck. Just as I'm contemplating telling Amber to ask her parents, she comes walking in with two grocery bags.

"You need some help with that, babe?" I ask, but it's like she didn't hear me. "Amber? Amber?" I say more forcefully.

She snaps out of it. "Huh?" I look at her suspiciously.

"Are you a'ight?" I ask.

"Oh. Yeah, I'm alright. Just thinking about something my mom said when I talked to her on the phone."

"I was asking if you needed help. Do you have any more bags in the car?"

"Oh, no. No. No, this is it, but you can go ahead and put this up while I hop in the shower?"

I get up to help and she hurries off to the bathroom, seemingly flustered about something.

I finished putting up the groceries but saw she didn't get any steak sauce. I went to grab my car keys from the bedroom and notice her satin panties laying on the floor, in front of the bathroom door. "She must have been in a hurry to shower," I say to myself.

As I go to pick them up, I notice the crotch is wet and completely stained. I put the soiled panties to my nose and take a whiff. I can smell her womanly essence and can tell that she has nutted on herself.

I take a step towards the bathroom door and I'm about to open it, when I hear moaning. I slowly twist the knob and place the door ajar. I can see her silhouette through the glass shower door. Amber has one leg on the side of the tub, with her hand moving feverishly over her twat. I can tell that she was eagerly fucking herself with two fingers. Every now and then, she would pull them out, so she can vigorously rub her clit.

I watched for three to four minutes, until she brought herself to a violent climax. So spent, that she has to sit down in the tub while the water rains down upon her. I quietly close the door. I wonder what had her so worked up that she came in her panties and still felt the need to play with herself in the shower. I made a mental note to ask her about it later.

Right now, I have bigger fish to fry. I grab my car keys, text Amber to let her know I'll be back in a couple hours, and I leave the house on a mission. I have to get a bag by any means necessary.

Chelsea Johnson

I pull up to Jason's crib after I went to my boyfriends' house for a quick shower. I changed into a black Bebe top and a red Bebe skirt, with no panties. When I walked in, both Jacorey and Jason were in the living room playing 2k. I can tell they are gambling because I see twenty dollar bills on the floor between them.

"Ok. There she goes," Jason says excitedly.

I hold up the blunt wraps and the Newports.

"Bet that. What's up? You gone twist one up for us," Jacorey asks as I sit down on the love seat next to him.

"Sure. Where's the Loud at?" I ask. He reaches on the coffee table and tosses me a bag of some strong smelling bud.

"That's Tru OG. Twist one up and spark it. A nigga ain't smoked one in almost two hours," Jacorey complains.

I start to buss the bud down and twist up the blunt. Two minutes later, we had the blunt lit and in rotation. I hit it twice, and my body started to tingle. My clit started to throb. Every time I smoke some Loud, I get horny as hell. Today was no different.

I lean over and whisper in Jacorey's ear. "Why don't you put the controller down and come play with this pussy."

He turns my way. Eyes glazed and chinky, looking sexy as hell. "Hold up. I got one more quarter left. You know we gambling. A nigga got to get that bag."

I smacked my lips. Fuck it. If he don't want to come get the pussy, I'll go get the dick. I grab the ponytail holder out my bag and tie my braids up. I reach over his lap and stick my hand in his gym shorts.

He sits back and looks at me with bewilderment, as I find what I was looking for. His dick felt hot in my hands. I stroked him twice before I placed him in my mouth. "Hmmm," I moan. The taste of his dick has my coochie cooing. Jacorey didn't have the biggest dick I've ever seen but it's one of the fattest, and by far one of the tastiest.

At first, he tries to play it cool. Still attempting to play the game, while I'm topping him off. *No sir.* When I'm sucking dick, that's the only thing that's going to be on his mind.

I take him deep, letting him molest the back of my throat as I hum around his shaft. He drops the controller. He leans back and relinquishes control.

"Ohh shit, Chelsea. Damn, girl, that shit feels good," he sighs as I bob my head, making sure to keep his cock wet and saturated.

I look out the corner of my eye and see Jason staring at me put in work. With the dick still in my mouth, I get off the couch and position myself on my knees, with my ass in the air. From Jason's vantage point, I know he can see up my skirt. Nothing but ass cheeks and a fat ass pussy on display.

My shit is leaking something serious. I can feel my juices running down the back of my thighs, as cold air brushes against my sex lips. I slyly peek back at Jason as I dip under Jacoreys dick to tackle his nut sack.

Jason has gotten off the couch and now is on his knees, shorts just low enough to free his dick. I could tell from a quick assessment that his dick was big enough to get the job done. Acting as if I was oblivious to him joining the fun, I continued to wolf down Jacoreys meat.

I feel Jason's hand slide up under my pussy and rub my clit. I let Jacoreys' dick fall out of my mouth.

"Ohhh shit," I hiss as he stuffs his whole length into my greedy twat. I squeeze Jacoreys dick as Jason begins to pound into me, digging in my box with powerful strokes.

"Damn, Chelsea. This some good ass pussy. Your shit wet as motherfucka," he declares, as I use my walls to massage his shaft. Jacorey grabs my ponytail, pulling my head back and placing his dick back where it belongs. A bitch like me was in heaven. Stuffed with two dicks, it didn't take long for me to cum. When I did, my whole body convulses. I screamed but my screams were muffled, due to a mouth full of cock.

For the next hour and a half, I let them niggas fuck me into total exhaustion. One time, Lakiesha calls while I have Jacoreys dick in my mouth and Jason's dick up my ass. I listen as he lies to her about what he's doing and who he's doing it with. I suck even harder, eager to make him cum while she's on the phone. He hangs up moments before his hot, sticky treat pepper sprays my taste buds.

After our session, I snatched the rest of the Loud they had and got ready to leave. I see I have a missed call from my boyfriend, Bobby, and one from Tammy. As I'm walking out the door, I check myself in the mirror to make sure I'm stain free. I call my bestie to see what she wanted.

***

Tammy Taylor

My phone rings the familiar ring tone "Freak a Leek" by Petey Pablo. *Now she wants to call.* "What's up bitttccchhhh?" I answer.

"Shit, hoe, you know me, just got my tune up for the day."

Yeah, I do know you. I listen to this fake ass bitch tell me about her day at the salon.

"What you got going on today?" She finally asks after she gets winded talking about herself.

"Oh, I ain't on shit. I just left my lil boo spot. I had to beat the nigga off with a stick. This nigga ate my ass and pussy for an hour straight. Bitch, I'm still light headed," I joke.

"I know that's right. Gotta eat the booty like groceries," she caps.

"What you bout to do?" I ask, eager to get her off my line.

"I don't know yet? I see Bobby's ass hit me up, too. I'll probably swing by there and see if he'll break a bitch off some bread."

I had to laugh to myself. This girl is a natural born user. Bobby was her boyfriend and she treats her jumpoffs better than she treats her man.

"Well, girl, let me... Oh, before I forget. That's why I called. I wanted to invite you to a kick back party at that rap nigga Lo-Life's crib on Friday night. That bitch gone be lit. You know he just bought that twelve bedroom mansion in River Oaks. It's RSVP only."

"What? Oh, hell yeah, a bitch going. What you gone wear?" She ask excitedly.

"I don't know yet, but you know your girl gone put that shit on. It's going to be a lot of heavy hitters in the spot."

"Shit, I already know. Bitch, I can't wait."

We talked a little more about what we were going to wear. Then we disconnected as I pulled up to my cousin Wacco's trap in the Oaks.

Wacco is a known Crip and OG of his circle of Hoovers. Every time I pull up, it's always a group of thirsty ass niggas outside the spot. Wacco's a shot caller, so they never sweat or disrespect. Even though Lo-Life is a high ranking Blood, him and Wacco came up in the streets at the same time and had a lot of respect for each other. So much so, that Lo-Life was willing to take Wacco on tour with him because he knew he needed certified shooters in the squad.

I walk in the trap and notice two of his lieutenants in the living room, bagging up hard and soft. They look up, acknowledge me, but don't speak, as they went right back to doing what they were doing.

"Where's Wacco?" I ask. The brighter one nods his head towards the bedroom. I make my way over there and open the door. Why I didn't knock first?

I don't know but I walk smooth in on Wacco getting his dick sucked by a big bitch named Shanquell. Shanquell goes to my church and was the daughter of Sister Bernice and Brother Ford. She comes off as a goody two-shoe, but Wacco has her on her knees, in front of the bed. With one foot on the bed and one foot on the floor, he's feeding it to her Captain Morgan style.

With both hands behind her back, Wacco has her head gripped with both hands, fucking her face like it's a fresh batch of pussy. I close the door and wait for him to finish up. Even though I just had my pussy thoroughly ate, seeing Shanquell gobble down dick has my juices bubbling.

I'm not about to disgrace myself by fucking with one of my cousins' underlings, so I squeeze my thighs together and wait on him to finish getting his nuts vacuumed.

A few minutes later, the door opens and out comes Shanquell. She sees me and jumps in shock.

"Hey, Shanquell girl," I greet.

Even though she has dark brown skin, I still see her blush when she realizes it's me. "Umm. Hey, Tammy," she answers meekly, while putting her head down, trying to get out of there as fast as she can. The front of her shirt is saturated with spit, no doubt from the sloppy top she just administered.

Before I know it, she's out the door and Wacco is coming out the room. "Oh shit. What's up, lil cuz? What brings you through my neck of the woods?" he asks.

I hate that I seen what I seen. Now I can't get the sight of his big black dick out of my mind.

I shake it off. "I came to rap with you about Friday night. I want to go over the whole play, to make sure everything goes according to plan."

He looks annoyed. "Come on, Tam, you ain't got to triple check me. I told you I got you. I'ma make sure everything goes according to plan."

"I understand that Wacco, but still... Can you indulge a bitch, and just go over everything one more time?"

He sighs. "A'ight, lil cuz. Let's talk."

I walk with him into the room and we go over every detail of Friday night. Yeah, it will be a night for everyone to remember.

Yolanda Cooper

"Hello? Girl, I'm almost there. Hold your horses," I tell my girl, Jamie, as I make a right on her street.

"Did you remember to grab the Goose?" She asks.

"Of course, I got the Grey Goose. Plus, I picked up some wine coolers, too." I parked in front of her house. "Bitch, I'm outside." I disconnect the call and make my way to her front door.

Jamie had been my friend since my stripper days. She and I were both stripping at Gold Diggers, but she was just doing it to get through college. She never looked down on me for staying, and I loved and respected her for it.

Tonight, we were having a "kick back" as the youngsters call it. Just us girls, Jamie, me and three of our home girls from the good ole days. Everyone was in charge of bringing something. I had to bring the Grey Goose, which was our preferred drink, when we were in the club.

I walk in and see all the girls in the living room, chatting it up. Jamie stood up to give me a hug. Jamie, on all accounts was a bad bitch. A five foot four inch red bone, brick house, with hazel green eyes and an ass that would make Buffy jealous. That's not all that made her a bad bitch, though. She graduated college with a Masters in Accounting and a Bachelors in Business Management. She had lucked up and hooked a wealthy trick and convinced him to invest in her. She made sure he didn't regret it. Now she owns a commercial real estate company and also has a chain of tax offices.

"Heyyy, Yum Yum," she sang. As she hugs me, she slaps my ass and watches it jiggle. That was our traditional greeting. I hug her back and return the gesture, smacking her ass and watching it wobble.

She turns to the others. "Yum, I know you remember Meme, Jewlz and Honey, right?"

I turn to the three ex-strippers. "Hey y'all. Of course, I remember them," I say as I sit down.

We speak about our new lives and we discuss those from our past. About an hour into it, Jamie's doorbell rings. She gets up to answer it. In the state I am in, I am not prepared for who enters.

Stepping through the foyer, smelling like Kenneth Cole Black, dressed in a white and green Gucci tee, with some all white Gucci shorts, accented with some white and green Gucci loafers was Jamie's twin brother Ja'Quell, standing at six feet two inches and built like an NFL running back. When I tell you this nigga is beyond fine, that would be an understatement.

Then, he had the nerve to bring two others with him that were sexy ass hell in their own right. I think every piece of pussy in the living room was weeping for attention. Ja'Quell and I used to flirt heavy back in the day, but nothing serious. He had wanted me to leave Saint, but that wasn't going to happen. I hadn't seen him in years, but looking at him now, I can tell he has bossed all the way up.

"Oh, if it isn't Yum Yum," he chided in that sweet and sultry voice of his.

I blush like a schoolgirl. "Quell? How you doing, baby? Your sister told me you had moved to Atlanta."

He licks his lips, while staring into my eyes. "Yeah, I did. Atlanta got some fine ass women, but ain't shit like my Texas girls."

"I know that's right," Honey shouts, while giving Jewlz a high five.

"Plus," he continues. "I have some business ventures up there that sis helped me cultivate."

I had heard that Ja'Quell was low key worth close to two million dollars, legit money, not to mention, what he had in the game.

When I was coming up, Quell was the type of man every hood bitch wanted, sexy as fuck, hustled hard and stood on his ten.

"I heard you're married now," he said, while nodding towards my wedding band.

All of a sudden, I felt self conscious about my marriage. "Yeah, I got married a few years back. He's a good man. He treats me real well," I confided.

"Yeah, but does he fuck you like you need to be fucked?" He asks.

I look away. "Come on, Quell, you ain't supposed to ask a married woman that."

"Boy, what's wrong with you?" Jamie scolded him. She was the big sister by three minutes and you could tell.

He put his hands up in mock surrender. "A'ight, A'ight. My bad. I brought you ladies something."

The other gentleman he brought with him left and returned with bags of edible arrangements. Each of us screamed like kids on Christmas, while opening up our bags.

"Yolanda, can I speak to you for a second?"

It wasn't often Quell used my government, so that definitely got my attention. We excuse ourselves and went into the kitchen.

"Look. To be honest with you, you've been on my mind the whole time I was in the A. You can ask my sister. Every time I called home, I would ask about you. I know you're married and I don't want to ruin anything, if you're happy. But... Here's my card. If you're not, give me a call. I would love to take a shot at making you happy."

I couldn't help but to smile as I took the card. "I'm not going to promise anything, but... We might can link up soon," I say as I kiss him on his cheek. His intoxicating scent is invading my nostrils.

"I hope so," he whispers as he leaves me standing in the kitchen, panties soaked and sticking to my crevices.

For the rest of the evening, I couldn't keep my thoughts in check. Images of Ja'Quell and I having hot, passionate sex, dominate my mind. I leave Jamie's house and contemplate calling Quell to quench my thirst for some delicious cock. Instead, like a good little wife, I go home and put this pussy on my husband.

***

Derrick Cooper aka DC

It's been so long since I've been on the Nawf side of Houston, I tell myself as I turn into Coke Apartments in 5th Ward. Even though I'm East up till my feet up, my pass is good everywhere I go, especially in Coke apartments.

My homie, Blade, has been home for about two weeks now and has been itching to peel a nigga shit back for that bag. Even though I consider myself a jack of all trades, my nigga Blade is a straight up demon. Ski mask or bare face, he's coming for your shit.

When I was leaving Jr's crib earlier, Blade hit me up and told me he had a nice lick for me. Of course, I'm trying to see what the numbers read.

I pull up and park the truck on "D Block," right in front of the generator. As soon as I hop out, I notice a dice game going on. I contemplate shooting, but think better of it. Shooting dice is one of those things you intend to spend only minutes doing, and before you know it, you've been at it for hours. Right now, time is money.

I walk through the breezeway on my way to Blade's apartment and bump into a neighborhood bitch by the name of Dick Tracy. Now legend is, Dick Tracy once made two different niggas cum in less than three minutes, just off the head. Every time I slide through, she always finds a way to push up on me.

I would have sampled her goods, but she was just *too* aggressive for my taste.

As soon as she sees me, she reaches for my dick, cuffing my shit. "Damn, DC, when you gone let a bitch devour that snake you got between your legs. They already told me you in the ten and up club."

I gently move her hand out the way. "Tracy, your throat ain't deep enough to devour this motherfucka," I say, as I walk up the stairs to Blade's apartment.

The last thing I hear is, "You don't think fat meat greasy, huh? Try a bitch out, and I guarantee, you ain't gone want nobody else lips wrapped around your dick, once Dick Tracy gets a hold of it." I laugh as Blade opens the door.

"What it is Blood?" I ask, while performing our handshake.

"You already know. Bloody ways and Bloody days," he responds as he lets me in. We sit in the living room and get straight to the bidness. *Just the way I like it.*

"Check game, DC. Have you ever heard of that nigga Ja'Quell Peters?"

I think for a second before I respond. "It sounds familiar, but I can't be for sure. Why?"

"A'ight, well about 4 years ago, Quell and a couple of niggas hit old school Smitty for five birds and two hundred thousand dollars. They kicked in Smitty's spot, laid everybody down, and then vamped out with the stash. Well, everybody died but Smitty. Of course, Smitty being the OG that he is, never told the authorities who did it but you know the old head never forgot."

"A'ight, I'm hearing you, Blade. But where do we come in at?" I was eager to get down to the good part. The part where we get paid.

"I'm getting to that D. A'ight, so Ja'Quell has been in Atlanta this whole time, making some major moves, but he still has his hands in the streets. Through Smitty's people, they found out Ja'Quell's about to make a major move to purchase fifty keys. He plans on taking half back with him to Atlanta, and leaving half in Texas with his team down here in Houston."

My ears begin to perk up. That's the type of lick a nigga wait his whole life to hit. "So what? We hit the nigga after he makes the purchase?" I ask.

"Naw. We hit the nigga while he's making the purchase. That way we hit for the fifty keys, plus the 1.2 million dollars he's bringing to cop."

"Hold up. Hold up. So you saying, you and me gone run down and hit this nigga, Ja'Quell, and his plug, just the two of us? Bro, I know they not 'bout to have all that work and money without having extra security," I point out.

"That's the thing. They've been dealing with each other for so long, they only keep one man a piece with them when they make a transaction. Usually, Ja'Quell would send his right hand man, but due to the size of the purchase, he's going himself."

I sat back and worked the play through my head. "So. What do we have to give Smitty?" I ask.

Blade smiles. "That's the best part. The old head only wants what they took from him, five birds and 200k."

"So that leaves us with forty-five bricks and a ticket to split two ways," I calculate. My palms begin to itch like crazy. My arms get goosebumps, thinking about what this type of lick meant. I look Blade in his eyes. "So we have it overstood, we the only two leaving up out that bitch, right?"

"Ain't no other way," he answers.

"So, when is the play going down?"

"Saturday night," he says, while grabbing the bag of weed to twist up a blunt.

"I'll be ready," I say, as I get up, ready to make a move.

"Look, pull back up on Friday so we can run everything down. I think we should grab two of the lil homies, let them get their feet wet. Plus, we ain't really got to give them much. A couple stacks and a half a bird a piece should be good."

I open up the front door and look back at him as he goes to light the blunt. "That's a bet, and Blade, not a soul homie."

I closed the door and made my way to the truck. As I drive out of the apartments, I start to ask myself, could I trust Blade to pact fair once we slumped everybody, or should I look to be the only one that's leaving up out that bitch alive? *Only time will tell.*

Chapter 3
Tuesday

Charllessa Johnson
Damn. I'm about to be late for work. I grab my keys off the counter and double check myself in the full length mirror as I'm heading out the door. It's already 7:30am and I have to travel across town to get to work by eight o'clock. I'm the manager of a telecommunications company. The pay is decent, but my perks come with the endless supply of young delicious dick to devour.

Our company was one of those companies that regularly employed young adults in college or fresh out of college.

So, it wasn't out of the ordinary to see a new face on the job every week. Whenever that happened, I tried to make sure I was the first one to break them in. After I'd had them a couple times, I'd let the rest of these thirsty women get the scraps.

"That tramp Jessica better not be in my parking spot," I mumble, as I pull into the employee parking lot. To my relief and delight, I see my spot is unoccupied, as it should be.

After parking my car and hustling my way through the lobby, I finally made it to my office with three minutes to spare. I sit down and begin working on my daily duties.

Knock. Knock. Knock. I look up and see Jessica's head poked into my office.

"What's up, Jess?" I ask, slightly annoyed. It seems like no matter what, she always finds a way to interrupt my day with some nonsense.

"I got these census reports for you. Oh, and Regional called. I think they want you to attend a meeting on Friday."

"Ok. Well, thank you," I say, ready for her to depart.

"Oh, before I forget. We have a new hire."

I lift my head up. A new hire could mean some fresh meat for me to eat.

"And who is that?" I ask, maybe a little too enthusiastically.

Jessica's nosey ass picked up on my tone, and with a smirk, she said, "I'll send him in."

A couple minutes later, in walks a living God. I take one look at the man and almost cum in my LA Perlle panties. He had to be about six foot one, two hundred twenty pounds. He has a golden brown hue to him and a smile that lit my office up. I nonchalantly scan the front of his dockers and *Yes Lord*, the man looks like he has some serious trunk in the front.

He approaches my desk as I stand up to greet him and shake his hand. "How are you doing, Mrs. Johnson? My name is DaVon Miller."

I grab his hand and feel my coochie snap, crackle and pop. "Well, it's a pleasure to meet you, DaVon, and welcome aboard." I sit back down as he takes his seat. He sits with his legs wide open and I can't keep my eyes from landing in his crotch every fifteen seconds.

"So, DaVon, tell me about yourself. What made you choose our company?"

He leans back in his chair, wets his lips, and says, "Well, Charles is my first cousin and umm, he used to tell me about the perks he received while working here. He talked about it so much, I used to dream about it in my sleep."

I couldn't contain my smile. Charles was the first one at the job to get a taste of this vintage snatch. No doubt, the perks he was referring to were this wet ass coochie and this tight ass mouth.

"So, Mr. Miller, you came to work up here, especially for the perks?" I ask seductively.

He looks me dead in my eyes. "I've been dreaming about these perks for a long time. I just hope that my work performance will ensure that I get the same type of perks my cousin, Charles, got."

"Hmm. Well, I will say this. Your cousin Charles was a workhorse, who didn't mind putting in overtime to make sure the job was superbly done. If you are willing to exhibit that same type of work ethic, then I can assure you, you will receive every single perk there is to receive." I look down at his crotch to let him know there were no misunderstandings on what was being discussed.

"Well, I guess I better get back to work," he says as he stands up, his sizable erection on display.

As I see him to the door, I whisper. "How about you meet me after work so I can go over your work assignment with you?"

"Sure thing," he answers, as I shut the door behind him.

Lord have mercy, that man has my kitty cat throbbing. His cologne permeates the air in my office and my juices are flowing nonstop. I can't wait until after work. I'm a give his young ass exactly what he came looking for.

My phone beeps, letting me know I have a notification. I see I have a missed call from my husband. *I wonder what his trifling ass wants.* I pressed down on his number and hit call.

***

Rev. Lucas Johnson
"Hello? Hey, baby. I was just hitting you up to see if you dropped my clothes off at the dry cleaners this morning. Huh? Why not? Why were you late? A'ight, well I'm at the dog park and won't be home until later. Yeah. A'ight, love you. Bye."

I need this day to be my lucky day. "Welcome to Raceway Dog Park. How can I help you today?" The petite, cute white woman asks, as I step towards the counter.

"I would like to place a one thousand dollar bet on dog number five at twelve to one odds." Even though the winnings wouldn't cover the whole sixty thousand, it would at least knock off a chunk of it. I grab the ticket and race to the stands.

After the race was over, I was a thousand dollars poorer. I make my way to the ticket booth to place another bet. I still had $5,000 left from what I took from the church Sunday, and I intended on gambling all of it.

I'm so much in a rush to grab the ticket before the next race, that I don't see the man until I practically run him over. *Smack.* He almost falls, except someone grabs him and prevents his fall.

"Damn, my bad playa," I begin.

"Lucas? Lucas Johnson, that's you?"

I can't believe my eyes. "Lucky? Mannn, I know that ain't Lucky 400," I state.

Lucky is an old friend of mine from the sandbox. His mom was an old hoe and his daddy was a con man. Growing up, Lucky's parents never paid for anything. All their bills were paid off scams his dad ran.

His dad ended up getting killed and his mom ended up going to jail for stabbing a bitch up on the blade. Instead of putting Lucky in foster care, they shipped him off to Waco to stay at his grandmother's.

"Damn, man, what you been up to?" I ask.

"Shit, dawg, running the long and short. Right now, I'm going toe to toe with Uncle Sam, and he's losing," he boasts.

"Oh yeah, what you got cooking?" I was definitely intrigued.

"Ever since that Covid hit, the government been giving away money, dawg. That shit's so easy, it's scary. All I need is someone's info and I can have Uncle Sam clear a check for 100k or better. The lowest is twenty bands," he proclaimed.

Now he had me all ears. "So what's the requirements?" I ask.

"Look, if you can get me someone's Driver License, Social Security card, and if they got a bank account, that will be even sweeter. I can guarantee you at least a hundred thousand dollars for us to split two ways. If the account has more than ten thousand dollars in it, then the pay will go up."

This is exactly what I needed right now. "So, how long before they pay out?" I ask.

"Well," he says. "It depends on how fast you want the money."

"Shit, I need it like yesterday, dawg." I wasn't hiding the fact that I was desperate for a pay out.

"Well, in that case, I can put in a rapid return for you and you will get it back in two to three days."

"That's perfect." Now, I just have to figure out whose info to use. "Look, Lucky, I'm going to fuck with you on this, dawg. Give me your number and I will have the info to you by tonight or tomorrow morning," I tell him, as he repeated his number to me. I save him in my contacts.

"If you get me that info tonight or tomorrow morning, I will have the money in your hands by Saturday night. Guaranteed."

We shook hands and I left the dog park, feeling a hundred times better.

Now that I had a legitimate solution to my problem, I couldn't waste any time on anything else. I'm racking my brain trying to figure out whose info I could get in this short amount of time.

Then, it was as if the good Lord shined down on me. My phone rang. I look at the screen and see my secret lover's number pop up. Somewhere, my conscious was screaming at me. What I was doing was just plain wrong. Just like always, my comfort outweighed my conscience. "Hello?" I answer.

"Heyy, Sweetie," she replies.

"Are we still on for tonight?"

"Of course, baby. Matter fact, I'll be at our spot a little early."

"I'm at the dog park right now, but I'm heading home to take a shower. After that, I'll be heading up there."

" Ok. Well let me finish up over her and I'll make my way to you," she says. I finish up the call, and head to the house to get myself cleaned up. I really do care for her, but when it comes to my family and well being, she's just another bitch in my book.

***

Lucas Jr.

Fuck it. I've made my mind up. I'm just going to come clean to Amber about the whole DC situation. Her people got money, so I know five thousand dollars ain't shit to them. If she were to ask them, I know for sure they would give it to her.

I hate coming to her job. A lot of chicks on her job are messy as hell, and every time I came up here, Amber and I would have a fight about some bitch saying I shot at her.

Walking through the lobby, I noticed the smiles, but I wasn't going to fall for it today. I need to make sure Amber wasn't in one of her moods. I catch the elevator up to her floor and notice her manager, Alexis, is riding with me.

Alexis is an older chick. I wasn't sure exactly how old, but I know she is in her late forties. Be that as it may, she's still sexy as hell though. Five feet seven inches tall, caramel skin, nice set of titties and big wide booty, she kind of reminded me of Taraji P. Henson.

"How are you doing, Lucas?" She politely greets me.

"Oh, I'm cooling. Getting ready for this summer break," I reply.

"I know that's right. It's rare to find a black man who's doing something positive with his life. I respect that about you, Lucas. I tell my older women all the time, when we see a young black man taking care of business, I feel like it's our duty to help ensure that he is comfortable and secure enough to keep doing his thing. I know a lot of times, black men turn to the streets, due to financial strain. So, as a successful black woman, I find joy in relieving that strain so he can continue to move in a prosperous and positive path," she explained.

"That's deep," I admit. "I wish more women had that same point of view."

The elevator door opens up and I allow her to exit first, watching her ass move in her business skirt. She must feel me watching because she looks back and smiles as she disappears around the corner.

I approach Amber's cubicle and think I overhear her telling someone, "I don't know yet. You have to be patient, I've never done that." She must have heard me approaching because she hurries the person off of the phone. "Oh, I have to go. My boyfriend's here." She hangs the phone up. I can't put my finger on it, but something about Amber has changed over the last couple days.

"Heyy, baby," she smiles as she greets me.

"Hey," I reply. "I just came up here to see my baby one time. Plus, I need to holla at you 'bout something."

"Oh ok. So what's going on?" She asks.

"Umm. Well before you trip, just know that I know what I did was stupid as hell, and it will never happen again, but I need you to ask your people for five thousand dollars."

Amber's face tightened. "What in the world would I need to ask them for five thousand dollars for?"

I went ahead and told her everything. From me grabbing the pack, to my car getting broken into, to the deadline being Sunday to pay him back.

She listens to my whole spiel, looks at me and says, "How stupid can you be? You know damn well you're not built like that, and you…"

"Wait. Wait. What?" I ask indignantly. "What the fuck is that supposed to mean? I'm not built like that?"

"You know exactly what I mean, Lucas. You're an athlete. You're in college, and you've got your whole life ahead of you, and your stupid ass wants to go fuck it up by trying to be a drug dealer. Dude, that's ass backwards," she yells.

I notice that we're starting to make a scene. "You know what Amber? You got it. Forget I even pulled up. I'ma handle this by myself," I say over my shoulder as I leave her standing in her cubicle.

Man, I can't believe she tried to play me like some soft ass nigga. She's supposed to be my girl. I walk through the front door and make it to the parking lot as I hear someone calling my name.

"Lucas. Lucas."

I turn around and see Alexis jogging out of the building, trying to catch up.

"Look, I'm sorry about causing a scene back there, Alexis. Please don't take it out on Amber," I reason.

"Oh no, it's alright. Umm. Look, I overheard your conversation, and I think I can help."

"Really?" I say with skepticism.

Alexis begins to look around the parking lot. "How about we sit in your car so we can discuss it."

"Sure," I say, and we both get it.

After we close the doors, Alexis goes on to tell me how she meant what she said about respecting and admiring what I was doing with my life. She also goes on to say that she feels I'm a very handsome man, and even though she's nearly twice my age, she would love to be able to take care of whatever needs I have.

I sit in disbelief as I listen to her proposal. Finally, I ask, "What needs do you think I need met?"

She bites her bottom lip, reaches for my Gucci belt, and says, "Well, for starters, I see you're extremely stressed right now, and I feel you need the stress sucked out through your pee hole." Her expert hands had my cock free, and before I knew it, her hot mouth was devouring my member whole.

Wet sucking sounds fill the car as Alexis slurps and swallows. Spit saturates my balls. "Cum for me, daddy. Make momma swallow that nut. Fill my belly up," she begs. "Ummm. I need to taste that cum all over my tongue." She bobs her head as I recline in the driver seat. My balls are wet, soggy, and aching for release.

"Shit. Eat that dick. Suck the stress away, momma," I urge as I grab the back of her head, not giving a damn about her weave.

Gulp. Gulp. Gulp. Gulp, was the sound of my dick violating her mouth.

I remember how Amber had insinuated I was soft. I wrapped Alexis's hair around my fist, and fuck her mouth with complete abandonment. No restraint.

Awk. Awk. Awk. Awk. She grabs ahold of my thigh and squeezes, as I show no mercy at all. I take my aggression out on her throat, as I skull fuck her. My balls tighten and I feel my legs tremble.

"Shit. Here it comes, baby. Swallow it all," I command. "Awww fuccckkkk." My ass comes off of the seat and I shoot hot nut down her throat. Like a seasoned slut, she gobbles it down and continues to nurse on my cock head for more. "Shit. Whooo. Girl, you wasn't bullshitting. A nigga needed that. For real, for real.

She giggles and says, "I told you, baby, I got you. Matter fact," she says as she reaches into her bra and pulls out four hundred dollars. "Here, this is for you. I'll have another six hundred for you when you come through and slang this fat ass cock up in a bitch." She cleans my dick off with some wipes she keeps in her purse, then tucks my dick back into my boxers.

After checking herself in the mirror, she opens the door and steps out.

"Wait," I say. "I hope this will stay between us. I'm not trying to fuck up what I got with Amber," I tell her honestly.

She looks at me and smiles. "Baby boy, this grown woman pussy you're about to be getting. Only mess I'm about, is the mess this dick will make when it spits all over my face. You don't ever have to worry about me telling your girlfriend anything." With that, she closes the door and heads back into the building.

I look at the four hundred dollars in my hand. I can't believe I just made my car note just to get some fire ass head. Then, I had six hundred more on the way to lay that pipe. If Alexis is down to pay like that, then I'ma definitely make this a regular thing. I just pray Amber never finds out. I put the car in drive and head home to get cleaned up.

***

Chelsea Johnson

"Ooohhh shiittt, babbyy. Eat that ass," I moan, while on all fours, ass in the air. My boyfriend, Bobby, has his tongue up my shit hole. Bobby and I have been together for almost a year now. Even though he's not the cutest nigga I've ever been with, nor has the biggest dick, he's by far the best ass eater, probably on the planet.

I cry out as he forms an "O" over my anal ring. With his lips, he sucks gently on my opening. This nigga is the only one I know that absolutely loves to eat a bitch pussy and ass like it's a fine cuisine. He spreads my cheeks apart and runs his tongue down the center of my crack, before he hardens it and fucks me like a miniature dick.

"Fuccckkk, baby," I moan as my asshole pulls his tongue in. I feel him dip under me and his tongue finds my nub. He begins to suck gently on it while his nose is lodged into my ass crack. I feel him inhale my scent and the intake of air has my asshole catching goosebumps. My coochie begins to weep. I hear him smacking on my snatch and I know it won't be long before I'm creaming all over the place.

My phone lights up. I would have ignored it but a familiar tune of *Bitch Better Have My Money* by my girl Rihanna alerts me of who it is. So, I elected to text, since I was otherwise occupied.

Me: What's up? Can't talk. Busy.

His reply came quickly.

Deacon Cooper: When can I get another round?

Me: When R U trynna meet?

Deacon Cooper: 2nite?

I already have plans for tonight.

Me: Can't 2nite. How bout 2morrow?

As I wait on a response, I hear Bobby ask, "Baby, who you texting?"

I look back at him and say, "What I tell you about questioning me? If you don't trust me, then maybe we shouldn't be together, Bobby." I hear him sigh. "Now finish up. I got to go to Tyra's to help her set her new apartment up."

Bobby hesitates like he wants to say something, thinks better of it, and sticks his face back where it belongs, between my ass cheeks.

Deacon Cooper finally responds.

Deacon Cooper: Tomorrow is fine. Meet me at the Marriott at 7pm. I'll bring five with me.

I smile at that. I drop my phone and reach back with my right hand. I pull Bobby's face deeper into my ass, as my left hand rubs my clit until I cry out, exploding all over his face. "Ohhhh shit. I'm cumming, Bobby! Fucckk."

Bobby sucks up the nut like a vacuum. My body shakes with intensity.

After the tremors subside, I get up and walk to the shower, leaving him jacking his dick to get his nut off. Look, it's not that I don't care about him or I don't respect him. He's just too passive for me. I need a man that's going to check me and put me in my place. Bobby is a nice guy, and bitches like me feel like nice guys finish last.

He holds down a decent job and treats me well, *so fuck it.* Plus, his head game is out of this world. Bobby does what I ask, when I ask and how I ask. He rarely questions me, and when he does, I check him and he slinks back like a wounded animal. I know he isn't the man for me long term, but I'm comfortable with him at this moment.

After I hop out the shower, I throw on a black Dior skirt with a red offset tee to match. I spray on some Chanel fragrance and grab my Gucci clutch as I head to the door.

Bobby is in the living room, watching YouTube videos on his phone. I walk up to him with my hand out. "I need some money."

He looks at me with furrowed eyebrows, but relaxes his face and asks, "You need money to go help your friend fix up her apartment?"

I look at him as if he's slow. "Bobby, if I'm asking you for money, obviously it's some things she needs help purchasing for her apartment." That explanation seemed to be enough for him. He reaches into his pocket and retrieves his wallet.

"How much, Chelsea?"

"Just a couple hundred, babe." I soften my tone.

He peels me off three hundred dollars.

I grab his keys and make my way out the door. As soon as I slide into the driver seat of his white Lincoln MKZ, I call Tyra.

"Hello?" She answers excitedly.

"What's good bitch? What's got you so excited?"

"Mannn. Where the hell you at?"

"I'm on the way right now. You know I had to get Bobby off my ass. Literally."

"I already talked to T Fatts. Him and KC on the way right now, so you better get your ass over here pronto."

"Girl, I'm on the way! I got some Loud I snatched from Jacorey's ass yesterday."

"Ok, bitch, bring it." She sang as she ended the call. I've been waiting to test drive that nigga KC for a minute now. He's a five foot eleven inch, two hundred fifteen pound Hershey bar, with drip that'll have a bitch creaming her panties just standing next to him. He's from Kansas City, Missouri, hence the name.

He had been in Houston for a few months now. When I first seen him, I was with Bobby on a double date with Tyra and her boyfriend, Perry, at Pappas. He was there with T Fatts and two nondescript bitches.

T Fatts and Tyra had been creeping for a while, so later that night, he had hit Tyra up and told her that his homeboy was trying to find out who I was.

We knew Perry was headed out of town tonight, so Tyra and I had set up our lil sneaky links. As soon as she confirmed Perry was on the plane, they were on the way. I was anxious as hell to see if this nigga dick matched his swag. I park the car in Tyra's driveway and notice T Fatts' Nissan Armada on twenty-four inch Asantis parked in the street.

"I see them nigga's are punctual behind this pussy," I say to myself.

As soon as I walk in the apartment, I notice not one, not two but three niggas in the living room.

"Wassup?" Dude #3 greets me as I step in. Tyra must have noticed the surprise look on my face.

"Hey, Chelsea. This is Karl. Karl, this my home girl, Chelsea. Everybody else knows each other."

Karl stands up to greet me. "How you doing, Karl?" I say as I take his hand.

"Nice to meet you," he responds as I take a seat next to KC. I have to admit. Karl is kind of cute. He reminds me of a young Michael B Jordan. Apparently, they have plans to hit the gambling shack later on. T Fatts decided to just bring

Karl along to save an extra trip. I pull out the loud pack and put a couple in the air.

Twenty minutes later, T Fatts and Tyra disappear into the room. Being that she has a one bedroom apartment, that means KC and I have the living room to work with.

I don't know what KC has in mind, but I'm high and horny as fuck. I hope he isn't shy and can perform under pressure. KC's flipping through the channels, looking for Sport Center, while Karl's playing on his phone. *Fuck this.*

I reach for KC's belt buckle. He looks at me with a smile as he helps me unzip and pull his shorts and shirt off. Sitting in only his Polo boxer briefs, I slide my hand over the front, gripping his package through the fabric. My mouth waters as I reach within the elastic waistband, pulling out a thick, hot slab of cock.

I lower my head into his lap, rubbing his dick all over my face. Smearing pre cum on my cheeks, nose, and forehead. I inhale his scent. His nuts are fresh and clean, which make me even hornier. I open up wide, slowly stuffing him in. His cock tastes sweet to me.

I relaxed my throat and went to work, bobbing my head, while I jack his dick with fluid efficiency.

Slurp. Slurp. Slurp. His dick twitches and jumps on my tongue as I suck him in deep and hard.

"Ohhh fuck," KC moans as I cuff his balls, massaging them while I deep throat him with ease.

I pull him out of my mouth. "Sssss. Let me see this dick spit, baby," I urged as I put him back in.

KC grabs the back of my head and groans. "Aww shit, I'm bout cumm. Ughhhhhh." His dick backfires and my mouth fills with warm salty goo.

I swallow and keep swallowing until he has to pry me off of his pipe. I finally let his dick fall from my mouth and back up off of it. I watch it lay limp, still twitching, slick with my split.

"Damn. You the truth, girl."

I look up and see T Fatts standing over us, dick in hand. I quickly scan the room, looking for Tyra.

"She's in the room, with Karl," T Fatts says as he slowly jacks his beautiful black cock. Sensing my confusion, he continues, "I told her I wanted to sample this fire ass head I've been hearing so much about. From what I just saw, I know I won't be disappointed."

Still on my knees, KC scoots over and T Fatts takes his place on the couch. I grab his shaft, and lick from under his balls to the tip of his dick. I pop the head in my mouth and gently suck on it like the nipple on a baby's bottle. I stretched the loose skin on his cock and work my mouth like I would my pussy, loose on the way down, tight and on the way up. I turn my head sideways and work my cheek bones.

"Oohh weee. Suck that dick, bitch. Shiiittt." T Fatts howls as I chew him up.

There isn't a bitch alive that can eat a dick better than me. And at the end of tonight, T Fatts will know that to be the gospel.

"Oh shit. Damn. You bout to make a nigga nut already."

I pull him out and say, "Cum on my face, nigga. Spray me down with that shit," I beg.

As he stands up, I begin to nibble on his nut sack, while I jacked his slack.

"Aggghhh, here it comes. Awww shit."

I open up wide. Spurts of hot dick milk splatters my face, leaving me coated in cum.

"Gawd damn. Shit, girl. Whoooo." T Fatts staggers and falls back onto the couch. I smack my lips. I take my hands and rub his cum into my skin, like it's face cream.

Both he and KC look at me as if I'm a goddess. If I am, I'm the goddess of dick sucking.

"Now that both of y'all have had yours, when is a bitch going to get her pussy slayed," I ask.

The two of them spend the next thirty minutes fucking me into oblivion. As we rest, I hear Tyra taking dick from Karl all the way in the living room. So, of course, I want to try his shit out.

I convince them to take the show into the bedroom. As we walk in, we see Tyra with her feet planted flat on the bed, squatting over Karl's long curved dick, dropping her ass and making it clap. I watch as her ass jiggles and shakes, making my pussy wet with anticipation. I wonder what that curve dick do?

"Damn. That pussy looks good," KC says, causing Tyra and Karl to stop momentarily.

Tyra looks back and bites her lip. "Well, come get you some."

KC climbs aboard the bed and Tyra repositions herself, laying flat against Karl's stomach. I watch as they get in position. Tyra reaches behind her, grabs Karl's curved hook and places him at the center of her anal ring.

"Awww shit," she cries as the head splits open her asshole, inch by inch. Her shit box is stuffed to capacity.

I desperately need to taste some dick. I make T Fatts stand at the foot of the bed and drop to my knees. While I watch Tyra get double stuffed, I eat T Fatts alive.

"Oh fuck. A bitch feels full," Tyra screams as they begin to pick up the pace.

I rub my clit as I gobble T Fatts's cock. With his hands on my head and my eyes on Tyra, I get my face fucked unmercifully. Balls slap against my chin as I watch and listen to Tyra scream out her release.

"Ohhh fuck. Please, Jesussss. Oh my, I'm cummmiiinnngg."

KC pulls out and I get a bird's eye view of Tyra squirting cum all over Karl's nuts, while his dick is still lodged between her cheeks.

My body shakes violently as I cum right here on my knees. I feel T Fatts dick harden and his balls twitch. I wait hungrily for his sack to empty so I can drink his sweet cock milk. He didn't disappoint. My mouth fills and empties with each gulp. Now I crave Tyra's cum. Once I know T Fatts is useless, I get up and approach Tyra on my hands and knees.

With Karl still stroking out her asshole, I begin to slurp on her clit, playing with Karl's balls in the process. Every so often, I pull him out, suck on his slimy cock, then put it back in her ass.

Yeah, you might call me a nasty bitch, but I guarantee you, one night with me and your man will never be satisfied with you again.

The five of us spent the next three hours fucking and sucking in all types of different variations. By the time they left for their dice game, my pussy was swollen and my asshole was on fire.

I looked at Tyra, spread eagle, with her pussy hole blew open, and I smiled. If a bitch pussy can't close, that means she got done right. I hear my phone ring and I force myself out the bed to go answer it. I notice it's Bobby calling.

"Hello," I answer irritated.

"Hey, babe. What time are you coming home? My mom called. She says she needs me to grab some groceries for her."

I want to say *fuck your mom,* but instead, I say, "We're almost through over here. I'll be home in about twenty minutes."

"A'ight, baby. I'll see you then. I love you."

"I love you, too," I mumble, before getting off the phone.

I go into Tyra's closet and grab my hoe bag that I keep at her house. It has hygiene products with extra panties and bras. I take a shower and head on home. Even though I was royally fucked, I still might let Bobby suck on my pussy until I go to sleep.

***

Charllessa Johnson

I stare at the clock in my office, 4:58. Two minutes and counting until quitting time. I make sure all my paperwork is properly signed and stored away. I look through my office window and see employees buzzing about, like worker bees, trying to get everything done before the Queen emerges. My mind flashes. I see images of what I think DaVon would look like naked.

I imagine him having a nice long, wide cock that will have me creaming and screaming his name. My phone buzzes. I look down and see a text from my husband, letting me know that he made it home, but he's about to head back out with Deacon Cooper and won't be back until later. *Yeah right.*

More likely, he was on his way to go have sex with some woman, who didn't do a thing for him. A woman who didn't give him two beautiful children. A woman who's sex game probably paled in comparison to mine, but for some reason, he couldn't resist.

I don't even dignify the text with a response. Instead, I grab my purse, as Jessica pokes her head in my office. "Well, everything's done, boss lady? If you don't have anything else for me to do, I'm bout to bounce."

"Naw, Jess, you're good to go," I reply as I turn the lights off in my office. I'm usually the last one to leave, so I don't make it to the parking lot until 5:30.

I'm not surprised to see DaVon is the only one in the lot, besides me. I spot him on the hood of his cherry red 2023 Mustang GTO.

"Nice car," I remark as I open my driver side door.

"Follow me," is all he says as he jumps in his Stang and we take off. I'm curious as to where we are headed because we have passed up numerous motels. At the end of the day, I'm not tripping as long as the dick is worth the drive.

After twenty minutes of driving, we arrive at a set of luxury apartments on Richmond Ave. I follow behind him as he punches in his gate code. We park, and ten minutes later, we're walking into his stylish and fully furnished apartment.

"Nice apartment," I comment as I take a seat.

"Would you like something to drink?" he asks.

"Uhh. Sure, why not? What you got?"

He heads to the bar. "We have a wide variety."

"We?" I ask.

"Oh yeah, I stay here with my roommate, Jay. He's at his girl's house right now, so we don't have to worry about him," he explains.

"Do you have any Remy?" I ask.

"Matter fact, I do." He pours us both a shot and sits down across from me.

After a few minutes of chit chat, I cut to the chase. "Ok look, DaVon. I appreciate the hospitality. I really do, but I didn't come here to kick it. I came her to get fucked down. As you know, I'm a married woman, so I am on a time frame. Each time we do this, I need you to keep that in mind. Now, if you don't mind, I need you to show me to your bathroom. A lady needs to freshen up first. After all, I've been at work all day."

He gets up and shows me where the bathroom is located. I get in and make sure I scrub my most sacred areas. After applying Cocoa Butter lotion and my favorite fragrance, I come out the bathroom with only a towel on. DaVon greets me in nothing but a pair of black Cavalli boxers. That boy has the body of a Greek god, washboard abs with the v cut. My coochie begins to drip honey, and I know I'm in for a great ride.

He leads me into his room. With black curtains over the windows, the room is completely devoid of light, but I can still make out the outline of his dick, once he sheds the boxers.

I sit on his bed, still wrapped in a towel, with my hands around his fat, warm meat as it grows to my touch. I dip my head and scoop the tip of his cock into my mouth. Feeling the smooth velvet skin slide across my tongue, I shake my head like a pit when it locks on to an opponent. I lock on the dick, sucking hard, making my cheeks cave in.

"Oohh shit. Yessss. Suck that dick," he moans for the first of many to come. I begin to bob my head, while turning slightly to the left, then to the right. When I feel his slab is hard as concrete, I pull back, allowing it to fall from my mouth.

I take the towel off, lay flat on the bed with my legs wide and my soul opens up. I spread my lips apart and watch as he guides his stiff rod into the mouth of my slick, wet coochie. I feel the first four inches and know he's about to cause some damage.

With my hands on my calves, holding my legs open, DaVon deep strokes and pounds my kitty until my cum bubbles and runs down the crack of my ass.

I cry out, "Ohhh my Laawwrrddd. Shiittt," as my coochie creams all over his cock. My breast swings wildly as he continues to beat my box.

Squish. Squish. Squish. Squish. My cat is so wet and sloppy.

DaVon begins to tremble. I feel his dick jump within my womb.

"Aghhh. I'm bout to cum. Where you want it at? Where?" He pulls out and barely catches his nut in time.

I don't answer. Instead, I open up my mouth, and he knows exactly what I desire.

The first spurt hits my nose, but the second finds its target. My lips and tongue are drenched in cock snot. I grab his dick and squeeze him between my lips, pulling every ounce of cum from his loins. I suck his head like a granddaddy crawfish. I lick the side of his shaft. I lick under his balls. I even lick his inner thighs and I'm still hungry for more of his baby batter. He steps back, admiring me for what I am, *a cock crazed cougar!*

After he regains his composure, he begins to put back on his boxers.

I bite my bottom lip. "We're not done yet. Are we?"

He looks at me, chest heaving. "Of course not. I just need to get a drink real quick. Do you want one?"

"No, thank you, but hurry back. Remember, time frame."

DaVon leaves me in this dark room, coochie saturated, begging to be stuffed some more. I reach between my legs and keep my kitty occupied. He returns a few minutes later. Even though it's dark, I can still tell he's changed his boxers. Now, he has on black Fendi boxers. I think that it's peculiar, but hey.

With my legs still splayed open, coochie on display, Davon removes his boxers and crawls between my legs. He begins by kissing my inner thighs, sucking then biting on each spot of flesh he touches. Chills run up my spine.

He sucks on each one of my engorged sex lips, smacking as he pulls them into his mouth. It sounds like he's drinking a bowl of soup. I wind my hips as I feel his tongue slide between my folds, and then enter the same place his dick had just been a short time ago.

"Yesssss. Eat that coochie, baby. Make momma cum in your mouth."

DaVon attacks my pearl, sucking gently while flicking the tip of his tongue across its surface.

I arch my back, grab his ears, and hold on for dear life. My orgasm starts in my toes and works it way up.

His tongue moves in figure eights. He takes one thumb and slides it in my cunt, and plugs my booty hole with the other. My coochie erupts.

"Ohhh Lawrd Jesssuuus," I cry out as DaVon sucks my clit, while twisting his thumbs. The sensation has me delirious. I try to close my thighs, but he snatches them back open, refusing to release his hold.

"Ohh, baby, pleaaasseee. I can't take no more," I howl, but he isn't listening.

He lightly bites on my clit and I come harder than before. My essence squirts against his chin. DaVon tells me to turn over. I do as I'm told. He places me face down with a pillow under my stomach. I feel my cheeks separate and spread open. Something wet slides up and down my sweaty crack. I think he's looking for some back door action, but after rubbing his head up and down my slit, he drops his dick off into my coochie.

I don't know if I'm tripping, but his cock feels wider than before. My walls grip and pull at him. With a thumb lodge in my butt, he rides me hard. My cheeks jiggle and shake as he digs me out.

"Oh. Oh. Oh. Oh," is all I can utter as I cum again. My box is too wet, I begin to queef.

My face is buried into the mattress. "Gawd damn this some good ass dick." I can't help but to give him props as he continues to carve my coochie to shreds. DaVon is writing his name on my walls.

"Oh shit. Awww. Here it cums. Here it cums. Oh shit," he announces.

I'm too exhausted to move. I look back and say, "On my ass. Put it on my ass."

He pulls out, but instead of nutting on my cheeks, he pushes the head of his cock into my ass and fills it with gooey goodness. I'm so exhausted, I can't do anything but lay there as his sperm bubbles out, dribbles down my crack, flows through my sex lips, and creates a puddle beneath me.

I pass out and was probably sleep for a few minutes, until I heard DaVon coming back into the room. *Damn. When did he leave?* Still on my stomach spread eagle, I feel him get back in bed. *Hell naw. This boy gots too much stamina.*

He grabs me by the hips and pulls me back until I'm on my hands and knees. I feel his dick rest between my cheeks as he reaches under me and diddles my clit. I bite my lip and prepare for the sudden discomfort I was sure to experience.

I look back at him. "I don't want it slow. If you gone fuck me in my ass, then fuck me hard and fast."

He pushes in and I grit my teeth. Inch by glorious inch, I feel him bore through my rectum.

His balls tap against my pearl and I know he's all the way home. I feel like I need to shit. I brace myself as he pulls back and does exactly as I asked him to, fucking me hard and fast. "Fuck. Fuck. Fuck. Shit. Shit. Shit," I scream as I cum in waves. People don't think you can cum out your asshole. Let me tell you first hand, my asshole lubes and skeets all over his cock as he keeps on pounding.

"Shit," he yells as he pulls out, forcing me to turn around and catch the last nut of the day. Not much comes out, but I make sure I still leave him spotless. What? If you expect a man to eat your ass, then it better be clean. And if it's clean enough for him, then it's clean enough for me.

Thoroughly exhausted and drained, we lay in bed trying to catch our breath. I look at DaVon put on his silk Cavalli boxers and I smile.

"Boy, you got some out of this world sex game. A woman can definitely get used to that."

He smiles and then compliments me on how I took the dick like a seasoned pro.

"Can I take a shower before I leave?"

"Of course," he answers. While in the shower, I think about everything that just took place. I have to admit, that might have been the best sex I ever had in my life. I'm definitely coming back for more of that.

I get dressed and head out the door, I notice a picture of DaVon and someone that looks exactly like him. "Who is that?" I ask, pointing to the picture. "Oh. That's my twin brother, JaVon. We call him Jay."

"Jay, like your roommate, Jay?"

"Matter fact, yeah, he's my roommate," he says slyly.

I smile. "Well, hopefully he'll be here next time so I can meet him," I say as DaVon walks me to the door.

"Yeah, most likely he'll be here," he replies as I step out and he closes the door behind me.

I walk to my car, still sore from a good ole fashion bait and switch. I knew something was off about the whole thing, but to be honest, now that I've fucked both brothers, I'm not going to want it any other way.

I look at the time, 9:15pm. *Damn. Time flew by.* I start the car and head back home. I hope Lucas gets satisfied tonight because my coochie's closed for repairs.

***

Rev. Lucas Johnson

As I lay up in the motel room and wait on her, I can't help but to feel a little bit guilty about what I'm about to do. She and I have been seeing each other for a while now. I know it's wrong on so many levels, but I can't stay away. The pussy is excellent. The head is superb. Plus, she knows all types of freaky ass tricks in the bedroom. Hopefully, she won't ever discover what I'm planning.

I hear the door knob twist and she enters the room. "Heyyy sweetie," she says as she rushes in. I take a second to appreciate her essence, her beauty, her smile as she strips down to nothing. I'm already down to my boxers, so it's nothing for me to slip them off.

I lay back, stroking my dick as she gets on the bed and cat crawls between my legs. One thing I always loved about her is her passion for sucking dick. She places a pillow under my ass so I would be elevated. I open my legs up. She grabs a hold of my cock, stroking while she sucks on my balls. She grips it tightly and pulls upward, hard enough to make me raise my ass off of the bed.

"You know what I want," she declares.

I spread my legs and she dips underneath me. This time, spreading my ass cheeks so she can use the tip of her tongue to probe my asshole. She is the one woman, besides my wife, that can have me in this compromising position.

I feel her wet tongue caress my anal ring, and my dick grows another few inches. I feel her sucking, hear her slurping, and my toes curl. She is a stone cold freakazoid. I asked her once if she ever showed her husband how freaky she could be. She told me no, that she was scared to. Once a man sees his woman unleash a certain level of freakiness, he becomes self conscious and starts to question where she learned it from and if he is the only one enjoying it.

Once my salad was sufficiently tossed, she climbs aboard and rides me until she comes all over my dick and balls. We spend the next forty-five minutes making each other cum. Finally, she gets up and goes to the bathroom to freshen up.

While she's gone, I go in her purse and pull out her driver's license, social security card and checkbook. I take pictures of all the information I could, then send it to Lucky. He responds with a thumbs up emoji to let me know he received it.

After she returns from the bathroom, she explains that something has come up and that she will make it up to me.

"It's all good, baby. As always, I've enjoyed our time together."

She gives me a kiss and I wait fifteen minutes after she's left before I decide to leave. Now that the deed is done, I feel a lot better about my chances of survival. Then a thought crosses my mind. *What if Lucky doesn't pact fair? Or the check doesn't come when he says it will.* Naw, I've been knowing Lucky since the sandbox. Plus, he's an expert at this. He knows what he's doing.

My phone rings. I see it's a video of Sister Denise. I click to download. A video of Denise with her head stuffed between another woman's thighs pops up. The woman is gripping the sheets, writhing, twisting and turning as Denise sucks, slurps and devours her pussy.

My dick instantly bricks up. I look at the clock. Shit. It's almost 9:00pm. I go ahead and text Denise.
Me: R U still wit her?
Denise: She's eating me out right now.
Me: I'm on da way.

I know my wife will have a fit, but ain't no way I'm passing this up. I make a u-turn and head to the other side of town. Knowing Denise, she was at her cousins' apartment. Her husband thought her cousin was a devoted married woman. Little did he know, her cousin was the gateway for Denise. When she wanted to get loose and act a fool, that's where she went. If I'm lucky, I'll be able to pop both of them tonight.

***

Tammy Taylor
"Like I said, boo, it's going to be a surprise."
Slurp. Slurp. Slurp.
"Huh? Naw, I'm just sitting here watching TV, talking to you."
Slurp. Slurp. Slurp.
"That's probably the TV you're hearing."
Sluurrppp. I pull Mako's big, eleven inch, nutmeg colored cock out of my mouth as I struggle to talk to my lil side boo, Robert. It's not like I'm trying to disrespect him, it's just that, he called while I had my face stuff with a thug ass nigga's dick.

I sit up and jack him off slowly as I try to wrap up my conversation. "Look boo, all I need you to do is make sure you hide her phone the same night, before she heads out the door."

I feel Mako palm the back of my head, pushing me back into his lap. I did as instructed, stuffing him back in. The tip of his dick scrapes the back of my throat.

"Uh hmm. Hmm?" I mumble, as I try my best to answer Robert's questions.

I pull away and hold up one finger to let Mako know I just need one second.

"Yeah, boo. So we're all set? Remember, don't say nothing to no one. Ok, bye bye."

I hang up and throw the phone on the couch as Mako reaches for my head once again. With no protest from me, he had his monster cock back down my throat in no time. I was a beast on the head, but even I couldn't deep throat this nigga's dick. My eyes were watery, my cheeks were puffy and my lips were red as he clogged up my windpipe.

He pushes my head down, I struggle to breath. I slap and claw at his hand but he won't release his hold. I feel as though I'm about to pass out. He finally lets me go.

"Uggghhh, ughhh." I suck in great big gulps as I prepare to go back in.

Pushing my head back into his lap, Mako holds me in place as he fucks my mouth brutally. I become light headed. Choking. My oxygen supply is being stifled off. This is an enormous slab of cock. I pray he will cum soon, if not, I very well might choke to death. My pussy's on fire and my clit throbs like a broken ankle.

It seems as if Mako doesn't give a fuck if I died, as long as he gets his nut down my throat. I claw and scratch, praying he will allow me some reprieve. He grunts, groans and sweet deliverance. Hot cum singes the back of my throat and tongue as his balls finally empty.

As soon as I taste it, my own orgasm is triggered. My body shakes and trembles. I lock onto his cock with my lips and squeeze as my pussy implodes, skeeting cum all over the love seat. Rough and rugged is the only way Mako can get his rocks off.

The nigga's a six foot three inch, two hundred thirty-five pound beast in the streets. His copper tone skin and chestnut colored eyes would fool you, but Mako has a serious reputation as a Big Steppa. He fell out of Hunterwood Apartments, but has been terrorizing the city for years. Lucky for me, he was cool with my cousin Wacco.

Mako and I had been fucking around for about three months now. I was out on a date with this guy named Darius. We were at the movies, watching the new Black Panther flick, when Mako walks right up to me, talking bout he wants me, and any nigga standing in his way will get dealt with. Then the nigga had the audacity to stick his hand under my dress and slide his finger up and down my slit, pushing my panties all up in my crack.

I know he felt how soaked I was. My panties were sticking to my sex lips. The crazy thing about it, Darius was standing two feet away. Needless to say, I left with Mako right then, and later that night, he introduced me to his eleven inch monster.

Man, that boy was such a goon, the only way he got off was if pain and suffering was involved. When he hits me from the back, he wraps a belt around my neck and rides me like the Kentucky Derby. When I suck his dick, he makes sure he chokes me out, until he cums down my gullet. Sometimes the pain would transcend into one of the most intense orgasms I've ever had.

I struggle to catch my breath and my pussy vibrates and squirts small amounts of cum, as I lay back on the couch with my legs stretched open.

I look over at Mako. "Say, nigga. (He despises pet names) Everything is set for Friday. I will take care of my end, just make sure you and your boys take care of y'alls."

He grips the base of his dick and kneels between my open thighs While rubbing his dick head up and down my slit, he growls, "First of all, bitch, I'll always make sure my job's done. Just make sure the numbers are right."

A chill goes down my spine. This nigga legitimately scares me.

"Now, shut the fuck up and take this dick," he says, before slamming all eleven inches into my quivering cunt.

I cry out in pain as I feel that nigga all in my throat. With my legs pushed back, the only protection I had was to place my hands against his stomach to stop the abuse.

He reaches up with both hands, grips my throat and squeezes the oxygen from my body. I begin to see spots, but my pussy feels like a volcano that's about to erupt. I pray that if I die, I don't go to hell as Mako carves up my inside. Tears fall from my eyes as I have another earth shattering orgasm. I black out.

I wake up to Mako slapping me with what feels like a soggy banana. I open my eyes and see it isn't a banana at all, It's his semi erect dick. "Let me find out your ass can't take no dick," he smugly comments.

"It ain't the dick, nigga. Your ass wanna choke a bitch till she pass out. What you expect?" I reply defiantly. I'm not about to let the nigga throw shade on my sex game.

"Yeah. Yeah. Well, finish what you started."

I shake my head, grab his limp member, caked with my dry nut, and begin to lubricate him with my tongue. I take a deep breath. *Lord knows I'm bout to need every ounce of it.*

Yolanda Cooper

I pull into my driveway, see my husband's SUV, and instantly feel guilty. By all accounts, he's a good man and treats me well. I think about Ja'Quell and my body begins to tingle. It's something about a street nigga that does something to me. I enjoy being treated like a queen but sometimes a woman needs to be treated like a slut.

While I sit in my driveway, I text Ja'Quell.

Me: Hey big head. U busy?
He responds almost immediately.
Ja'Quell: Naw. I'm just at home kicking back.

Me:I thought bout what you said. I wanna spend some time wit u 2 talk bout it. When r u free?
Ja'Quell: Available right now
Me: Can't. Already home
Ja'Quell: I'ma B tied up next couple days. How bout we spend Saturday 2gether. I got a bidness meeting that night, but after that we can spend the night 2gether before I go back to the A.
Me: Bet C u then.
Ja'Quell: 4 Sho

I erase the thread from the conversation and put the phone back in my purse. I notice the Perc's I just purchased and contemplate throwing them away. Unbeknownst to my husband, I started back taking prescription meds. It started a while back. I had a minor car accident and had sprained my wrist.

Then I began popping them even when my wrist felt better. I just love the way they make me feel. Plus, when I'm on them, sex is ten times more pleasurable. I get less inhibited. I begin to do things I enjoy doing, but are reluctant to when I'm sober.

I scoop the little baggie of pills, place them in my bra and head inside. I walk in and see DC in the living room watching TV. He has on a white wife beater and some red and black gym shorts.

I try not to, but my eyes travel over his crotch, searching for his print.

He looks up and says, "pops is in the shower".

I stand motionless for a few seconds. I want so bad to taste his thick chocolate stick and for him to fuck me from the back as he calls me all types of nasty bitches and hoes. I need the type of dick only a certified street nigga can deliver.

Don't get me wrong, Dennis was a street nigga, but now, he's older and has tempered his edge. DC was still knee deep in the streets and still possessed that rage needed to fuck a bitch like me into a coma.

Sensing my trepidation, DC looks up and smirks. He squeezes his cock through the fabric of his gym shorts and I see his snake come alive. I watch as it grows until it's too big to stay confined. He reaches into his shorts and out flops his massive cock.

It baffles me on how the son can have a bigger dick than the dad. My kitty quivers and leaks down my thighs. I wet my lips with my tongue as I watch DC slowly jack his cock three feet away from me, while his dad is less than twenty feet away, taking a shower. Pre cum forms at the tip and my mouth salivates. I don't think I've ever craved to have a cock in my mouth so bad in my life.

"Just five minutes," he begs, as he sits there stroking.

My feet begin to move on their own. It's like I'm being hypnotized. My heart pounds in my chest. What if Dennis comes out and sees me on my knees with his son's dick in my mouth? The risk and fear of getting caught makes my clit pitter patter.

Just as I was about to drop to my knees, my husband calls from the room. "DC, do you still got some more weed?"

DC stuffs himself back into his shorts, while I make a beeline to the kitchen.

"Uhh. Yeah, I think I do, pops. Wassup, you trynna blow one?"

I hear Dennis respond. "Hell yeah. I'm trying to go that way before Yolanda comes home."

DC looks at me inquisitively. I make my way back to the front door.

"Shit, I think that's her pulling up right now." I hear DC say as I close the door then hop into my car.

I sit here, trying to catch my breath. "Bitch. You need to get a grip on yourself. You have a wonderful marriage. You bout to fuck all that shit up. What the hell is wrong with you?" I chastise myself as I grip the steering wheel.

I have been flirting with danger for some time now. DC and Ja'Quell were definitely not helping matters at all. I can't help what my pussy craves. I love my husband, but this isn't about love. It's simply pure primal need. I gather myself, pop me a Perc to calm my nerves, and head back into my home for the second time tonight.

This time, when I entered, my husband and his son were both sitting down watching TV. I notice the bag of weed on the coffee table, with some rolling papers beside it.

"Hey, baby," my husband greets me.

"Hey," I respond, not trying to make eye contact. Guilt consuming me.

"You trynna blow one with us?" DC asks as I shuffle by.

"Oh naw. She don't do drugs," Dennis answers for me.

"Oh that's good then," I hear DC state as I make my way into the bedroom.

I take another shower and prepare myself for bed. I know Dennis is going to want some when he comes in. He always does when he smokes some good weed.

About forty-five minutes later, Dennis crawls into bed, sniffing at my pussy. The Perc's have me geeked and freaked out. As I think about his son, I show my husband some of my inner freak that I've kept locked away. By 2am, he's out like a light and snoring like a Grizzley bear. I lay wide awake, thinking. The Perc's have my pussy percolating.

Even though my cunt is content, I still hunger for dick. With greed taking ahold of me, I slide out of bed, making sure not to wake Dennis up. I tiptoe through the house butt naked, until I arrive in front of DC's bedroom door. *This is it, the point of no return.*

I twist the door knob. DC lays across the bed in nothing but a pair of black boxer briefs, snoring lightly. I can't believe I'm in this room, while my husband lays sleeping in our marriage bed. I creep forward, standing over DC as he sleeps. I reach out and cuff his dick through the fabric.

His eyes instantly shoot open as he grabs my forearm. My heart skips. DC stares into my eyes for a few moments before he releases his grip, allowing me to fish his cock out. His meat feels so hot in my hands. My palms feel as if they're on fire, as I begin to stroke him slowly.

He starts to say something but I cut him short. "Shhh. Don't talk. Just let me get what I came for," I tell him as I lean over and slide him deep within my mouth.

"Shhhhiiitt. Fuck," he moans as I suck gently on his plum sized crown.

I place my hands at the base of his shaft and form a diamond, with his dick in the middle. I taste his essence on my tongue as his pre cum oozes from his piss hole. I begin to bob my head while at the same time popping my ass to the music in my head, just like the good ole days at the club.

My coochie wants so bad to ride his fat ass dick, but I don't want to risk it. Right now, it's all about eating his cum. DC scoots up, grabs a hold of my weave and wraps it in his fist. I know what's coming and I eagerly await it.

With my feet on the ground, bent over, ass in the air, DC tightens his grip and begins to fuck my mouth vigorously. I brace myself, popping my ass to each stroke as his enormous cock impedes my breathing. My pussy drips profusely.

"Eat this dick, you nasty bitch," he says and I cum instantly.

Small squirts shoot from my pussy and drip down my thick thighs. I can't remember the last time I came from sucking dick. I moan around his cock, trying to suck the soul from his tip. His body gets tense then begins to tremble.

"Aww shit. Here it cums, bitch. Here it cummmmsss," he growls and his ass lifts off the bed. His balls erupt and my mouth floods with cum.

I gulp down everything and keep sucking. He quivers, dick softens while still in my mouth. With a soft "pop," I pull it out and lick him clean. I kiss lightly on his balls as I talk to him.

Muah. "Long as we (muah) keep this (muah) between us (muah), you can have this anytime you want." Muah.

I tuck his dick back in his boxers and leave him in bed speechless. I creep back to my room, praying that my husband is asleep. I crack the door open. *He's still sleep.* I tiptoe past the bed and head for the bathroom to brush my teeth and gargle with mouthwash. Now that I've had a taste of DC's dick, I know things will never be the same. I love my husband and don't want to hurt him, but I have to have his son's cock in my life. *What am I going to do?* I drift off to sleep, *now* fully sedated.

Chapter 4
Wednesday

Lucas Jr.
"Jr, I don't know what you want me to say. Of course, I'm upset. You put, not only yourself, but both of us in danger. What if DC decides to hurt me to get at you? Huh? Then what?"

Amber was in rare form. It was a little after noon and we had been going at it ever since ten this morning.

"I already told you Amber, I apologize. It was stupid. I don't know what I was thinking, alright, but arguing bout it won't change shit. We need a solution." I don't know how many times I can tell her the same thing.

She looks at me and shakes her head. "I won't lie to my parents, Jr. If I ask Daddy for five thousand dollars, he's going to want to know what it's for. I will tell him the truth and he's not going to give it to me," she confesses.

That's one thing I hate about Amber. She has to take the moral high road with everything.

"Why the fuck would—? You know what? Fuck it," I scream in frustration. It feels as if she's working against me instead of with me.

I go to our mini bar and fix myself a stiff shot. I need something to help calm my nerves before I say something or do something stupid. I'm thinking about hitting Alexis up and seeing if she will shoot me the bread, but I decide not to. I haven't had the chance to put that dick on her yet and the chances of her giving me the money without that, is slim to none.

By now, I was officially tuning out everything Amber was saying, but that didn't deter her from saying it. With my hands over my face, I shake my head and try to drown out the noise.

I didn't even realize she was standing next to me until she slapped me on the shoulder. "Are you ignoring me, Jr?"

I look at her with confusion. "Huh? Naw, I'm not ignoring you."

"What did I just say then?" She asks.

"You just asked me if I was ignoring you. Duh," I retort.

"Not that, stupid. Before that?"

"Look, Amber, I'm not trying to argue bout this shit. I asked for your help because you're my girl and I thought I could depend on you before anyone else. Obviously I was wrong. Now, can you please allow me to sit and think for a second?"

She looks like she wants to say something, but instead, she gets up and heads in the kitchen.

"What would you like for lunch?" she calls out.

I think about it. Even though I'm really not hungry, I reply, "Fish and fries." I hear the cupboards open and close as she grabs the necessary utensils.

I sit and worry. I honestly don't know what to do. I debated on calling pops and seeing if he could talk to Deacon Cooper. Maybe the deacon could talk to DC about letting me make it. Hell naw. I can't do that. That's like the ultimate bitch move. Then, I still might owe him at the end of the day.

All types of scenarios play in my mind, but none of them seem plausible. I pick up my phone and text Alexis.

Me: I know we got plans 2 C each other Friday, but I was wondering could we c each other now.

Alexis: Friday is my only off day this week, so no, boo. Friday is the soonest I can meet. Something wrong?

I want so badly to tell her I need sum help but my pride won't let me. Well, at least not until I drop off that dick.
Me: Nothing wrong. Just feenin for sum of dat.
Alexis: (smiling face emoji) Well, let me send u something to hold u over.

Thirty seconds later, a video arrives. I open it and up pops a pussy so fat, it looks like a ten dollar hamburger. I watch as a pink vibrator slides between her folds, dancing on her clit until white cum pours out of her pussy hole. I hurry up and send the video to my email and erase all of the evidence.

I place my phone on the coffee table and pick the remote control up, flipping through the channels. Next thing I know, there's a loud knock at the door.

Amber peeks her head out of the kitchen. "Are you expecting somebody?"

I shake my head and get up to go answer. I look through the peephole. My heart drops.

Derrick Cooper aka DC

As I pull up to Jr's apartment complex, I finish giving Blade the whole run down. How I fronted Jr. the pack. How I had him followed and had his car broken into to steal the pack back. I even tell him how Jr's girl's ass and pussy is so fat, that a nigga has to get a piece of it.

Blade can't stop laughing. "So what's up, Blood? Once you pop that, is you gone let a nigga get a sample or what?"

I look at the nigga like he's stupid or something. "Nigga, of course. You know I ain't cuffing no bitch."

"Already," he responds as we find a spot to park. We hop out, head to their door, and knock. At first, I think they ain't home, but then I remember seeing Jr's Charger, so I knock even harder.

Finally, he opens up. "Wh- what's up, DC?"

"What you mean what's up? Nigga, I came to check on the progress on my paper."

"But you, you said I had until Su Sunday. I'm still working on it," he stammers.

"First off, nigga, I ain't trying to stand out here and talk about it, so let me in so we can talk about it further."

He reluctantly steps aside and we walk in. As soon as we cross the threshold, the aroma of fried fish hits my nostrils and I immediately get hungry. I look to the left and observe Amber in the kitchen. She sees me and instantly adverts her eyes, but not before I catch her blushing.

Blade and I take a seat in the living room. As Jr. decides to join us, I remark, "Damn, Amber. That sure smells good. Can a brother get a plate?"

She pokes her head from out the kitchen and says, "Of course. What type of host would I be if I didn't offer? What about your friend?"

Blade quickly answers, "Hell yeah, a nigga wants some of that." I'm not sure if she caught his meaning.

"So, Jr., what kind of progress are we making on that bread?" I ask. I notice he keeps wiping his hands, so I know he's nervous as hell.

"Uhh. To be honest, DC, I got about twelve hundred dollars on me right now, but I got some things lined up this week, so I should have that to you by Sunday."

I smile at that. "So. You got twelve hundred dollars on you right now?"

He nods his head "yes." I stick out my hand. He gets up, heads to the bedroom and returns with the money.

I count it out. "Appreciate it, nigga. I'm pretty sure you'll have the other thirty-eight by Sunday."

He nods his head as he sips on his glass. Couple minutes later, Amber comes out with the plates. I contemplate making her serve me first, but I let Jr. have this one. I take notice of what she has on. Some green boy shorts, that wasn't doing much to hide that fat ass monkey or the two basketballs she was dragging around.

Her nipples are poking out her top. I know she's thinking about this heavy ass dick she had in her hands a couple days ago. She sits down next to Jr, as she eats her plate of fish.

"So, Amber, you didn't have to work today?" I ask.

"Oh no. I usually have Wednesdays off."

"Where you work at?" Blade asks.

Amber gives a look of uncertainty.

"You don't have to answer that, Amber," I assure her.

She thinks about it. "Naw, it's alright. I work at the resource center downtown."

"Oh yeah? My relative Brenda works down there," Blade informs her.

She perks up at hearing that. "Brenda? Light skin, short, with the pretty eyes? That's your people?"

"Yeah. That's my mom's sister's daughter," Blade tells her, and just like that, the tension is lifted. After we get done eating, Amber puts away the dishes and excuses herself.

"Let me let you men handle y'all's business. I'm pretty sure y'all have a lot to discuss," she says as she walks toward the back. I watch that ass jiggle with each step, and my dick begins to rise.

After ten minutes of bullshit conversation, I tell Blade that I'm headed to the restroom.

Last time I came over, I seen how the set up was. You could either enter the bedroom from the hallway or you could enter it from the bathroom.

I entered the bathroom from the hallway and locked the door behind me, even though I was confident that I would not be interrupted. I crack the door open and see Amber bent over, putting panties in the bottom drawer. Even from this distance, I can see her pussy swallow up the material of her boy shorts.

I groan to myself as I stalk her down. I grab her by the waist. She jumps in shock as she feels my dick against her ass cheeks.

"Oh my God, DC. What are you doing? You know Jr.'s in the living room," she whispers angrily.

I bite her ear and growl, "Fuck Jr., this gone be my pussy from now on. That nigga owes me and I want you as payment." I grind my dick into her ass and she emits a moan.

"DC. P-please. We can work something else out," she pleads as I push her forward, forcing her to hold on to the dresser.

"I want you to keep your hands on the dresser until I tell you what to do with them," I order, as I yank her boy shorts down to her knees. I open up her ass cheeks and lick up and down her crack. Her body trembles and she moans again. Damn. She's got a greasy ass pussy!

"Pleeaasee don't do this, DC," she begs.

Smack. I smack her on her ass and watch her cheeks jiggle.

"Bitch, shut the fuck up. I told you, this my pussy now. I'll do what I want with it until the debt is paid. Until then, this shit belongs to me."

Smack. I slap the other cheek. She grips the dresser even tighter.

I stand up and take my sweats and boxers off. I look in the mirror and see the look of anticipation on her face. She sees what's in store for her. I let my dick rest between her cheeks as I talk to her.

"You want this dick, then put it in yourself."

She reaches back, and with her small hands, she finds me and grips it tightly. She positions my cock at the mouth of her pussy.

"Good girl," I whisper, before I slam it home.

"Agghhh fuucccckkk," she screams out as I open her wider than she has ever been before. I grab a hold of her wide hips and dick her down with strong powerful strokes. She reaches back to try and get me to ease up. No dice. I slap her hand away.

"Bitch. What. I. Tell. You? Put. Your. Hands. Back. On. The. Dresser," I growl as I gut her open.

She cries out. "Ohh my Gawwddd. Shit."

Her walls choke at my dick and I can tell, she just nutted all over me. I look down to verify, and yes, white cum cakes my dick like icing on a donut. I keep pounding.

Her knees bang against the dresser drawers. Her ass cheeks clap and slam against my abs. I pull her off the dresser and push her onto the bed, never once breaking our connection.

While I'm still lodged in her, I have her lay flat, closing her legs tight. My thighs rest on each side of hers. I grab her by the neck like an unruly pit and I dig in. Nothing but her ass and the bed moves with each stroke.

"Bitch, I'ma fuck this pussy whenever I want, however I want, with whoever I want."

She hears that and her cunt starts to contract. She cries out again. "Ohh fuck. Christ. I'm cummminnnggg."

I look down and see what looks like piss, squirting from the back of her pussy. Never once do I let up. I need to make sure this pussy has my name on it.

I pull her by the waist, but keep her face in the mattress. I lift one leg up and hit that shit at an angle. Nice and steady strokes, taking the time to conserve my energy. I spread her right cheek apart, watching my sledge hammer knock down her right wall.

"Ohh shit. What the fuck are you doing to me?" she cries out as another violent seizure takes ahold of her.

I pull out until just the tip is in. "You want some more of this dick?"

"Yesss," she whispers.

"Bitch, I can't hear you. Do you want some more of the dick?"

"Yes," she cries out, louder this time.

"Well beg for this dick then," I order her.

"Pleeeasse, DC. Give me that dick. Please."

With a smile on my face, I slam back in, balls tapping her clit. She cums again. I slide back, letting my shit fall out.

"Turn around and lick this motherfucka clean."

She obeys, like I knew she would. I stand and watch her take ahold of my dick in her tiny little hands. She licks and sucks, trying her best to handle what I have to offer. I know, in due time, she'll be able to master it.

"Lay back," I instruct her.

She scoots her ass back, then lays flat with her legs wide open. I stare at her sex lips. They look battered and bruised. Her cunt is bright red and leaking fluid.

"You better keep them motherfucking legs open," I warn. I slide back in and her breath catches in her throat. I grab her shoulders and work my hips at a steady pace, giving her just enough dick, with each stroke. I whisper in her ear, "Is this pussy mine?"

She nods her head, but still says, "yesss."

"Who does this pussy belong to?"

"Ohhhh shit, baby. You."

"And who am I, bitch?" I put a little more power behind the strokes now to let her know who runs this pussy.

"Ohhhh. DC. This pussy belongs to DC," she cries out as her body is trembling.

"Who's Jr?" I ask, picking up the pace. She acts like she doesn't want to answer. Now I'm back to beating her twat in. Her pussy is so saturated, I hear it squelching as I break her back. "Bitch, who is Jr.?"

"Ohh shit. Fuck Jr. Fuck Jr. Fuckkkk Juunnniiiiooorrr," she yells as she cums harder than she ever has in her life. I pull out and start to jack off. She doesn't need any instructions. She positions herself with her head back and her mouth wide.

"Agghh. Agghh. Gawd damn," I howl as I shoot across her face and all over their bed.

I sit back breathlessly, watching her lick my dick clean. She sees me watching her and puts her head down. I pick her chin up.

"Why you got your head down?"

"Cause I've never cheated on Jr.," she admits. "I love that nigga and, and I know shit will be fucked up between us now."

I don't really care about their relationship status. Only thing I care about is making sure that fire ass pussy is on demand, so I don't respond.

Instead, I say, "Look. I'm bout to go back out there and my nigga Blade's about to come in here. I want you to show him the same love you just showed me."

Amber looked genuinely hurt. I guess she thought what we did was some exclusive shit.

"Damn. That's how you gone do me? Y'all about to run a train on me, while my boyfriend's in the living room? Does Jr. know this shits going on?" She had the nerve to ask.

I'm usually not the one to dirty mack anybody but, "Check this out, Amber. Jr.'s a bitch. Straight up. To be honest, I could have fucked you in front of him and he wouldn't have done shit about it. If it wasn't for the fact that he can't pay his debt, this would have probably never happened. But I'm glad it did. You got some grade A pussy and I plan on hitting that on the regular." She looks away, probably ashamed because she knows I told the truth. "Tell me you don't want this dick again, and me and my nigga will leave right now." She remains quiet. "I thought so," I say as I get up to leave.

Before I go back in the bathroom, I look back at her. "I will always keep it real with you, Amber. The real is this. I like to have fun with my bitches. That means threesomes, trains, swaps or whatever. You can keep your boyfriend, but when you're with me, that's what's going on."

I walk out of the bathroom and see Jr. and Blade sitting quietly. Blade has his Glock .40 sitting on the coffee table.

Jr sits quietly with what looks like tears forming in his eyes. No doubt, he heard me putting the pound game down on his bitch. *Oh well.*

I gave the Blade the head nod to let him know he's next. He disappears into the back. I sit down next to Jr., smelling like his girlfriends' pussy. The nigga is either really mad or really scared because he can't stop shaking. I grab Blade's Glock and sit it on my lap. I don't need the nigga getting any bright ideas.

Fifteen minutes later, I hear Amber moaning as Blade's pounding her back out. Each time she screams, Jr flinches. He balls his hands up into a fist while we listen to his girl scream, "Fucckk. That's my ass. You're fucking my ass." I got to give it to him though, he sure knows how to pick a fine piece of ass.

***

Lucus Jr.

I watch DC get up and go to the restroom. My gut tells me something isn't right.

"Say, mane. Where'd you meet your girl at?" Blade asks me.

"Huh?" I hear the question but I'm not understanding the reason for asking.

"Your girl, Amber? Where'd you meet her at? I ain't gone front. The bitch bad," he has the nerve to say.

"We went to school together," I mumble as I keep counting the minutes that DC has been gone. My legs begin to bounce. I'm getting anxious. I get up.

"Where you going?" He asks.

I look at him with indignation. "I'm gonna go check on my girl," I say with authority.

He reaches in his waistband and pulls out a gun. My heart drops to my nuts.

"Naw, homie. What you finna do is, sit right here and wait till she get done? Relax, she's a big girl, she can take care of herself."

With the gun in his right hand, he pats the sofa with his left, indicating where he wants me to sit. I've never felt so weak and powerless in my whole life. I hate myself for putting my girlfriend in this predicament.

Then I start to reason. Maybe I'm overreacting. Maybe, what I feel is taking place, isn't. I *need* DC to return soon. Ten minutes go by and I hear someone moan. I write it off as my mind playing tricks, until I hear it again. Then I hear the unmistakable sound of skin slapping, grunts and moans coming from the bedroom. My anger becomes inconsolable.

I swear to myself, DC will pay with his life for raping Amber. Tears well in my eyes as I hear her scream in agony. I look at the gun on the table and I contemplate making a move for it. *Fuck it.* If I get shot in the process, it would be better than having to sit here and listen to my girlfriend suffer.

Then I hear her scream out. "Fuck Jr." My heart shatters. I would have thought it was just my imagination, due to the stress of the situation, but not only does she say it again, but Blade makes a comment about it.

"Damn, homie. You ready to captain save that hoe and she screaming fuck you. Uhm. Uhm. Uhm." He shakes his head, as if to say, "That's a damn shame."

My whole body is numb. I can't believe what I'm hearing. I can barely breathe. I feel like I'm about to have a heart attack. I put my hands over my face and I allow my tears to fall. I want DC to just kill me and end the pain. I listen to their sex noises until it sound as if DC finally busses his nut.

Five minutes later, he emerges from the room with a smug look on his face. I want so desperately to go back there and confront Amber, ask her why she said what she said. Before I can move, Blade gets up and makes his way to the back. I close my eyes and try to shake the thoughts from my head. It's no way this shit is happening right now.

DC grabs Blade's gun off the table, and there goes any chance of retribution. I sit silently fuming as we listen to Amber's screams as Blade has his way with her, also. At that very moment, if I had a gun, I'd kill everyone in the house, including myself.

"Don't worry, dawg. I'm not gonna take your bitch from you. She's yours. I'm just gonna play with her from time to time."

I don't dignify his comment with a response. Instead, I sit back and plot my revenge. Everyone involved will pay, I vow. Twenty excruciating minutes pass until Blade emerges from the bedroom shirtless. "Ohhh weee, boy. That bitch got some A-1 snappa," he brags, as if I'm not sitting here. He slaps me on the back and I cringe.

DC stands up. "Well, Blade. Let's gone make a move," he says as they both make their way to the door.

Ten minutes after they depart, I sit motionless on the couch, too angry to confront Amber. I hear the shower running and I wait. She finally appears from the room in one of my Purple Label Polo shirts, with no panties underneath.

She slowly and timidly tip toes towards me. She sits down, folding her legs up under her. I still can't look at her.

"Look, baby, I'm so sorry, but I felt like I had no choice," she pleads. "I hope you know that I love you and I don't want this to be the end of us."

I take a deep breath and rationalize. None of this would have happened if it wasn't for my fuck up. I couldn't believe that Amber felt she had to do and say those things to protect us.

"Please, baby, look at me," she begs. "Say something."

She grabs my face. I struggle to look her in her eyes.

"Baby listen. We will get through this. Love conquers all. Just please don't hold what happened today against me."

I look her in her eyes. "I'm so sorry, baby. None of this would have happened if I didn't get that pack from him. It's me that needs forgiveness." Tears ran down my cheek as we both cried.

Tears soak through my Purple Label Polo as she held on to me until we both fell asleep in each other's arms.

***

Chelsea Johnson

Wednesday had finally arrived. As soon as I left school, I texted Deacon Cooper to make sure we were still on. He hurriedly texted me back to confirm.

Me: So what time u want to meet?
Dennis: R u going to be busy around 8-9?
Me: Well I'm bout to go shopping, which reminds me. Can I get an advance? (praying hands emoji)
Dennis: Well that depends.
Me: On what?
Dennis: How well you will perform 2nite.

Instead of texting him back. I send him a video of one of my greatest performances. I let this guy at my school named Dajuan record me sucking his dick. The only thing was, it had to be on my phone. I don't know if it was due to the fact I was on camera but he was shooting his load off in 1:37 flat. Deacon Cooper took a minute to respond, probably because he was watching it more than once. Finally, he pops back up.

Dennis: Send the app

I knew it. That's some of my best work. Ain't no way he would be able to deny me after seeing that. I sent him the app info, and two minutes later, I had five hundred dollars in my account. With what I'ma peel Bobby for later, this should make enough for a decent shopping trip.

By 6:00, I was pulling up to the Galleria. I spent a couple hours shopping, copping me a new Dior dress, some matching gold and black velvet pumps, and a new Fendi clutch. I contemplate getting my hair redone now, but once I have the good Deacon's dick down my throat, his hands will be all over my head, fucking up my hairdo. *Fuck that.*

Feeling hungry, I head to the food court to grab me some wings and fries. After ten minutes of eating, I catch the eye of a cute Hispanic dude, with his girlfriend next to him, ordering their food. I couldn't tell if she was cute or not, but I could tell she's black. I take a wing, stick it in my mouth and suck the meat off the bone suggestively.

He licks his lips. I know I have him. I nod towards the men's restroom, to let him know I would be waiting. Luckily, the men's restroom is deserted. I chose the stall that was furthest from the door, went in and waited. Less than five minutes later, I hear someone enter.

"Lookout, mami? Where you at?" He says in a South American accent.

I open the stall and wave him in. He comes in and shuts the door. I sit on the toilet and pull him towards me.

"What's your name?" He asks. I start to unbuckle his belt.

"I need to see the product before I buy it. So to speak," I say as I pull out his meaty cock. It wasn't the biggest, but it was definitely doable. I began to stroke it while I talked to him. "My name is Chelsea."

He moans as I continue to work his shaft. "Is that your girlfriend out there?" I ask.

"Sssshhh, yea. Yeah, that's my girl," he responds as I use my other hand to play with his nuts. I begin to jack his dick faster, my fist gripping his shaft like a python.

"Does she like sucking your dick? Does she like licking your nuts? Does she eat your cum like her favorite flavored ice cream?" His cock jumps in my hand.

"Agh. Agh. Agh. Agh," he groans as my hand moves with a blur.

"I see you like black bitches, huh? Well let me let you in on a secret. This black bitch right here, will eat the dick off your body, and then ask you for seconds!" I whisper while looking up at him.

His eyes shut tight, his mouth opens up as he howls. "Fuccckk. I'm cummmiinnngg."

I drop my head down, cover his cock with my mouth and accepted everything he had to give me.

"Hmmm, mmmhh," I moan around his dick as it twitches and jerks in my mouth. I pop him out and leave it hanging in front of me. I grab my phone. "Put your number in. I'll call you this weekend," I say while I'm face to face with his deflated dick.

We agree that he should leave the restroom first, but not before he makes me promise I'll answer when he calls.

I wait five more minutes until I emerge out of the restroom. I walk past his table as I make my way past the food court. I hear his girl say, "Damn, Juan, your food's almost cold." I smile and keep moving.

Once I leave the mall, I call the Deacon to let him know I was done shopping and needed to freshen up. He tells me not to worry about it, he's reserved a room for us and I can just meet him there. He also has reservations for a restaurant and wants to take me out. I don't understand why he would want to risk someone seeing us, but fuck it. He's paying to play.

I pull up at room 282. As I step in, I see shopping bags from Saks sitting in the bed. I pull the contents out and see a red, slip on, Michael Kors dress, with some red and gold Bottega heels. "Oh, he's definitely getting the fuck of a lifetime tonight," I tell myself as I hop in the shower.

By the time I get out, Deacon Cooper is sitting on the bed in a double breasted, navy blue suit and some Navy blue Gators.

"How'd you like the dress?"

"Are you kidding me? I love it, Deacon."

That puts a smile on his face. "Well, you're not a little girl anymore, you're a grown woman, so I figure you need to start representing yourself as one," he informs me. He looks at his platinum Yacht Master Rolex. "I'm going to wait in the car, we have reservations for 8:30. It's 7:50 right now."

"I'll be quick," I interject.

Dennis leaves me in the room to get dressed. I make sure I'm smelling good, looking good, and feeling even greater. I pop me a Molly before I leave the room. I know when I pop one, I become a whole nother monster, and tonight, I need to make sure that, besides his wife, I'm his go to when he opens up his wallet.

I slide into the passenger seat of his SUV. As soon as my body feels the A/C, a chemical reaction from the drug takes place. My clit begins to throb. My nipples are hard as granite. My body begins to heat up, despite the vents blowing snowballs. I squirm in my seat. I wore a thong because I know, once the Molly takes effect, my coochie will start to bubble and I will need something to catch the drip.

"Are you alright?" Dennis asks, obviously noticing that I keep fidgeting in my seat.

I rub my thighs. "Ssss. Yeah, baby. I'm sooo alright. I'm just a lil hungry." My mouth waters.

"Well, we'll be at the restaurant in about twenty minutes," he replies, clearly missing my true intent. I grab at his zipper.

"Twenty minutes is way too long. I need a snack." I fish his rod out of his slacks.

"Oh shit, Chelsea," he moans as I slip his flaccid dick between my lips. I suck him hard three times and his meat is fully erect. I grab the base, pull the excess skin back, and take him deep down my throat. "Ohhh shit. Suck that dick, baby girl." I bob my head, making sure I suck on the tip each time I get to the top. I reach between my legs and push my thong to the side so I can get at my clit. My shit is so wet, I know I'll be having to throw my panties away before we even make it to the restaurant.

I feel the car come to a stop and realize we must be at a light. I choke and gag a little as I attempt to deep throat all eight inches of his delicious, scrumptious cock.

Beep. Beep.

"What the—? Shit. Chelsea, don't move."

"Hmmm?" I mumble, mouth full of dick.

"Your dad's right next to us," he panics.

"Mmm hmm?" I know this nigga ain't just say that my dad's right next to us.

"A'ight, look. He wants me to wind the window down. Just keep doing what you're doing," he urges.

I do what I'm told. Sucking and slurping for all I was worth, while the Deacon winds the window down so he can talk to my dad.

***

Deacon Cooper
"Shit. Chelsea, don't move."

I'm sitting here getting the best head that I've gotten in a while and I hear a motherfucka laying on the horn. I look to my left and see my best friend's Escalade. He can't really see me because I'm behind tint, but he knows it's my whip, just like I know that's his.

He winds his window down and tells me to do the same. Shit. I got an idea. I tell Chelsea to keep doing what she's doing. Dad or not, ain't nothing bout to stop me from getting this top grade head. Plus, as long as her head is in my lap, he won't be able to see her below my window seal. Well, that's the plan anyway.

I wind the window down halfway. "What's up dawg? What's going on?" I feel Chelsea's spit drip down the side of my balls. I grip the steering wheel as she attempts to deep throat my whole cock.

I'm bout to head to Rays Gambling Shack on the south side," he tells me. "What you got going?"

I grunt, feeling Chelsea bury her head even further into my crotch. She's trying her best to trap by balls between her teeth, lightly biting down, while she sucks on each one. Goosebumps crawl up my spine. I can barely manage to speak. "Shit. Um. I'll probably. Probably, uhmm. Damn," I blurt out, while wincing.

"What's wrong with you, nigga?" He asks suspiciously.

"Dawg. My stomach's doing flips. I think I ate some bad pork this afternoon," I lied.

My balls are tight as hell and feel as if they're about to pop. She sticks my dick back in her mouth while massaging my sack.

My toes curl in my Gators. I'm praying the light turns green before... Before. "Ohhh shiittt," I grit my teeth as I explode in her mouth.

Just like a good little girl, she swallows every drop, just as her dad tells me, "A'ight, bro. Well, get you some rest or something. I'll catch up with you later tomorrow."

I nod my head and wind the window back up, just as the light turns green. Chelsea continues to suck gently, while I drive us to the restaurant. *Jesus. This girl will be the death of me.*

I've never met a woman who could suck cock like her. My heart is still beating at 100mph. Man, that was too close for comfort. I can only imagine what Lucas would do if he saw his precious little girl with eight inches of beef down her throat, especially if it's attached to his best friend.

"Damn, that was close," I tell Chelsea as I park.

"Shit, tell me about it." She has a smile on her face. Let me find out that shit turned her lil ass on. I open the door to get out, but she yells, "Wait."

I shut the door. "What's wrong?" She leans back in her seat, reaches under her dress and peels off her black laced thong.

"These motherfucka's are no more good," she states as she shows me how soiled they were. Her cum was all in the crotch area. So while I damn near had a heart attack talking to her dad, this lil bitch is gobbling my dick and bussin a fat ass nut. *Yeah, she is definitely going to be the death of me.*

After she reapplies her makeup, we head in and have a nice dinner. Well I do. Chelsea barely eats anything, but she's insatiable. She wants to crawl under the table and "finish the job," as she puts it. As much as I may have wanted her to, I was a regular at this establishment, and there is something else I want to do.

When we get back to the room, I let her have her way with me. Now, I'll be the first to admit, that young woman wore me out till exhaustion. She played with my flaccid dick, trying her best to get it back to full attention. I had came four times in two hours. It would be nothing short of a miracle, if she would be able to get a rise out of me.

I know I passed out because when I awoke, Chelsea was gone. I look at the clock, 12:15am. *Damn. My wife is going to kill me.* I jump in the shower to take a quick wash off. Ten minutes later, I'm rushing out the door, headed home to my wife and kid.

***

Rev. Lucas Johnson

I look at the watch. It's 8:15. I'm supposed to meet Lucky at 8:30. I pull up to the light at Wallisville and SouthLake Houston Prky. I look to my right and see Dennis' Yukon at the light. Beep. Beep. I honk the horn to get his attention. At first, I don't think he hears me. I roll my window down and wave at him. Finally, he lets the window down, but only halfway.

"What's up, dawg? What's going on?"

I can tell something isn't right with him. I'll put him on the same play with Lucky, once I see that it's successful. "What you got going on?" I ask.

He's about to answer but his face tightens and he looks like he's in pain. He tells me his stomach is fucked up due to something he ate earlier, so I let it go. The light turns green and I promise to catch up with him later.

Now I'm on the freeway headed to the South, but something about the conversation with Dennis keeps bothering me. I can't put my foot on it, but I can't shake it either.

Finally, I pull up to Rays off OST in 3rd Ward. Rays has been up and running for thirty years now. Some cats even say that the Mayor of Houston used to stay up in Rays, shooting craps, back in his younger days.

I park my Escalade next to Lucky's money green Maserati. I step out and make my way through the parking lot. I pass a black sedan, and can't help but to look inside, after I notice the car's rocking slightly.

Right there in the front seat, is an old high school friend of mine named Sheryl, with her head in the lap of a kid that looks young enough to be her grandson. I shake my head. No doubt, she was paying him off for a hit of crack or a shot of dope.

Sheryl was a widely known dopefiend, who dibbled and dabbled in just about any and everything. When she was younger, she was easily one of the top three baddest bitches in school. To be completely honest, she could have made a legitimate claim to have Charllessa beat back then.

When Sheryl was 17, she started messing with a thirty-four year old cat named Catfish from 4th Ward. Catfish used to pick her up after school in his candy red '84 "El Dog," taking her back to his hood and fucking her young brains out.

Rumors started to surface that Catfish had her smoking premo's and soon had her running trains with the young niggas out his hood, that went to school with us.

Once the word got out, Sheryl felt so ashamed that she dropped out of school and disappeared for a couple years. When she popped back up, she was a full blown addict, sleeping on the streets and turning tricks for nickel rocks.

I watch as lil man is pumping so hard into her mouth, the car is rocking as if they're having sex. Suddenly, he tenses up and unloads into her mouth. I shake my head and keep on pushing into the gambling shack.

As soon as I enter, I smell that familiar scent of stale smoke and green money. I see Lucky at the pool table, shooting craps. I make my way over.

"Bet two hundred dollars I hit six or eight before I hit five or nine," he tells another hustler named Jim Bo. Jim Bo puts the two hundred dollars on the table.

"That's a bet, lil nigga. All craps."

"Fa sho." Lucky rolls them and they land on ace deuce. Jim Bo picks up the money.

"Bet back?"

Lucky pulls out a knot. "Fuck it. Bet a band."

Not wanting to look like a chump, Jim Bo put down the thousand dollars. Luck looks up at me and smiles.

"Lucas, if you wanna get paid, better hop on the Lucky train." With that, he let's them fly. "Tre tre." Luck picks up the thousand dollars.

Now it was his turn to ask, "Bet back?"

Jim Bo reluctantly places another thousand dollars down. Lucky rolls again. This time, they land on "six deuce."

"Fuck," Jim Bo yells.

Lucky asks again, "Bet back?" Jim Bo waves him off.

"Just shoot nigga," he growls.

Luck picks the dice up, shakes them and says "Now the real. Two three, like Jordan." The dice tumble, flip and land on "ace four."

"Don't nobody move but me," Lucky screams out as he rakes everyone's money up. Once he has the table cleared, he sits the dice down and says. "Pass em," letting the next man in rotation get his shot off.

He nods towards the bar and I follow. "What's good, Luck? I see you still got a mean jumper with them dice?" We order some drinks.

"Yeah, you know, dice are like dope. It's all in the wrist." We receive our drinks. He takes a few sips, then begins.

"Look, I wanted to lace you up on the progress. I went ahead and shot that info you gave me to my people. They made sure they processed the application and they received an email this afternoon saying to expect the money by Saturday. *Thank you Jesus.* I tried to contain my excitement.

"So how much total?" I had to ask.

"They were able to utilize a few provisions, which allowed us to get even more. The loan will be two hundred eighty thousand. That's a hundred forty for each of us. I'll take care of the team off my end," he notifies me.

I pump my fist in the air. A hundred forty thousand for fucking a bitch and taking a picture of her info. *Only in America.* I shook Lucky's hand. "Bet. Just let me know when and where you want to meet up Saturday," I say as I make my way to the door.

"You ain't staying?"

I look back. "Not tonight. I need to head home and spend some time with the misses."

He laughs at that. My hands were shaking from pure adrenaline and excitement of a much needed pay day. I didn't even want any pussy. I went straight home for the first time in a long time.

Chelsea Johnson

I walk out the shower, expecting Dennis to be ready for another round, but much to my dismay, he's out like a light. Laid out, mouth open, drooling like a baby. I reach down, grab ahold of his dick, and squeeze. *Nothing.* The Molly has my pussy on fire. Only thing that will put it out is if I get stuffed with more cock.

I step outside to get some fresh air and hopefully cool down. As I walk down the stairs, I notice a red SUV swerve into the parking lot. You can tell by the "Drill Music" coming from the speakers, the occupants have to be young niggas. I stand on the steps, waiting to see who emerges.

Seconds later, all four doors open up, along with a cloud of smoke. It's hard to tell, but it looks as if all four of them are cute as hell, or at the very least doable. By the looks of it, it seems as if they are heading out somewhere, but rented a room for the night. Most likely, so they could have a place to bring their conquest for the night.

The Molly I popped earlier has my mind spinning with thoughts of letting all four of them have their way with me. Having all three of my holes stuffed while the fourth one waits his turn. I wait until they go inside the room until I make my way downstairs. With each step I take, I drip more and more in anticipation. I can hear my heart beating through my eardrums.

Knock. Knock. Knock. I knock on the room door and wait. It doesn't take long for one of them to open the door.

"Uhh. Wassup? Who are you?" The driver asks, while checking me up and down.

I contemplate telling him the truth, but the type of shit I wanted done to me, it would probably be best if I lied. "Breanna. My name is Breanna. I just moved from Waco. Do y'all know where I can get some good Loud at?"

The driver thought about it for a second, then he reluctantly says, "Shit, we got some Loud. You can blow one with us if you want."

Of course I had to play a little hard to get. "Uhh. I don't know. What if y'all try and rape me?"

The driver's smile turn into a frown. "Rape? Baby girl, only time we take from a bitch is when we take them shopping or take them on trips. Me and the guys, we're playas. We ain't on no creep shit."

He sounds really offended, so I clean it up. "My bad, I didn't mean to offend you. It's just, I'm a little bitty bitch and all y'all niggas look like y'all two hundred plus."

"Naw, I understand." He turns around and walks back in the room, leaving me to make the choice to follow or not. Of course, I do.

When I walk in, all the others are already on the bed, in the process of twisting up. "What y'all charging for an eight," I ask.

The driver, who I later learn is named Swisha, says, "We ain't gone sell you nothing. If you want, you can just kick back and blow with us, until we head out."

I look at Swisha. "You sure? I don't want y'all thinking a bitch on some bum shit. I can pay for what I want," I assure him.

The front passenger, who they kept calling Zay, jumps in the conversation. "I can dig that. You an independent woman. That's wassup, but we some boss niggas, and if we can't afford to let you smoke for free, then we ain't them niggas we claim we are."

I can't argue with that. I make myself comfortable, sitting at the edge of the bed. I introduce myself and learn the other two are named Juice and Aloe. All of them have sex appeal and I'm pretty sure they could smell how wet my pussy is.

Zay twists up the first blunts and we put them in rotation. About half way through, my pussy is aching so bad, I can't stand it. The weed and Molly have me on *ten*. I catch Juice looking up my skirt, so I part my thighs to give him a better view. He looks around to see if anybody sees what he's witnessed. I start to rub my neck as if I'm sore.

"Your neck hurt?" Aloe asks, biting the bait.

"Ahh yeah. I had got into a bad wreck about three weeks ago and it gets sore from time to time," I lie.

"You want me to give you a massage?" I look at him as if he just had the most brilliant idea ever.

"Sure."

They all get up and make room so I can lay down.

"Get some lotion out of my purse," I tell Swisha as Aloe positions himself on top of me. Swisha brings me a bottle but it isn't lotion. "Boy. This is K-Y," I tell him with a smile. I catch the looks and I hope they will take charge soon because I need to feel stuffed.

Swisha finds the cocoa butter lotion and applies it to my back as Aloe begins to rub me down. I know my skirt is flipped up because I can feel the material of Aloes sweats rubbing against my bare ass cheeks. I imagine him sliding between my ass crack, I close my eyes and let out a soft moan.

That's all the encouragement they need. As my eyes are closed, I feel something wet, poking me in my nose. I open my eyes to see Swisha's purplish colored dick head, smeared with pre cum at the tip. With my face flat on the mattress, I open wide and allow him to ease his cock into my mouth.

I clamp down with my lips as Aloe pins my head down into the mattress, while his homeboy fucks my face, nice and slow. With one hand holding my head in place, Aloe uses his other hand to somehow remove not only his sweats but his boxers also.

I feel him guide his dick as he slams what has to be a good seven to eight inches deep into my pussy. I cry out as I'm finally getting what I want. Aloe pulls me up by the hips and begins to pound into my box. I let Swish's dick fall out my mouth so I can tell Aloe what I need.

"Beat this pussy up, nigga. A bitch trynna cum on this dick." He grips my hips even tighter as he tries to touch my heart with his dick. "Agghh fuck. That's it. Beat. That. Pussy. Upppppp," I howl as he beats my box down. I reach up under me so I can play with his balls.

"Ohhh shit. I'm bout to nut. Fuck," he announces, right before he pulls out and cums all over my ass. I feel his warm nut dripping down my cheeks. I reach back, smear my hand in it, then I lick my palms clean.

Now that we are no longer shy, it's time for some real fun. Aloe stands back and announces. "Mannn. This bitch got some snap back."

I feel Juice taking his place. I reach for Swisha's dick and place it back in my mouth. Juice pushes through and hits the bottom of my pussy. Swisha grabs my head with both hands and fucks my mouth just as hard as Juice is fucking my pussy.

"Ohh shit. Oohh shit. I'm bout to nut. Agghhhh. Swallow all this shit." He floods my mouth with his sweet nectar. My cheeks balloon and I need time to swallow it all. He withdraws and slaps me across the face, with his wet, limp noodle. Drops of cum splash against my nose and lips.

"Ohhh. I'm still hungry. Please, somebody, feed me more dick." Now my craving has me possessed.

"Open wide." I did as told and opened up to receive him. "Keep your mouth all the way open. I don't want to feel your lips around my dick," he says as he pushes his rod over my tongue and down the back of my throat.

I immediately begin to choke. "Awka. Awka. Awka." My airways are clogged. Snot is coming out my nose.

"Now suck that dick, bitch." I'm so glad to be able to wrap my lips around his cock, that I cum all over Juice. My pussy begins to make noises. Squish. Squish. Squish Juice leans into me, sawing away.

We get so turnt up, the four of them never make it to wherever it is they were headed to. I finally got what I desired. All three holes stuffed, with one on standby. I even let Swisha piss on me in the shower, while I lay in the tub, rubbing my clit until I exploded.

I leave them in the room asleep. As I get in my car, I could barely sit down. Like Ice Cube said, *Today was a good day.*

Chapter 5
Thursday

Charllessa Johnson
"I need to tell Dominique, her numbers have dropped for the last two consecutive months," I tell myself, as I go over the departments' numbers for the quarter. I run across DaVon's numbers and can't help but to think about the work him and his twin brother put on me the other day. My coochie heats up and begins to tingle. I rub my thighs together. I look down into my lap. *Down girl.*

I need to set something up with him soon. This time, though, I'ma let him know, him and his brother don't have to hide the fact that they're switching. I've never had two men at once but that's all that's been on my mind lately.

Knock. Knock. I look up and see Jessica poke her head into my office. Jessica's been with the company for a while now. She became my top assistant soon after she started and has been everything I could've dreamed of. She's the only one I trust and knows just about every affair that I've had at the office. Shit, once I test drive them, I throw her the keys so she can take them for a spin. Even though she gets on my nerves, I consider her a friend.

"Heyy, Boss Lady. Are you going to lunch?" I look at the clock. It's already lunch time.

"Naw, I'm a stay back and finish this paper work," I tell her.

"Wellll. Can I have lunch in your office?" I look at her inquisitively. "It's been a while," she pleads. I think about it. *Why not? I need the company.*

"You just got to be quick. I got to finish this paperwork," I say as she steps into my office, shutting and locking the door behind her. I take a second to admire her beauty. Jessica is a cute lil thing. She has the body of a young Vivica Fox, with a face that resembles Monica. She walks around my desk. I roll my chair back to give her room to work.

I spread my legs apart as she drops to her knees. Even though I'm not technically into women, I messed around and let Jessica eat me out one day after work. Ever since then, she's been dining on my fat cat from time to time.

She pushes my skirt back and rubs my thighs while inhaling my scent. "Umm. You smell so good, boss lady," she tells me as she places my thighs on the arms of the chair. With my legs jacked up and wide open, she curls her finger behind the thin material of my thong panties and pulls them to the side, exposing my slit, hole, and clit.

"Damn. You're soaking wet, aren't you?" Her voice is husky as she sucks in my left meaty sex lip.

I look down and see her pretty face between my thighs. The mouth on my coochie waters. "Shhhhiiittt, girl. Eat momma's coodie cat," I moan as she licks me from the bottom of my slit, to the top of my clit. I can hear the wet sucking sounds as she traps my clit between her lips, pulling on my nub through her teeth. "Oh my Jesus, Jess. Damn you, girl. This shit feels too gooood."

She has me grabbing the arm of the chair, trying to get away from her oral onslaught.

Two fingers slide within my cunt. I lose my breath as her digits tap against my g spot. My juices cascade around her fingers and down her wrist as she snacks and smacks on my snatch. "Oh my. Oh my Gawd. Damn. Giiirrrlllll." That's all I could say as I felt my orgasm about to build? I grab the back of her head, working my hips against her tongue. Her right wrist twisting like she's working a lock. Her left thumb lodged deep within my booty hole. She pulls hard on my clit and I reward her with a mouth full of yummy cum.

"Oh Jesus. I'm cumming. I'm cumming. I'm cummmming," I growl as my body shakes and my cum squirts over her lips. She struggles to sop it up, as my orgasm never ceases.

"Ooh. Ooh. Ooh," I pant, trying to catch my breath, too weak to say anything.

Jessica opens up my ass cheeks and begins to lightly lick me clean, from the crack of my ass to in between my folds. She even sticks her tongue inside of my coochie, lapping up every mouth savoring morsel.

Once I'm sufficiently clean, she kisses my cat before pulling my thong back in place. She stands up and wipes her face off with the back of her sleeves. My legs are still propped up on the arms of the chair. My coochie's still splayed open. I look at her in amazement.

"Girl. You keep eating my coochie like that, and you gone turn an old woman out," I had to confess to her.

She looks at me, bites her bottom lip and says, "I sure hope so." I smile. "Do you need anything else before I go?"

"Oh lord no, girl. You got me ready to go to sleep up in here. I need to finish this up." As she leaves, I watch her booty bounce in her skirt, my mouth begins to salivate. I tell myself that next time she eats me out, I'ma return the favor. *Why not?* One good head deserves another.

My office phone begins to ring. "Hello? Yes. Go ahead and patch him through. How are you doing, Mr. Reynolds. Yes, I'm aware, and I'll be there. Yes. Yes. Ok. I'll see you then. Goodbye." I hang up, feeling as though something is off.

Mr. Reynolds is the head of operations for our company. Apparently, he and a couple of the board members of our company were having a meeting and I'm instructed to attend. I'm not sure what it's about. Maybe it's a promotion? I sure hope so. I know, for the most part, our production has increased ten folds since I was promoted to General Manager. Yet and still, it's something unsettling about the meeting, but I guess I'll have to wait until tomorrow to find out.

Thirty minutes later, DaVon knocks on my door and pokes his head in. "Hey, Lady J," he chimes. I instantly get wet all over again.

"Come on in," I offer. Images of him and his brother sexing me down start to invade my thoughts. My clit starts thumping. "Go ahead and have a seat."

"Well actually, I'm not going to be long. I told my brother that you wanted to meet him and he's just as eager to meet you. The only thing is, it will have to be tonight because he's going out of town. Unless, you want to wait until next week."

I bite on my bottom lip, full of indecision. "Well, I don't want to keep him waiting. I guess we'll meet tonight. Right after work, of course. My husband usually makes it home from his daily affairs around 9-10pm."

"That's perfect," he assures me. After we chat for a while longer, he excuses himself and I get back to finishing my paperwork. In my forty years plus of living and sexing, I've never took on two men at once. I'm trembling with anticipation. I look at my watch, 1:45pm. I can't wait until check out time.

***

Derrick Cooper aka DC

"I wonder where's Yolanda?" I ask myself as I sit on the couch, watching Menace. I'm at the crib all alone. I know pops is at the detail shop, but I notice Yolanda's been gone most of the days lately. I thought for sure, after she woke me up that night with that top of the line neck job, she'd be back for more. Now, she's never at the house. *Oh well.*

I grab my phone and log into my Gram. I scroll through and see I have a message from an older white woman. I click to open up my DM and I smile.

Her name is Tiffany Battle. She was one of the teachers on the unit I was on. I used to be in her class watching her prance around with her pants jacked up all in her pussy. Even though I was in the "jack game," I never had jacked off in a public setting. Yet and still, it was something about her that did it to me.

I made sure that I had me a corner desk? I tore a hole in my pants, right there in the crotch area. That way, when it was time, I could pull my dick out through the hole and jack off with my pants still on. It wasn't uncommon in the pen to see three or four different dudes jacking off to the same officer, or in this case, same teacher!

The first day I jacked on her, she was sitting at her desk doing paperwork. She must have caught my hand movements because I saw her eyes move and then land on mines. A lot of so-called "jackers" are scared of the eye contact. Honestly, it's not worth doing, if she's not watching.

I noticed that her breathing became labored and she had stopped writing. Her thighs began to open and close, while she nonchalantly eyed my dick being stroked. I wasn't backing down. I stared her right in her eyes and dared her to do the same. When she licked her lips, it was over with.

I came all over the floor. Nut was all under my desk. She bit her bottom lip, smiled and continued doing her paperwork. I'm not sure if anyone noticed but I didn't give a fuck. If they got burnt up looking at my dick, then that's on them. One thing I did know, though. I was hooked.

As we were being let out of class, I thought for sure she would probably get on my ass or tell me don't do it any more. Instead, all she said was, "See you tomorrow, Mr. Cooper."

As the days turned into weeks and the weeks turned into months, our little thing became *our* little thing. Suddenly, it was finally time for me to go home. On my last day of class, she told me she would get in touch with me, but I blew it off. Most people kept jail things in jail, and once they get to the world, they forget all about you.

I seen she was logged on, so I hit her in the DM.

Me: What's going on, Ms. B. I see you stayed true to your word.

Ms. B: Heyy, Mr. Cooper. Yeah, I told you I would get in touch. How has being a free man treated you?

Me: Oh everythings good. I'm still getting used to being out.

Ms. B: I'm glad you're doing ok. I hope you're not being a bad boy, like you used to be in my class. (smiley face emoji)

Me: Naw. You know that's only for jail. Speaking about that, why you never said nothing?

Ms. B: Well, I've always been infatuated with black men, and it's something about you that does something to me.

Me: What are you getting into today?

Ms. B: I don't have anything planned. Why?

Me: Well send me your # and we can do something about your infatuation.

Ms. B didn't waste any time sending the digits. I call and we set something up for later that evening.

Yolanda Cooper

I exit the freeway and make a left on Aldine Bender. I don't have any business over here, but my main pill plug has to re-up so I'm forced to come and score from some dude named Baby D in Haverstock Apts. Haverstock, or the "Stock Yard," as they call it, is one of the most dangerously notorious apartments in Houston. Just a month ago, there was a gang shooting where three people ended up dead.

I pull into the apartments and see all types of people walking around, crack heads, dealers, kids, prostitutes. It seems as if the whole apartment complex was out and about. I had to wave a couple dealers off, who approached my car talking bout, "What you looking for?"

I find Baby D's apartment, park and go to the door. Knock. Knock. Knock. Nobody answers. I look around and hope that no one decides to come talk to me. I just want to grab my pills and go. Don't get me wrong, I'm no stranger to the hood, or the ghetto, but this ain't my block, so anything can go down.

Knock. Knock. Knock. Finally, someone opens the door. The sight of him takes my breath away. Standing in front of me is a six foot one, sexy ass chocolate, thugged out, hell of a man. Baby D has that smooth, Hershey chocolate complexion, and a taper fade with spinning beehive waves. He looks like he's annoyed, until he appraises my appearance.

He cracks a smile. "You must be, Yummy." I nod my head and he steps back to allow me entry into his spot. He shuts the door behind me. "So. What you looking for?"

I sit down and respond. "I need some Roxy's, and if you got some, Narco's. I need some tens.

"How many?"

I think about it. It's no telling when my connect will be back in play, so I figure I might as well stack up, while I have the chance. Plus, I wouldn't want to make the trip back over here, anytime soon. "Can you handle twenty each?" I ask.

He laughs. "Baby girl, I can handle two hundred each, if that's what you're paying for."

"Well. In that case, give me thirty each. How much is that gonna be?"

He looks at me and cocks head to the side, as if trying to contemplate something.

"Well, I charge fifteen dollars apiece for the Roxy's and ten dollars apiece for the Narco's. So that would be around seven hundred fifty dollars, pill for pill, but umm," he licks his lips suggestively. "I'll wave the fee if you let a nigga get a taste of that."

That's why I love street niggas. They are so forward and direct with what they want. I cross my legs. "And what exactly do you mean by get a taste?" I say seductively.

"I'm trynna see if that pussy is as yummy as you look," he boldly replies. I sit back and think about his proposal. I have the seven hundred fifty dollars, but looking at his lips, I can't help but wonder if he can have me cumming all over them. If he can, that will definitely be a plus. *Why not?*

I put my bag on the ground and stood up. I unbuckle my BCBG daisy duke shorts and pull them off slowly. Baby D never takes his eyes off me as I slowly peel off my pink and black laced thong. I sit back down on the couch, lean back with my legs cocked up, bent at the knees, and spread open. "Dinner's served."

He makes his way over to me, dropping to his knees. He grabs my left leg and places it over his right shoulder. I reach down and spread my pussy lips, exposing my hardened nub.

Baby D sucks on my clit like it's a freshly picked strawberry. "Ohhh yesss. Show me what you can do. Eat that pussy up" He sucks on each of my sex lips, smacking on them like a plate of ribs. He peels the skin back on the hood of my clit and uses the tip of his tongue like a windshield wiper.

"Agghhh. Aghhh. Shit. Damn, boy. You gone make me cum," I cry out as I feel a massive orgasm coming. He pulls back. "Wh-what you doing? Why you stop?" I ask, clearly flustered.

"Turn around. Hold on to the back of the couch, and put your knees on the cushion." Anxious to get my nut cracked, I did as I was instructed. Smack. My left cheek stings, while it jiggles. Smack. Now my right cheek burns. He rubs his middle finger from the top of my slit, to the bottom of my ass crack.

I look back. "Come on, baby. Stop playing with it. Finish me off. A bitch needs that nut." I'm begging him now. He spreads my globes apart, exposing my small pinkish brown, crinkly asshole. I feel his tongue massage my ring. "Ohhh shit. Ohhh shit. That's feels good, baby. Eat that ass up."

Baby D covers my anal ring with his mouth, and while he sucks on it, he also uses his tongue to penetrate my backdoor. I claw at the back of the couch. I feel him reach up under me and diddle my clit. My coochie overflows. I work my ass, twerking on this niggas face, while he eats my booty like he's starving.

Once again, my orgasm is on the brink. "Oh my gawd. Oh my gawd. I'm finna cum, baby. I'm finna cum." I plead, but once again, the nigga backs off it. Now I'm pissed.

I smack my lips and look back at his ass. "Nigga, what the fuck? Why you keep stopping? A bitch was almost there."

Baby D had his dick in his hands, stroking slowly. I look at it and I'm disappointed. Even though it's thick as a soda can, it's maybe six inches tops. A bitch like me is used to fucking with the heavy hitters, eight inches or better. Six won't do shit but piss me off.

"Nigga. What you think you bout to do with that? You said you wanted a taste, not the whole meal," I point out.

"Yeah, but that ass taste so good, a nigga need that wrapped around his dick." *Ass?* I'm not a stranger to anal sex, but this nigga's dick is way too thick, and my little bitty asshole can't handle that.

"Hell naw. Your shit too fat, dude. Fuck no. Why don't you just use the other entrance." I need that nut so I'm willing to compromise.

Baby D reaches up under me and starts back playing with my clit. "Naw, baby girl. I want that ass," he says, as pushes the tip of his plum sized dick head through my barrier.

"Hold up. Hold up. Hold up, nigga. Damn." Before I could finish, he has managed to push his whole head in. "Awww shit. What the fuck? Nigga, your shit fat as hell."

My shit felt like it was on fire. The walls in my ass were holding on for dear life, squeezing his cock like a juice maker. I cry out as he pushes another inch and a half up my dookie shoot.

"Ssshhhh. Take that dick like a big girl," he taunts. "All that ass you got back there, I know you can handle this lil ole dick." He begins to saw into my bowels.

I look back and see his cock is pulling my asshole inside out, every time he backstrokes. My booty hole is wet and I begin to moan. The pain has morphed into intense pleasure.

"Yeahhh, that's it. Take that dick, bitch," he growls.

I reach down and play with my pearl. The nut I've been searching for comes roaring back. Before I know what's happening, it hits me like a runaway train.

"Ooohhh my fuckkkiiinnn gaawwddd. I'm cuuummiiiinng," I scream as my whole body convulses. My asshole locks on to his dick, choking the life out of his cock, while my pussy squirts nut all over the couch cushion.

"Agghh shit, bitch. I'm cumming. I'm cumming." I feel his warm goo singe the inside of my ass, as he fills me to the brim.

My orgasm resurges and my pussy squirts again. I cry out. "Lord Jesus help me." Damn, that was one of the best nuts I done ever had.

Baby D keeps his dick in my ass until it softens up. He unplugs and watches as the cream oozes out, running down the back of my legs. He slaps me on the ass.

"Damn, girl. That was definitely worth every pill," he huffs. I had to look back to make sure my asshole was still intact.

"Can a bitch get a washcloth? Please?" After I wipe myself clean, I get my pills and head to the car. That boy got me walking like I got a stick up my ass. I slid into my driver seat and immediately felt the after effects of a good ass fucking.

Halfway home, my phone rings. It's Ja'Quell. I can't help but smile as I answer the phone. We talk about our plans for Saturday and he alludes to things he plans on doing to me. Then he hits me with a bombshell.

"I want you to go back to Atlanta with me." *What?* I can't believe what I'm hearing. "Look, Yolanda, I know you have a husband, but I want to build a family with you. I've had a crush on you for years. I've always felt like you didn't fuck with me back then because I didn't have my weight up. Well, now I'm bossed up, and all I need is a queen," he says with sincerity.

My heart aches for him. Truth be told, Ja'Quell is my dream man. The only problem is, I'm not the woman he thinks I am. I literally just got my ass blew out, by a nigga I just met today, for some pills I'm addicted to.

I take a deep breath. "Look. Ja'Quell, you know I fuck with you the long way. To be completely honest with you, I've felt something for you for years. I would love to be your queen, but... But you know what? Alright." I throw caution to the wind. "A'ight. I'll go back to Atlanta with you."

"That's what I'm talking bout," he yells so loudly, I had to pull the phone away from my ear. "I'll come and scoop you up Saturday. We'll kick it before my meeting, then right after that, we can spend some time together. First thing Sunday morning, we'll head out east."

We talk for a few minutes, then I see Dennis is calling. "Ja'Quell, I got to take this. I'll call you later."

"Hello. Hey, baby. Yeah, I'm out right now. I'll stop by the shop on my way back. Alright, sweetie. I love you, too."

I'm sure I'll go to hell for the shit I've been doing lately. Now I'm about to run off and leave my husband.

What if me and Ja'Quell don't work out? Then I just did all this for nothing. My head starts to hurt. I pull out one of the Narco's and down it with a sip of water. Not much after, I'm floating on cloud nine, and all is right in the world.

Lucas Jr.

"How much?" I ask Butta as I turn the gun over in my hand. After that incident at the crib with DC, Amber and Blade, I wasn't bout to get caught lacking ever again.

"Well. It's brand new, in the box. Plus, I'll give an extra clip for five hundred dollars total," Butta pitched.

"Bet." I pull out the money and pay him for the Glock .21. Since that day, I've had dreams of killing DC and Blade. I feel like that's the only way for Amber and me to be safe. I really don't know if I'll be able to do it, though. I don't think I've killed anything in my life, but roaches and rats.

I hop back in the car and call Amber. It rings three times and goes to voicemail. I try again. Same results. I put the car in drive and head home to our apartment. Even though she's at work, she usually answers. I scroll through my phone and contemplate hitting my lil side bitch, Jasmine, but I'm really not trying to hear her mouth. After I get my nut, I be trying to leave, but she's always asking me what I got going on with Amber. Talking bout, I need to drop Amber and go with her. *Yeah right.*

I come home and jump in the shower. Afterwards, I twist up some loud and smoke me a blunt. I look at the clock, 2pm. Since it's Thursday, Amber usually gets off at 3:30 or 4. I call her cell phone once again, no answer.

"What the fuck?" I decide to call her job.

Alexis answers Ambers' office phone. "Hey, Alexis, what's going on?"

"Nothing much, baby. Is Amber going to be ok?" she asks in a hushed tone.

I sit up straight. "What do you mean, is she going to be ok? She's at work with you," I say, not liking how this is sounding.

Alexis replies. "Umm. She *was* at work earlier, but she left for lunch and called in sick. She said she ate something that didn't agree with her, and it had her throwing up, as well as diarrhea. I gave her the rest of the day off. I'm surprised you didn't know that."

"I uh. I just got in. More than likely, she will. Oh wait. There she goes calling my cell right now. I got to go," I lie.

I didn't need Alexis or anyone else to know Amber and I wasn't on the same accord. I hang the phone up and try to make sense of what is going on. I call Amber's phone once again. Voice mail.

Now I'm getting extremely aggravated. Where the hell is she and why hasn't she called? I twist another blunt up and take it to the head. I must have dozed off and woke up around 5:30. Amber is in the kitchen cooking.

"Heyyy, baby," she greets me cheerfully.

"Wassup? You just got home?"

"Umm. No, not really. I got home about thirty minutes ago. I seen you was sleep, so I didn't want to bother you. I'd gotten sick at work, and when I went to throw up, my phone dropped in the toilet. I was at my mom's waiting on it to dry, while she fixed me some food and gave me some medicine."

So I was worried for nothing.

"I'm cooking some chicken and dumplings. Do you want anything extra with it?" she asks.

"Naw, that's cool." I'm relieved she has a perfectly good explanation for everything.

I want to tell her about the gun, but decide not to. I know she'll overreact and worry about the wrong thing. Plus, when I kill DC, I need her to be able to have deniability. After we eat, we spend the rest of the day lying around and watching movies.

Derrick Cooper aka DC

It's 5:30pm and I'm sitting in front of Carl's BBQ, waiting on Ms. B to pull up. I know she's not familiar with this side of town, so I triple checked with her to make sure she has the address correct. Still, I can't help but to wonder if she's gotten lost.

Just as I'm bout to call her, I see a purple Chevy Malibu turn into the parking lot. I text her to let her know it's me in the Denali. Once she locates me, I tell her to follow me as we make our way to Coke Apartments.

Since Blade and I need to sit down and go over some key details for the lick Saturday, it just makes sense for me to take Ms. B over there for our lil session.

As we both park and get out, I can't help but to admire her body. Ms. B's a fifty year old white woman, with a petite body, a nice set of tits, and a bubble butt. She's rocking some short denim shorts, a white Old Navy shirt and some lime green flip flops.

A lot of eyes are glued to her, as she makes her way through the projects. I don't know how much experience she has when it comes to taking black dicks, but she's about to get more than she can handle.

As we approach the door, we hear loud music, as if Blade's throwing a party. I knock on the door. A few seconds later, it opens up, but it isn't Blade that greets us.

"What it do, big homie?" One of the young homies named Gator answers the door. He's rocking some red gym shorts and a black wife beater.

"You know what it is, Blood! Bunch of Bickin back." We shake hands.

Ms. B and I enter the apartment and I notice it's about five of the homies in here shootin' dice, or playing on the game system. Weed smoke fills the air, while Finesse 2x fills our ears. I can tell Ms. B is definitely nervous by how she clings to my side. Plus, the homies are looking at her like she's fried chicken and it's chow time.

I had her sit on the couch, while I went to find Blade. As soon as I walk in the bedroom, I notice Blade is wrapped in a towel, still wet from a shower. "Nigga, put some clothes on, we ain't in the pen no more," I joke as he looks up with a smile.

"Yeah, if we was in the pen, a nigga might not even be able to have a towel to dry off with, especially on Ferguson Unit." We both laugh as he heads to the closet to get dressed. I turn my back to give him some privacy.

"Nigga, you missed it," he yells from within the closet.

"Missed what?"

"The lil freak hoe. Blood. That bitch pussy too good. A nigga might have to cuff that."

I laugh at his comment. "Mannn. Stop with the bullshit. You know only thing we cuff is the bucks." It was his turn to laugh.

"Yeah, you right about that. What's good though? Why you so early?"

"Oh shit, yeah. Do you remember Ms. Battle?" I ask him.

He looks at me and ponders the question. "Ms. Battle? Ms. Battle? Oh shit. You talking bout the teacher?

"Yeaahhh. The teacher," I answer.

"Oh yeah, I remember her sexy ass. What about her?"

"She got at a nigga on the Gram earlier today, talking bout fucking with a nigga, so I brought her ass over here."

"What? Where she at?" He couldn't contain his excitement.

"She's in the living room, but look. We got to take her slow. I don't know what type of timing she on, but you know me, I'm a set the alley oop up," I assure him.

He rubs his hands together. "Mannn. I use to jack that dick, thinking bout that sexy ass white woman," he says, almost to himself. He looks up, as an idea strikes him. "I got some liquor, if you want to loosen her up a bit. When she's ready, you can bring her back here. Just let me know when you seal the deal, and I'm a slide up in here."

"Bet," I confirm, as we shake and I head back into the living room.

Ms. B is sitting, watching two of the lil homies play Madden, while the homie Gator's sitting next to her. No doubt, he's trying to slide his young ass up in her drawers. If I'm not tripping, it looks like she's enjoying the conversation.

She sees me and straightens up. "Hey, Derrick," she chimes.

I nod my head, as if to say, "wassup."

"Do you want something to drink?" I make my way to the kitchen.

"Sure. Why not?"

I pour her a stiff shot of Crown and Coke, while the lil homies twist up another blunt. They offer her a hit, but she refuses. Twenty minutes later, I can tell Ms. B is loose as a goose. She no longer gives off that nervous energy.

I notice that her legs, which were crossed, are now gaped wide open, as she laughs and plays with the homies. I catch a couple of them licking their lips, as they eye her gap. A couple times, she catches them looking, but doesn't speak on it. No doubt, she must feel flattered by the attention. I figure it's now or never.

I whisper in her ear and tell her to follow me, as we make our way to the bedroom. I close the door behind us, but don't lock it.

"I like your friends," she slurs, obviously buzzed from the alcohol.

I want to correct her and let her know, niggas like me don't have friends, only associates, but I decide not to.

"Yeah. They say they like you too," I shoot out there.

"Yeah? Really? They said that?" She asks as I'm coming out my clothes. I get down to my boxers as she gets down to her bra and panties. I lick my lips and tell her to come finish the rest.

She walks over and squats down in front me so she can remove my boxers. As she peels off my waistband, my heavy dick pops out and hangs inches away from her face. I hear her catch her breath, as she gets her first close up view.

"Lord have mercy. This is a big ole cock," she whispers as she takes it into her small hands.

I look down at her, as she plays with it. She looks amazed at the weight and size of it. "Do you think you can handle all that?"

She bites her lip. "I don't know, but I'ma sure try, Bubba." She then stuffs it in her mouth.

Damn. Her mouth is so wet and warm. It feels like a pussy sucking on my dick. She slowly begins to work her neck, bobbing up and down as my cock grows to its full potential. She pulls back, my dick flops out.

"Oh my. Your cock is just absolutely gorgeous."

"Well. Let me see you make it spit up," I tell her as I grab the back of her head, forcing my length down her throat. "Shhhhh. Suck that big ole black dick," I urge, as she bobs her head even faster. I feel the crown of my cock, scratching the back of her throat, but I want to see if she can take it all.

"Deep throat that shit for me, baby. Let me see you make it disappear."

Ms. B grabs ahold of the base and slowly works my shaft down her throat, inch by inch, until finally, all ten and a half were missing.

I can't believe it. In all my life, she is the only one that has ever been able to down the whole thing. She pulls back, and as soon as my slimy cock is dislodged, she gasps for air.

"Fuck," I groan as I watch her struggle to catch her breath, chest heaving. I look at her with new found respect. She just earned her a permanent spot on the team.

After she steadies her breathing, she grabs a hold of my dick, smearing it all over her lips. "Damn. I'm already in love with this big black cock," she confesses, as she begins suckling on the head. She jiggles my balls with her free hand, while placing tender kisses all over my shaft.

"Stand up. Take your bra and panties off."

She wastes no time getting to it. Now, she's standing in front of me, booty ball naked. Her pussy hairs are trimmed and tits sag a bit, but she's still sexy as hell to be fifty years old.

"Lay in the bed," I instruct her, as I jack my dick to keep it ready. She lays back, legs spread, pussy lips wet with anticipation. I crawl between her legs, grabbing my dick at the base, running it up and down her slit.

She moans, "Fuck me with that big black cock. Yesss. Fuck me like the whore that I am."

I slam down. She howls as if she's being stabbed. "Aghhhhh fuckkkk." I pull back and begin stroking, hitting her with only six to eight inches at a time. "Oh my gawd. Oh my gawd. Oh my gawd," she pants as I give her what she came for.

"You love that black dick, bitch?"

"Oh, I love it."

"I said. Do. You. Love. That. Black. Dick. Bitch?"

"Oh yes. I love it. I swear," she screams as her body shakes and her pussy contracts.

I look down between our bodies and see my black dick covered in her white cream, and I know she's had her first nut of the day.

I slide another three to four inches in and put her in a bear hug, while never breaking stride. Her pussy's so wet, I feel her saturate my balls with her juices. I bite her on her ear and growl, "This my pussy now. My shit. I own this. You're my slave now. You hear me?"

"Oh my gawd. Yessss. I'll do whatever you say. This is your pussssyyy," she cries as she cums again, digging her nails into my back.

Squish. Squish. Squish. Her pussy hole talks to me, while my dick talks back.

"Open them legs up." I grit my teeth, while pounding away. She uses her hands, grabs at the back of her thighs and opens herself up wider. I grab her by the throat, squeeze as I dig deep off into her well. Our body's are clapping together as I roar," Bitch, I own this pussy. You gone do what I tell you, when I tell you."

Her eyes roll back in her head. The headboard's putting dents in the wall. My nuts are boiling hot. I feel them about to pop. Her pussy snaps at my dick, trying to milk me dry as her own nut explodes.

"Agghh shit. Here it comes." I climb out of the pussy and straddle her chest, jacking my dick. "Agghhh ssshit. Damn," I groan, as my cum shoots out and splashes against her open mouth.

Out of breath, I let my cock fall and lay on her chest. It twitches and spasms, as I watch her smile. She reaches up, takes ahold of her tits, and places my dick between them.

"Fuck my tits," she says, as she licks her cum stained lips. I slowly stroke between her globes.

I notice the door creep open. The lil homie Gator peeks inside and gives me the "wassup" signal. I nod and watch as he slides into the room. I see Blade about to come in behind him but I hold up one finger to let him know to hold up. *One at a time.*

I grab Ms. B's head and slowly feed her dick as Gator creeps around the bed. I know, due to the fact she has a mouth full of cock, she can't see that we're not alone. She'll soon find out. Gator undresses.

"Open your legs up," I tell her. She obeys without hesitation.

"Look at me," I command, and once again, she does as told. I wind my hips and she sucks my cock with zeal, stroking it with her soft hands.

I wait for the moment of realization. I feel the weight of the bed shift as Gator gets into position. Her eyes become buck, as she feels the lil homie slide his dick up in her well fucked cunt.

"Relax," I coax, as I continue to feed her. "This my pussy now. Remember?" I wait on her response. "This my pussy right?" She nods her head. "Well my lil homie likes you and I want him to love this pussy like I love it."

She closes her eyes and enjoys the sensation the homie is giving her. After a while, he picks up the pace and begins to power fuck her, while I continue to feed her that dick.

I hear him yell, "Damn. I'm bout to bust." He pulls out and cums all over her tummy. After wiping his dick off on her pubic hairs, he makes his way out of the room.

"Send in the next one," I say. Now that we all have an understanding about what's taking place, I can be blatant about it.

Blade enters next, already shirtless and down to his boxers. "I want some of that ass," he says.

I roll off of Ms. B's chest. I scoot down to the edge of the bed, sitting with my feet flat on the ground. I make Ms. B stand in front of me. I lean back and offer up my dick. She bends over at the waste and places my cock back where it belongs, in her mouth.

Blade grabs some petroleum jelly from out the drawer. He takes a glob of it and applies some to the crack of her ass. With two fingers, he pushes in and uses them to coat the inside of her rectum. Then with the rest, he covers his dick until it is slick and shiny. Once he's lubed and ready, he punches the crown of his cock through her sphincter.

"Ohh my lord," she cries out, squeezing my dick for dear life.

"Take that black dick like a good lil white slut," I whisper in her ear. "You're a whore that loves black cock, ain't you?" She nods her head yes, and Blade pushes another few inches in.

"Agghhhh fuuck," she cries out again.

I grab my dick and slap her with it. "Look at me. Look at me, bitch." She looks up with tears in her eyes. "I don't want to hear no more crying. Put this dick in your mouth and take that cock up your ass like the good lil slut you are." She nods and stuffs my dick back between her lips.

Blade begins to pick up the pace. I watch her ass jiggle and shake as he pounds into her.

"Say, Blood. This bitch gots a real tight ass," he boasts, as he tears into her backdoor.

She moans around my dick as she listens to Blade talk about her as if she's not there.

"Here it comes, bitch. I'm finna cum on all in your fluffy white ass," he growls as he unloads. "Aghhh shit. Fuck." Blade pushes all the way in, leaving nothing for the cum to do but seep out the sides.

Ms. B's body shakes and I know she came once again. Blade pulls out, slaps her on the ass with his dick a few times, before he puts his boxers back on and leaves the room. Soon after, all the homies in the spot, make their way to the room to get a taste of the "school teacher."

We fuck her in every way imaginable. At one point, we have every hole she has filled with dick. Once we're done, I see her to her car. It's dark outside, but she's no longer nervous about being in the hood.

"I had fun," she states, as she sits in the car. I notice her crotch is soaked.

"Me too. Next time, though, it will just be me and you," I assure her.

She smiles brightly. "I would love that." She closes her door and drives off.

I make my way back to Blade's spot so we can map out the lick. One thing's for sure, Ms. B's earned her spot on the squad. Who would have thought, a fifty year old white woman could handle the dick like a champ?

***

Tammy Taylor

"Is that? Damn, it is that bitch," I mumble to myself, as I see Chelsea and her boyfriend coming out of Giorgio's.

"Heyyy, girl, I didn't know you were gonna be here," she sang, as we hug each other.

"I didn't plan on it. It was a last minute thing. I came to get my lil cousin, Skeet, the new Jays's for his B Day." I nod in Bobby's direction. "Hey, Bobby," I greet him. He nods his head, without looking, and begins playing in his phone. Chelsea looks back at him, looks at me and then rolls her eyes.

"Girl, I'm so tired of him," she whispers as she grabs my arm and walks us out of earshot. "So. I know you're excited about tomorrow night," she starts, as we step into a Victoria Secret.

"Of course. This is the party of the year. That nigga Lo-Life's about to go on tour and rumor is, he might pick some people from the party to go on tour with him. My cousin Wacco's already got a seat reserved on the bus."

Her face lights up. "Bitch. You for real? Hoe, put that on something."

I look at her and say, "I put that on Jackie." She knows when I put it on my momma, it's ironclad. She muffles a scream.

"Girl, that changes everything then. A bitch has to make sure she makes an impression." I know by impression, she means she needs to find a way to wrap her lying lips around Lo-Life's dick.

"Yeah, most def," I respond, as I browse for a cute set of bra and panties. We discussed the party a little further. Then the bitch has the nerve to ask if I heard from Scott lately. It's been a few years since his ass went to jail. I'm still fucking his brother, from time to time, but I could give a fuck less about him. Matter fact, the last time I heard Scott's voice, he had called from jail and I happened to have his brothers' dick in my mouth. While he was on speaker phone asking Byron if he heard from me, I was swallowing a mouth full of Byron's cum.

"Naw, I haven't heard from him," I confess.

"Damn, girl. I thought y'all would still be rocking. Y'all were in love."

I grit my teeth. "Well. You know, shit changes. People change. Over time, we just grew apart," I say as I pay for my purchases, eager to get away from this no good, lying ass cunt.

"I can feel that," she says, as we make our way back to where Bobby is standing, still playing with his phone.

"A'ight, girl. Well, I'll catch up with you tomorrow," I say, as I make my way to the exit. "Bye, Bobby," I add as an afterthought. He nods his head, never taking his eyes off the phone.

As I hop in my car, my body's trembling and my hands are shaking from pure rage. It takes every ounce of humility for me not to expose that bitch for the fraud she is.

I put the car in drive and headed to my cousin's spot to give lil Skeeter his Jays. As I pull up to the apartments, I receive a text message from my boo, Robert.

Robert: Hey.
Me: Wassup, boo. U miss me?
Robert: Of course I do .When can I c u?
Me: I'll be busy all the way till Sunday. I'll C U 4 sho then.
Robert: (sad face emoji) A'ight. Got u 2morrow tho.
Me: I know u do, boo.
Robert: ttyl.
Me: Bet.

I park and hop out. My cousin, Skeet, is Wacco's little brother. He's only seventeen but his lil bad ass already has a name in the streets as a certified steppa. I've been hearing a couple people whispering about how it is supposed to be him that killed some Blood at a party three weeks ago.

Today is his birthday, so Wacco's throwing him a get-together with close family and friends. They didn't do big party's because they have too many open beefs with niggas all over the city, and if you throw a party, inviting everyone, then it's no way you can monitor all your ops.

I walk in and can barely see. Weed smoke pollutes the air. I find Skeet posted on the balcony with some of his homeboys. I walk up on him. "Heyy, lil cuz. Happy birthday."

He takes the shoes and smiles, showing off his gold and diamond teeth. "Appreciate it, cuz." I can tell he's lit off the liquor. I gave him a hug and felt the nigga palm my ass.

"Boy. What the fuck? Your ass is drunk as hell." I step back. "I'ma let your lil bad ass make it with that." I head back inside.

"Damn, she got a fat ass," I hear one of his homies say, as I make my way back in.

The music drowns out the rest of their conversation. I head to the kitchen to grab something to drink. Wacco's posted up, no shirt, filling cups with what looks like blueberry jungle juice. Images of him getting his dick sucked pops in my head. *What the fuck?*

Something is seriously wrong with me. Not my cousin. I shake the images, grab my cup and find a corner to dance in. About two hours later, I'm tore the fuck down. I walk outside so I can get some fresh air. Once I feel the cool night air, I instantly throw up. Urgghhh. Urgghhh. Urgghhh. I throw up everything I ate today, but I feel a whole lot better.

Still, I'm fucked up. I grab some gum out the car and take off walking. I see a dice game going, so I decide to stop and watch. My bad ass lil cousin, Skeet, is shooting, with a pile of money in the pot. "Bet I 5 or 9," he calls out.

One of his homeboys takes up the challenge. "That's a bet to you."

Skeet shoots and rolls a 7 on the first roll. "Fuck," he yells as his homeboys picked up all the money. Skeet notices me for the first time. "Oh shit. Wassup, cuz? You shooting?"

"Boy. I don't know how to shoot no dice," I slur.

"Say, cuz, you a'ight?"

I wet my lips. "Yeeaahh, I'm gucci. Just a lil tipsy."

He taps his homeboy on the shoulder. "Say, I'll be back. I need to make sure my people straight." His homeboy acknowledges him and Skeet gets up and takes my hand. We start to walk.

"Where we going?" I ask.

"We gone chill until you sober up. This ain't the right hood for you to be walking around like that," he says as we approach a Washateria. As we step in, I notice we don't have anywhere to sit. Skeet helps me hop onto one of the washing machines. Since I have a skirt on, I'm self conscious and keep my legs closed as he stands two feet away from me.

"Why you looking at me like that?" I say, noticing the hungry look in his eyes.

"Like what?" he asks innocently.

"Like you want to eat a bitch alive."

He chuckles. "Maybe I do."

My pussy begins to tingle. It has to be the alcohol because images of Skeet eating my pussy start to cloud my mind. I squeeze my thighs together tightly.

"Boy, you trippin. You're my relative. Ain't no stupid shit going on."

"Yeah, we related. But not by blood. Your auntie married my uncle."

"What that mean?" I retort.

He closes the gap between us and grabs me by my thighs, yanking them open. "That means, a nigga can eat this pussy all night, if you let me." He kisses me on my inner thigh and I moan. My pussy's calling for him and I feel powerless to stop him.

"Hold up. This ain't right, Skeet," I say, unconvincingly.

He pulls me forward, until my ass is hanging off the edge of the washer. He puts his mouth over the crotch of my panties and sucks hard, extracting the juices from the thin cloth. This niggas acting like a straight up animal, and that has my kitty gushing.

With his gold and diamond teeth, he rips my panties and begins to devour my snatch. "Ohh shit. Damn, boy. This shit. This shit. Ooohh it ain't right," I cry as Skeet alternates between sucking on my clit and sucking out my pussy hole. He squeezes on the back of my thighs, as he feasts on me like he's possessed.

I feel his diamonds graze my clit and I cum hard. "Ohh Gaawwdd. I'm cumming. I'm cummmmminngg," I bellow out as my thighs shake and my pussy secretes. Skeet doesn't miss a beat, he keeps sucking, licking and slurping as he unbuckles his pants.

"Get down," he says as he pulls me off the washer. My legs are so weak, I almost fall. He turns me around and pushes me forward. My chest is pressed against the washer, my skirt flipped up, exposing my bare ass cheeks. Smack. He slaps my right cheek, and I moan in anticipation. "Open the legs up," he growls.

I spread my legs apart. His dick head slides past my folds and penetrates my opening. "Ooohh weee. This shit ain't right, Skeet," I claim, as he begins to dig in my guts. With my tits pressed against the top of the washer, my thighs banging against the sides, Skeet fucks me for all he's worth.

He holds on to my hips. I feel him all in my stomach. "Oh no. Oh no. I'm finna cummm. Shit, I'm cummmmingg." I grit my teeth, trying not to alert the whole complex. My legs are shaking and about to give out on me. Skeet must have sensed this and begins to fuck me even harder, forcing me up on my tip toes. I struggle to take the pounding. My juices are running all down my legs.

I reach back and push against his abs, trying to ease the pressure but he just keeps beating my inside loose. Finally he starts to grunt. "Agh. Aghh. Aghhh. I'm bout to cum."

"Not in me. Don't nut in me." He pulls out and jacks his dick. I turn around, but my legs are so weak, I just slide my back down the washer, until I'm sitting on the dirty ass Washateria floor, bare ass with my swollen, wet and dripping pussy on display.

I look up at Skeet as he stands over me jacking his dick feverishly. "Oh shit. Here it comes. Fuck. Catch this shit, cuz," he demands. I am too exhausted to do anything but tilt my head back and open my mouth up to receive his blessing.

Skeet's dick begins to jerk and cum splatters all over my hair, dripping down my forehead. "Fuck. Fuck. Fuck," he pants, as his balls drain and his cock is depleted. After he's emptied, he sits down and leans against the washer next to mine. He struggles to catch his breath.

"Happy birthday, nigga," I say, and he chuckles.

"Now, that was a way better gift than them Jordan's." After we clean ourselves up, I make him promise not to tell anybody, but only after he makes me promise that we will do it again. I head home, thinking how crazy life can be. Friday is one day away, and I can hardly wait.

***

Charllessa Johnson

Finally. I lock up the building and head to my vehicle. I see DaVon's parked and waiting for me to follow him home. It doesn't take us long to get there, but my panties are already sopping wet with anticipation.

As we park and head upstairs, I notice a couple strange looks from some of his neighbors. I know how it looks, older woman with a much younger man. *Oh well.*

"So. Your brother's anxious to meet me, huh?" I ask as he inserts his key.

"Yeah. He's been bugging me about it ever since he missed your first visit."

Little did they know, I knew exactly what transpired the last time I came to visit. He and his twin brother ran a bait and switch on me and didn't think I would notice. Now, the jokes on them because I loved every minute of it. And now I want, no scratch that, I *need* to see if I can handle both of their delicious cocks at one time.

DaVon opens the door and walks in. His twin brother's in the recliner, shirtless, drinking and watching what looks like an episode of "Power." It amazes me how identical they look. Only difference between them I could tell, is their sex game, and even that is subtle. JaVon stands up to greet me.

"How are you doing, Mrs. Johnson?"

"Boy, please. Call me Charllessa, or just plain ole Charley," I tell him as I shake his hand.

"A'ight then, Charley it is. Would you like something to drink?"

I think about it. "Sure. How bout a cranberry Vodka?"

He wets his lips. "Coming right up."

I take a seat on the couch and begin chatting it up with DaVon.

Once JaVon brings me my drink, I turn to his brother. "You know I like to be fresh and clean, so if you don't mind, I'd like to jump in the shower."

"Oh yeah, I forgot. Of course," he concedes, as I make my way to the bathroom. I make sure I scrub every nook and cranny, and once I dry off, I lotion up and add a light touch of my fragrance. I know I'm pressed for time and I don't want to waste any being bashful. I decide to greet the brothers the same way I greeted the world, completely nude.

The first one to take notice is DaVon. "Damn, girl," he exclaims, as he appraises me from top to bottom. JaVon follows his line of sight and gets an eyeful himself.

"Look, fellas. I know y'all were both responsible for that incredible time I had last time. Even though it was underhanded, I'm not upset at all. Matter fact, I would like y'all to be my first experience with two men at once." I want to be as direct as possible.

Both brothers look at each other, then shrug their shoulders like, "why not?" I walk into the living room as they begin to get undressed. I can't help but to try and compare the two. JaVon appears to be a little bit thicker, whereas DaVon had him on maybe a third of an inch. Both men were packing nice sized cargo, and my coochie was already beginning to slobber on herself.

DaVon takes the lead and pulls me towards him. He sits on the couch, with his semi erect penis in hand. I know what's expected, so I sit down on the coffee table, lean over and take him into my mouth.

"Oooh ssshit," he moans as I begin to pop his head, in and out my jaw.

I feel his brother spreading my cheeks apart, blowing cool air into my booty hole. He licks around the rim, before pushing the tip of his tongue inside. My coochie quivers and begins to run profusely. My mouth waters. The saliva drips down the sides of Davon's cock, as I use my right hand to jack him off slowly. JaVon takes two of his fingers and jams them up my cunt. My coochie massages his digits and I moan around DaVon's dick, while his brother rims me out.

Without warning, JaVon snatches his fingers out of my snatch and pushes them through my anus. First he sticks in one, then with little reluctance, he works the second finger in, down to the knuckle.

My asshole clenches around his fingers as he begins to finger fuck me slowly. My coochie's juices are overflowing and I desperately want to fill it with cock.

Suddenly, JaVon slaps me on the ass. "Turn around."

I let DaVon's dick fall from my mouth and stand up, with my back towards him. JaVon pushes me back. His brother grabs my hips and sits me down onto his lap. Slowly, I feel the crown of his cock at my back doors entrance. I cringe, preparing myself for the pain to come.

"Agghh ssss. Fuck," I hiss and grit my teeth as DaVon's fat ass cock, slices my booty hole open.

Once I feel his pelvic bone kiss my ass cheeks, I know he's officially balls deep. I feel as though I need to take a shit. I have to be careful. It's been more than a few times when Lucas has had me shit on his dick after an intense round of anal sex

JaVon pushes my legs back and has me position my feet flat on his brothers' thighs. With his brothers' dick sticking out my ass, JaVon peels the hood of my clit back and starts to suck on my pearl tongue. I cry out for mercy.

DaVon grips me under my thighs and lifts me up just enough to have some room to stroke, while his brother continues to slurp on my nub. Never have I felt so much pleasure and pain at the same time. All you can hear is Davon's balls slapping against the mouth of my coochie and the wet sucking sounds of his brothers' head game.

I grab JaVon's head and pull him further into my crotch. "Oohh shit. Ooohh shit. I'm bout to cum. Yes. Yes. Yessss, I'm cummmmiiinngg," I howl, as my cunt explodes.

My asshole locks onto DaVon's cock. Cum runs out of my coochie and flows through the crack of my ass, wetting DaVon's balls in the process. I'm literally seeing stars.

DaVon keeps stroking until my orgasm subsides, then we lay still. His dick is still lodged within my bowels. I try desperately to catch my breath, but the "terrific twins" have other plans.

JaVon squats down and positions the head off his dick at my opening. With one push, he spreads my folds apart and tunnels through my warm and wet cubby hole.

"Ohh my Jesu. I'm so full," I cry out.

This is the first time in my forty years plus that I've been double penetrated. DaVon lays still, while his brother works to establish a rhythm. My whole body is tripping. My nerves are on fire as the brothers both begin to saw into me.

"Ohhh Lawrd. I don't want it to ever stop. I want to feel this forever," I howl as my body begins to shudder.

JaVon reaches down with his right thumb and flicks at my clit. That does it. "Oh fuck me. Oh fuck me. Oh fuck me, I'm cummmmiiinngg." My body locks up, as my coochie squirts all over JaVon's pelvic area. Clearish, white fluids, drips off JaVon's dick and splashes onto his brother's balls below. My orgasm has yet to cease.

"Ohhh please. Ohhh please. Oh my gawd. I'm still cumming," I bellow as my snatch continues to spray.

"Damn, girl. You a freak," JaVon says, as he pulls out and stands up before me. His brother pushes me forward. Now I'm sitting straight up on that dick. JaVon takes his wet, slimy, cum soaked cock and pushes it through my soft pillowy lips. My tongue caresses his crown. With both hands behind my head, he begins to fuck my mouth, much like he just did my coochie, while his brother tears into my asshole.

"Ohhh yeah. Here it comes. Here it comes. You want it in your mouth?" JaVon asks.

I nod my head and mumble, "Mmm hmm." He tilts his head back, looks at the ceiling and roars. Bittersweet dick milk floods my mouth, expanding my cheeks until I swallow and gulp it down.

JaVon sits at the coffee table and pulls me forward so that his brother can stand up in it. Now on his feet, with me bent at the waist, DaVon grabs my hips and beats my asshole to a pulp. I reach under us and massage his balls as they swing wildly.

"Ohhh shit. I'm bout to cum. Where you want it at, Charley?" I pull off of him, turn around and stuff his shitty dick in my mouth, just as his cum splatters against the back of my throat.

"Mmmm mmmh," I moan around his cock as it twitches until it's completely flat and my tummy is completely full.

"Damn, girl. Oooh shit," DaVon says breathlessly. "You a beast, for real."

I smack my lips and say, "You ain't seen nothing yet." I look at the clock. It's already 7:45pm. "I got about another forty-five minutes to an hour, so let's see what else you boys have to offer."

We all three head into the bedroom. This is the first time I've ever had two dicks in my coochie at the same time. I guess being brothers, they didn't have a complex about sex.

Once I finally leave, my whole body is sore but I have awakened something in me. I'm not sure if having one sex partner at a time will ever be enough. I'm just upset that I didn't try this years ago.

Chapter 6
Friday

Chelsea Johnson
"Oh, girl. You gone kill them tonight." I'm looking at my Dior dress laid out across the bed, with the heels to match. I know I'll be the baddest bitch at the party tonight. Facts.

I know Lo-Life's looking for people to take on tour with him, so I had to make sure I was on my A game. I just left Joy's and got my bundles put in. Now, I'm bout to shower, then beat my face to perfection.

Bobby calls himself trying to get some pussy before I leave. *Think not.* I can't mess this wig up, plus I need this pussy to snap back like a ball cap. My goal is to find Lo-Life and put this neck and this wet wet on him. Once he gets a taste, he won't dare go on tour without having me close by. My phone vibrates. I look down and see Deacon Cooper's number.

"Hello?"

"Hey, Chelsea. What do you have planned for this evening?"

"Well, I'm going to be busy all night, but if you're trying to link up, Saturday might be cool." Even though the good Deacon is paying, this is a once in a lifetime opportunity I'm not missing for anyone in the world.

"Oh ok. I guess I'll call you tomorrow then," he answers, sort of depressed.

"Make sure you do that, Dennis. I want to spend some time with you," I finesse.

"Will do," he cheerfully replies, before disconnecting the call. I really want to see if Deacon Cooper will drop down on a car for me. The last one I had, got vandalized, the windows shattered, holes in the frame. Plus, whoever did it put sugar in the gas tank. *Hating ass hoes.*

I was tired of having to share a car with Bobby's worrisome ass. My dad was supposed to get me one, but he's dragging his feet, for some reason. I scroll through my contacts and call Tammy.

"Heyy, bitch," she sang out, as she answers.

"I'm almost ready. Where you at?" I ask, while getting ready to jump in the shower.

"I'm on Wallisville right now. I'll be pulling up at your crib in about fifteen minutes."

I hear someone talking in the background. "Who is that?"

"Oh. That's Brittany Moore."

"Huh? Say who? Brittany Moore? The same Brittany Moore that used to talk to Cal Wayne?"

Tammy took a deep breath. "Look, Chelsea. She ain't tripping, so neither should you. Lo-Lifes's her cousin on her daddy's side, so she gone get us in the room with him," she reasons.

Brittany and I were somewhat cool, until she found out her nigga, Cal Wayne, ate my pussy one night, while she was at work. The dumb ass nigga texted his homeboy, bragging about how a bitch ate his dick off the bone, not knowing, that same homeboy was trying to fuck Brittany. So you know what happened next. He showed Brittany the text messages. It just so happens that right before that, Cal Wayne had supposedly given her a STI. So when she found out the nigga ate my pussy, she went around telling people, I burned his stupid ass.

Of course, the nigga's dick never even seen my pussy, much less touch it. That didn't stop the rumors from spreading, though.

"I'm good, T. As long as she ain't on no hating shit, then we gucci," I assure her.

"That's a bet then, girl. She's chilling. I'll see you in like twenty minutes." She hung up.

I tossed my phone on the bed and hopped in the shower.

Twenty-five minutes later, I come out smelling like fresh rain. I walk in the bedroom with nothing but a towel on. I see Tammy reclining on the bed in a pair of sweats and a Houston Texan t-shirt. She must have noticed the look on my face.

"Girl. You think I'm bout to let you see what I got planned for you hoes? Uh Uh. Try again," she laughs.

She doesn't want me to see her outfit and switch up mines. It was still early, so I knew she had time to boss up. "Where's Brittany's trifl— My bad. I'ma keep that to myself. Where's Brittany at?"

Tammy shook her head? "Don't start Chelsea. You promised you was gone chill. She's in the living room."

I look at her like she done lost her fucking marbles. "What? You mean to tell me, you have that bitch alone with my man, in my house?" I'm about to activate on her ass.

"Girl. That nigga Bobby ain't even here. He left as soon as we pulled up," she informs me.

"Left? Where the fuck he done left to?" Bobby has me all types of fucked up. He knows I need the car to go out. I don't like going anywhere without my own form of transportation.

I look for my phone but can't find it. "You seen my phone?" Tammy stands up and starts to look around.

"Naw. Where did you last have it?"

"I threw it on the bed, right before I hopped in the shower."

"It wasn't no phone on the bed, when I came in," she claims, as we both begin to look for it.

"Let me see your phone real quick." I dial my number and wait to hear the familiar ringtone. The phone isn't in the room anywhere. I walk through the apartment repeatedly calling my number. Still nothing.

I dial Bobby's number and see the contact name Robert pop up. Robert is Bobby's government name. *Why is his number in Tammy's phone?* He doesn't pick up. "What the fuck?" I scream in frustration. I try to dial his number again. Still nothing. I try to dial mine. Same result.

I give Tammy back her phone. "Um. Say, T, I don't mean to rush, but we still got to get ready," the bitch, Brittany, has the nerve to say.

Tammy looks at her and then looks at me. "I know you were supposed to follow us to the party, but shit, you might as well ride with us. Ain't no telling where that nigga Bobby went. We need to get to the spot, though, so we can get ready."

Fuck. I'm not missing this party for nobody. Begrudgingly, I go and finish getting dressed. I'm so pissed at Bobby. Any other time his lame ass will answer. *All of a sudden?*

Thirty minutes later, we're in Tammy's car, headed to Brittany's apartment, so they could get dressed. While on the way there, Tammy is texting in her phone, and I can't help but wonder who she's talking to. I want to ask her why she has my nigga's number in her phone, but I don't want to fuck up our night. First thing tomorrow, though, she and I will have a serious talk.

Brittany stays in a section of Houston called Greenspoint. Her apartment is nicely furnished and smells like jasmine. I walk in and see pictures of her and Cal Wayne, and I can't help but smirk. That boy sure knows how to suck a pussy. I make a mental note to get a dose of that, sometime in the near future.

I sit in the living room, waiting patiently for them to get dressed. I've never been a hating ass bitch, so I have to give credit where credit is due. Both of them hoes are killing it.

Brittany has on a yellow and red Cavelli dress, with some yellow Louboutin pumps. Tammy is rocking a sky blue and white, strapless Fendi dress, with some white Fendi open toe heels. They are both giving me a run for my money, but I still feel as if I'm the baddest bitch in the room.

"Before we go, you know a bitch gots to get turnt up," Tammy says as she digs off in her purse and pulls out three Molly capsules. It has been a while since I took Molly, but this is definitely the occasion for it. "Wassup? You bitches down or what?"

I hold out my, and so does Brittany. Tammy looks at me and says, "You know what I like about Molly? You can take it a hundred times, and each time is just as fun as the first."

My heart skips a beat. Does she know about me and Scott? She couldn't have? I've been writing Scott every now and then, and he swears he never told her. I guess my paranoia is starting to get to me. With a stiff shot of Tequila, we all swallow our pills at the same time.

"Say, T, did Bobby ever hit back?" She pulls her phone out and checks, before showing me the screen.

"Nope. Still nothing."

"What the fuck?" I mumble, as I wait on the Molly to make me forget all of the pain.

***

Tammy Taylor
"Where's she at?"
"She's in the shower," he answers.
"You've got her phone, right?"
"Yeah. I got it."

"A'ight good. Don't forget, no matter what, don't answer when you see my number calling, or any number you don't know."

"I got you, but I still don't understand why."

"Just trust me. It's a surprise, boo," I tell him, while massaging his dick through his cargo shorts. I have been fucking Chelsea's boyfriend, Bobby, for a couple months now. I've often been on the phone with her, while her boyfriends' tongue has been shoved in my ass, or I was riding his face.

Don't get it twisted, though. Fucking Bobby doesn't even come close to evening out the score. "You want to taste it real quick?" I ask, while licking my lips.

"You know I do," he says, with hunger in his eyes. "Let's see how fast you can make me cum in your mouth," I challenge, as I head to the bedroom. I can hear the shower running as I lay on the bed, removing my sweats in the process.

Bobby starts to remove my panties. "Naw. We don't have time. Just eat that shit through the panties."

Bobby pushes my thong to the side and goes to work. First, licking between my folds, then sucking on each of my fat and meaty sex lips. He pops my nub into his mouth and begins to suckle on it like it's a thumb. He slides the tip of his tongue across the top of my clit. He pushes two fingers deep off into my box, curling them and stroking the spongy area on the roof of my pussy. M g-spot is crackling. Bobby is by far, one of, if not, the best bottom feeder on the planet. Not even four minutes in, I feel my nut begin to bubble.

My pussy juices splash against his lips as his girlfriend's cleaning out her nasty ass pussy, five feet away. "That's it, boo. Suck on that pussy. Oooh shit, make this pussy cum, baby. Make this pussy cum." My snatch is overflowing. Just knowing I have this bitch Chelsea's man's head between my thighs, literally sucking the cum out of me, while she's mere feet away, is doing something to me.

"Ohh shit. Oohh sshhiiit. Here it cums, baby. Here it cuummss. Drink it all down. Fuck. I'm cummmmiinnnggg," I squeal. Bobby opens his mouth wide, placing it over my whole pussy hole, allowing me to skeet straight down his throat.

I shake violently as I grip his head tightly, forcing him to drink up every drop. As soon as my tremors subside, we hear the shower stop running.

"Shit. She's done." He panics.

Jumping up, I hurriedly pull my sweats up, while he grabs her phone.

"Tell Brittany to come inside and wait in the living room," I tell him, as he's rushing out the door. Roughly, about five minutes later, Chelsea comes out of the bathroom, no doubt surprised to see me waiting for her, in her bed. My pussy's still sopping wet with my cum, and her boyfriend's saliva. I've been waiting a long time for tonight to come. She was my sister and she betrayed me, not just once, but every time she looks me in the eye and perpetuates the lie.

Now we're at Brittany's about to take these Molly's. It's only fitting that the same drug she used when she betrayed me, is the same drug she'll use when I get my revenge.

***

Charllessa Johnson

Friday has finally arrived. I don't have to be at the meeting until 10am, so I'm at the office making sure everything is running properly. I see Jessica, and I brief her on all of her extended duties, while I'm gone for the day. Since she started working for this company, she's been one hell of an asset. Honestly, I don't know what I would do without her.

"So, what do you think it's all about?" she asks.

"I don't know," I honestly reply.

"I think it's a promotion," she suggests.

I just smile at that. "Well, you should be good, but if anything goes wrong, then you know you can reach me on my cell."

"Do you want me to umm. Well, you know, before you go?"

Even though I'm wound up tight and could use a good nut, I have to take a rain check. "Naw. I'm ok. But thanks anyway." A thought comes to my mind. "Jess, you have been an asset to this company, as well as a great friend. Now, you know, I've never done. Well, you know, but I would like to try, the next time we have an opportunity."

Her smile lifts and her eyes sparkle. "I would love to be your first. But let me let you get ready," she says, as she gathers her things.

Twenty minutes later, DaVon pokes his head in my office. "Hey, Boss Lady."

I can't help but to smile, as I remember the life changing experience he and his brother performed on me last night.

"How are you doing, DaVon?"

"I hear you're heading to get a new promotion, which will probably mean you're heading to a new location. I just want to tell you that no matter where you're working, my brother and I are at your disposal."

My flesh forms goosebumps. Just the thought of having two sexy, big dick slanging brothers at my beck and call, was enough to make me cream in my panties.

"Well, DaVon, I'm not sure if it's even a promotion, but if it's that and they happen to move me, then I'm very pleased to know that the three of us can still get together to make magic."

He can't contain his smile, as he leaves me to my thoughts.

I continue my paperwork until 9:00. I lock my office up and I make my way downtown. Since I am ten minutes early, they make me wait until I'm summoned. I'm nervous as hell. "Mrs. Johnson," the cute Hispanic receptionist asks.

"Yes?"

"They will see you now." As soon as I walk in, I instantly know this is not about a promotion. The CEO of our company, Mr. Zalensky, is stone faced. He points to an older gentleman to his right.

"This is our company attorney, Mr. Shandler, and this," he points to a young Hispanic man, "is Officer Martinez. He's with the Harris County Sheriff's department."

I'm taken back. "Sherrif's Department? What? I mean, I don't understand," I stammer.

"Well, just have a seat, and we'll explain everything to you." My whole body trembles as I take the empty seat. Mr. Zalensky hands me a file. "Do you know a woman by the name of Jessica Carter?

"Uhh. Yes, of course. She's my assistant," I answered. Hearing Jessica's name has me kind of relieved. If they're here behind something she did, well sorry for her.

"Ms. Carter filed a complaint against you about four months ago, claiming that you were using your position with the company to blackmail your employees for sexual favors."

My heart drops. I can barely breathe. My ears are ringing. I watch Mr. Zalensky's lips move, but I can't make out what he's saying.

Apparently, Jessica's been working as an informant this whole time. They claim she has been taking notes of employees' names, dates and time. They even say she has DNA evidence. Pictures of her giving me head in my office and wiping her mouth on her shirt sleeve, flash in my mind.

I put my head down. Tears begin to fall. My life is over with. I want to crawl under the desk and die. I keep asking myself, why? Why would she do this to me? I trusted her. I thought she was a true friend.

"Mrs. Johnson. Can you stand up and put your hands behind your back?" I look up and see officer Martinez standing over me, cuffs in hand. My body trembles.

"Oh no. Lord, please no," I sob, praying all this is just a dream.

Officer Martinez forcefully stands me up and turns me around. Once I feel the cuffs slap against my wrist, my legs give out and everything goes black.

I wake up in the back of a police cruiser, staring at the roof. Immediately, I begin to move around, trying my best to get comfortable.

Officer Martinez looks back over his seat. "Look who finally decided to wake up."

All I can do is groan in pain, as the cuffs tighten around my wrist, each time I move. "You know, at first, I couldn't understand what male employee would turn a female boss as fine as you in, for giving him some trim. Then I find out it isn't a man, but a woman. So of course, I wanted to know what her motive was. Shit, I know you're probably wondering the same thing."

I stopped moving, hoping he would deliver the news he eluded to.

"Well, do you? Do you wonder what her motive is?" He looks at me, waiting on my answer.

"Yeah," I croak, my throat hoarse from crying and screaming.

"Well, do you know a Charles, Charles Montgomery?" I think to myself. Charles? That's my first office fling, the twins' cousin.

I just nod my head "yes."

"Apparently, Charles is her baby daddy, and after the affair you and him allegedly had, he left her for an older woman. So, I guess she's blamed you ever since."

I can't believe this shit. Jessica's sole purpose for joining the company was to destroy me for introducing her man to the joys of mature, cougar coochie. My whole life is ruined because she couldn't handle her man stepping out on her. Why not get revenge on him? Why me?

My head hurts as I struggle to make sense of it. Not soon after, we arrived at the county jail. That's when I find out my charges, official oppression, coercion, and sexual assault. They set the bail at a hundred thousand dollars apiece, for a total of three hundred thousand dollars. I would need thirty thousand to bond out. I have the money in a secret account of mine. Ever since I realized Lucas was squandering money, I started to stash away cash for a rainy day. The only question is, who can I get that I trust to be able to go get it. As I'm sitting in jail, cold, hungry and scared to death, no one comes to mind.

***

Deacon Dennis Cooper

"Say, son, I'm bout to make a run real quick. I'll be gone for a few hours. When Yolanda wakes up, let her know I'll be back soon, and if she needs anything, make sure she calls me before I head back," I tell my son, Derrick, before I head out the door.

I hop in the car and check my Platinum Rolex. I pull my phone out and text one of my PYTs, Meesha.

Me: What's up. U ready?
Meesha: Go head n cum thru. I'm at my aunts' house in Acres Homes.
Me: Just give me the directions. I'll put it up in my GPS.

Meesha is the twenty year old daughter of an ex-police officer named Omar. Omar and I went to school together. We even played on the same football team for about a year.

Meesha is half white and half black, with green eyes. She's about five feet three inches and one hundred thirty pounds, with a shape like Vanessa Williams. I had caught her coming out the mall one day. After a nice lunch and three hundred dollars, I had her eating on my dick and balls for dessert.

Since then, I would hit her up, maybe twice a month. Since today is Friday and I don't have any major plans, I figured why not call her up? Now I'm on the way to pick her up and I can't shake this funny feeling. I exit Lil York and pull up to her aunt's crib. I text her to let her know I'm outside.

She exits the house in some pink and white tights, a pink baby tee, no bra and I seriously doubt she has on any drawers. She jumps in and her cherry blossom scent drives me crazy.

"Sooo. Where are we headed?" she asks, while I put the truck in drive.

"We can go grab a bite to eat," I suggest.

"That's cool. I need to stop at my cousin's house real quick, though."

Now look, I'm from the hood, so being in the hood doesn't make me nervous, but being in hoods I'm not from or have legitimate ties to, does.

"How long are you going to be?" I ask, as we turn into her cousin's apartments in Copper Tree.

"I won't be long," she assures, as she hops out and disappears around the corner. I sit patiently in the truck, watching a group of kids play football. I notice they are dangerously close to my shit, so I pay them extra attention. My doors are locked, my windows are up but my music's low enough, I can hear what's going on outside.

I hear a loud noise and feel my truck shift. I check my sideview mirror. One of these bad ass lil motherfuckas done tackled another one right into the side of my Denali. I instantly hop out to assess the damage.

"Y'all kids need to watch what y'all doing," I scold them. I noticed a fist sized dent, just above my rear wheel well.

"Mannn. Fuck yo truck," the one that got tackled says, while the others laugh. I have a mind to take my belt off and whoop his lil bad ass, but I definitely don't want to cause a scene.

I turn around to head back in my truck but find myself face to face with the barrel of a pistol. My hands shoot up in the air. "Look, man, I don't want no problems," I pleaded.

"Give me your wallet and your keys. Matter fact, give me them Gators on your feet, too, nigga."

I hear one of the kids yell *"Sucka,"* as they run off giggling.

"Look, man. We ain't got to do all this."

Smack. Searing pain shoots through my face as his pistol splits the top of my left eye open.

"Agghhh fuck, man. A'ight. A'ight," I cry out, as I take my wallet out and hand it to him.

"Now give me the watch, the keys, and don't forget the shoes," he demands.

I do what I'm told, with blood gushing from the deep cut above my eye. "Lay face down. Put your hands behind your head."

There I was, face down and barefoot on the hot asphalt, in the middle of the afternoon, and no one moves to help me.

"Count to sixty before you get up. Anytime before that and one of my niggas who's watching will leave you stanking."

I do everything I'm told, and begin counting. I hear him start my truck up and peel out the parking lot. I can't believe I just got robbed in the middle of the apartments, in broad daylight. I count up to seventy, to make sure that I'm all the way in the clear.

I get up, dust myself off and head in search of Meesha's foul ass. Since I don't have a phone, or know where her cousin lives, I give up the search in less than twenty minutes. I take off walking to a nearby gas station. It's surprising how some people see my bloody face, and bare feet and don't even bother to ask if I'm alright. I guess this is a regular occurrence in these parts.

I plead with the store owner to allow me to use his phone and I call my wife, but surprisingly, she doesn't answer. I call my son next. Same result. She must still be asleep and his ass must be tuned into that game. I go ahead and call Lucas. He answers and agrees to come pick me up, but not before laughing at me.

"Nigga, I done told your ass about fucking with them young, ratchet ass hoes."

"Man fuck all that. Hurry up and come get a nigga, dawg. I'm out here barefoot," I tell him.

He laughs again, this time even harder. "I got you, dawg. I'm on the way."

I sit outside the store fuming. I swear to myself, if I ever see that nothing ass lil bitch again, I'ma snatch her ass up.

Lucas pulls up about twenty-five minutes later with a pair of shoes, some towels and some Peroxide. Even though I had to hear this nigga clown me all the way home, I'm happy as hell that I can count on him as a friend.

***

Derrick Cooper aka DC

"A'ight, Pops, I got you," I tell my old man as he makes his way out the door. Knowing him, he's probably on the way to some bitch's house. I check the time. I know he'll be gone for a few hours, at least.

I call Blade. "Whoop," he answers.

"What time you need me to come through?" I ask.

"Can you make it over here in about an hour?"

"Shit, I don't know. My old man just made a move somewhere." I have an idea. "Wait. Let me call you back. I'm bout to see if Yolanda will let me use her shit."

"Bet that," he says, before we disconnect.

I head into the bedroom to ask Yolanda. I tap on the door but she doesn't answer. I cracked it open, just a bit. There, laying spread eagle, in nothing but some tiny black, satin panties is Yolanda. Her panties are jacked to the side, stuffed into her crack. I can clearly see one of her sex lips hanging out the edge of the crotch band. I grab my dick as it begins to stir.

"Yolanda. Yolanda," I whisper. I hear the light snoring. *She's sleep.*

Damn, her pussy's fat as fuck. Her panties being jacked all in her ass crack is doing something to me. I take my wife beater, my gym shorts and boxers off. Now I'm in nothing but my socks as I creep up on her. I crawl into the bed, careful not to make too much noise.

I position myself over her, sliding my dick past her panties and through her folds. Her flower petals open up for me.

She moans out, "Oh, Ja'Quell."

Ja'Quell? How does she know that nigga? She has to be dreaming about him. I'ma have to keep a close eye on her now.

I lean in and punch all ten and a half into her hot, sticky cunt. Her eyes shoot open. I know she feels me all in her sternum. She instinctively reaches back, trying to prevent me from going any deeper. I grab her wrist with my right hand, and place my left on the small of her back, forcing her to toot that ass up. I work my hips and dig deep off in her pussy.

"Hold up. Hold up. It's too deep. Aghhh fuck," she pleads, as I dig her insides out.

I pull back, letting my dick fall out of her snatch. I grab the base and slide the tip up and down her slit. I tease her clit until she begins to like it.

"Put it in. Please, put it in," she begs.

"If I do, I don't want to hear all that crying. You hear me? You want this dick, you gone take this dick," I tell her.

"I'ma take it, baby. I promise, I'ma take it," she assures me, as I slide into her oven hot twat. With each stroke, I watch her ass cheeks jiggle and shake.

"Ooohhh shit. This pussy's good as fuck," I groan, as I watch my dick get swallowed up. I grab her throat and squeeze. Her pussy locks up around my dick.

"On my gawd. Oh my gawd. Oh my gawd. This dick is so gooood. I'm bout to cum. I'm bout to cum. I'm cummmiinnnnng." Yolanda's pussy lathers up my cock, spreading white froth all over my shaft. Her satin panties are sodden and soaked.

I pull out. "Come ride this dick." With no hesitation, Yolanda strips out of her panties and climbs aboard.

"Sssshit. This dick is soooo fucking big," she moans, as she slides down my pole.

I place her in a bear hug. "Hold on." With her knees in the crook of my arms and my hands locked around her back, I fuck her hard and fast. My nut sack and her ass cheeks collide, as I pound her into submission.

She screams out my name. "DC." Every so often, I stop and grind my pelvic bone into her clit, before I get back to gutting her like a pig.

Her pussy juices pour from her, cascading down. I can hear the wet smacking it causes when our skins slap at each other.

"Who fucks you better, me or my pops?" I growl. "Bitch. Who. Fucks. You. Better?"

"Oh my gawd. You do. You fuck me better. Damn. This dick is soooo goooood. I'm finna cum again," she cries out.

I push all the way in until the bottom of her cheeks sit on my balls. I rotate my hips, "stirring her pot", while she cums in waves. Her muscles contract like a heartbeat around my cock.

"Yeeeaaahh, that's it. Cum all over this dick. Wet these balls up," I urge, as she squeezes me tightly. Once I feel her orgasm subside, I go back to the pound game. Clap. Clap. Clap. Clap. Our bodies collide.

"Ooh shit, baby, pleeaasee. Cum for me. I need it. Hmmm, let momma taste that nut." Hearing her call herself momma, has my balls about to pop. My whole body becomes hot. My balls feel full and bloated, but my dick is ready to milk them.

"Aghh Gawd damn. I'm bout to cum," I yell. I release my hold and she jumps off me, just as the first spurt shoots out my dick head. Yolanda grabs my cock and places her mouth over it, as my second and third fills her jaws to capacity.

"Mmm mmhh," she moans around my dick, easily swallowing everything I have to offer. With a loud "pop," she lets it fall out of her mouth and begins to lap at my balls like a thirsty cat.

I look at her in admiration. "Damn, girl. I see why pops put a ring on it. You a straight up beast," I compliment, as she licks the cum off the side of my shaft.

"Boy. You ain't seen shit yet," she warns, as she stuffs me back into her mouth. Once she has me back on "ten," she turns around and eases back down onto my dick, reverse cowgirl.

"Damn," I moan, as she slides down my shaft like a knife through butter. With her hands on my knees, she begins to bounce that soft but colossal ass. I watch them cheeks clap and applaud. Each time, sounding like a pistol cocking back. She raises up, leaving only the tip in, then comes crashing back down.

We fuck hard for about forty-five minutes straight, until finally, she's exhausted. We both lay on her cum soaked mattress, breathing heavily.

"Say. I need to take care of something. You think I could use your car?"

She gets up to take a shower. Without hesitation, she looks back and says, "The keys are on the nightstand."

I thought for sure, she would put up a fight, but I guess good dick will get the job done. I grab the keys, hop in the shower, and make my way over to Blade's.

***

Yolanda Cooper

Damn, that boy's got a big ass dick. I'm in the shower washing my ass and it still feels as if he has his dick up in me. I look down and see my sex lips are swollen and red. I position the shower head, so the water can spray at my cat, soothing the slight pain from the beating it just took. I'm thinking about Ja'Quell and I'm starting to have doubts that I can be faithful to him. Here I am, married to a wonderful man, a man who treats me well and makes sure I'm financially secure. Yet and still, I just had his son's big ass dick, fucking up my insides.

On top of that, the other shit I'm in to. I honestly don't know if I can ever be a faithful housewife. I walk out the shower and allow myself to air dry. Feeling depressed all over again, I go into the kitchen, find myself a glass of wine, and pop two Narco's. I sit on my bed and daydream until I fall fast asleep.

***

Lucus Jr.

I'm outside of Deacon Cooper's house, waiting on DC to come out. I see the Deacon leave in a Yukon Denali. I know it'll be a while before DC will be able to move around. He uses his dad's truck to make his moves. I wait patiently with the Glock .21 sitting in my lap, fully loaded.

After plenty of thought, I've decided that killing DC is the only way Amber and I will be free of the burden. I hate myself for putting her through this. I text her phone and wait on her reply.

As I'm waiting, I see DC coming out the house. He looks as if he has a set of keys in his hands. I realize it's the Deacon's wife's car. I watch him get in and drive off. I get behind him and follow at a safe distance.

After about twenty-five minutes, we pull up in 5th ward, to some run down apartments. The name of the street sign says Coke. I assume that's the name of the complex. DC parks, hops out, and heads to an upstairs apartment. I take a deep breath and try to settle my nerves. I place the Glock in the pocket of my black hoodie and flip the hood over my head. I'm about to open the door to step out, when I see what looks like Amber's car pulling into the parking lot. My face drops. It can't be. I check my phone to see if I have any reply messages. Nothing.

My heart's trying to tear its way through my chest. I'm praying she's not in the car. The doors open up and my fears are realized. Out steps my girlfriend of almost six years, wearing a plaid skirt with a white polo collar shirt and some red and white Sketchers. She looks like a Catholic school girl.

I instantly grip the Glock in my pocket. My face becomes hard and hatred begins to bubble within my soul. "I know this bitch ain't playing the game like this," I say to myself. My eyes begin to mist, but I will myself to suck it up, as I watch her walk up the stairs.

She knocks on the door. Seconds later, Blade answers. He gives her a hug, lifting up her skirt and palming her ass, so the whole apartment complex can see. My heart is being torn to pieces. Now, I feel she deserves to die, also. *Fuck it.* Everybody has to go.

I wait about ten minutes after they go into the apartment, before I make my move. With the hoodie over my head and the Glock cocked and ready to go, I walk up to Blades' apartment door. I place my ear against the door to see if I can hear any conversations. It's quiet, except for the TV playing. I pull the pistol out and have it ready at my side.

I twist the door knob slowly and push it open. The living room is empty. I shut the door with haste, then take two deep breaths to steady my nerves. My hands are trembling, but I hold the pistol with purpose as I slowly make my way to the back of the apartment.

I hear the unmistakable sounds of sex, and my stomach turns. I continue on, until I get to what must be a bedroom door. I notice it's not completely shut, so I push it open ever so slightly. I can't believe my eyes.

My girlfriend, the love of my life, my soulmate is on her knees with DC and Blade on either side of her, dicks out, as she alternates between sucking each one.

"Mmmm. I can't wait to have both these monster cocks up in me at once," she purrs. She jacks on DC, while sucking on Blades' sizeable cock.

"We bout to fuck your ass till you can't walk straight," Blade brags.

"Your boyfriend won't be able to fuck you for a week," DC adds, as she stuffs his dick in her mouth now, while jacking off Blades. That's it. I'm about to kill all three of these bitches, when I hear someone coming into the apartment. I run and hide in the closet.

I hear what sounds like three different voices enter.

Voice #1: "Say Blood. OG Blade got the door open. I can see that lil bitch he got, chewing him and DC up.

Voice #2: "Hell Naw."

Voice #1: "Look. Look," he replies with excitement.

Voice #3 interjects, "Y'all niggas thirsty as hell. Bro already said he gone pass the bitch down once they get done with her. Y'all act like y'all don't have no hoes or something."

I hear Voice #3 go into the restroom, while the other two discuss some lick they have planned tomorrow. We begin to hear Amber wailing about how much the dick hurts but she doesn't want them to stop. Voice #1 and #2 decide to say fuck it and go into the room. They're hoping the big homies will let them in on the fun.

I contemplate laying everybody down, but think better of it. I don't know if any of the three young niggas got guns, and I don't want to start shooting and not be able to kill the big three. I want the ones responsible for my grief.

I exit the hall closet and run out the apartment, as fast as my legs will carry me. I sit in my car and sob. I can't believe Amber would do this to me. It's one thing to cheat. I could handle that, but sleeping with the enemy? This is betrayal on a whole nother level. My phone vibrates and I see it's a text message from Alexis, wanting to link up. I contemplate going, but decide to get a rain check. Instead, I go home and wait on my disloyal, deceitful ass girlfriend to show up.

***

Derrick Cooper aka DC

'Slurp. Slurp. Slurp. Mmm. I love both of these fat ass dicks."

I'm standing next to Blade while this freak bitch, Amber, tops us both. I knew she was a certified slut. She just needed a gangsta to bring it out of her.

"Get on the bed. Lay flat on your back, with your head hanging over the edge," I order. She kisses both of our dick heads before she stands up and shimmies out of her clothes. She definitely has one of the most perfect bodies I done seen. Everything is proportionate. I look at Blade to see which hole he wants first.

He gets in position, stuffing his dick in her mouth. I climb onto the bed, easing between her legs. I grab a hold of my dick, tapping her clit with it. Tap. Tap. Tap. Tap. Her clit swells and begins to poke out from under the hood. I push the skin back and let a big glob of spit land on her pearl. I take my thumb and rub her nub back and forth, up and down.

Her body begins to gyrate as her pussy becomes slick with moisture. Blade reaches up and tweaks her nipples, while he slowly grinds his cock down her throat. His balls rest on the bridge of her nose, knocking on her forehead each time he down strokes.

I place my cock at the mouth of her twat, waiting on the right time to slam it home. I rub her clit vigorously. She moans around Blades dick, clawing frantically at the sheets. Her breathing becomes shallow. I know she's on the verge of cumming. Right at the cusp, I slam all ten and a half into her box. She raises up like the Undertaker, forcing Blades rod to dislodge from her mouth.

"Ohh my Gawwdd." Her fist are balled up and her body is rigid, but her pussy is alive and squirting cum like a sprinkler.

I begin to slow stroke as she regains some composure. Blade grabs her ponytail, pulling her head back down. He stuffs his dick back in her cock holster.

"Yeeeaaahh, that's it, bitch! Cum all over that dick. Wet a nigga's shit up," I urge, as I push her legs back. I look down and watch as her sex lips expand, and my enormous cock rips her open.

"Let me get some of that pussy," Blade offers. I reluctantly pull out. Dick slimy and slick. "Get on your hands and knees," he directs her. She assumes the position. I sit on the bed in front of her with my legs spread and my dick standing straight up. Blade gets behind her, and with a hard shove, she has her face in my lap.

Blade waste no time, and begins to power fuck her. Her booty cheeks sound off. Clap. Clap. Clap. Clap. No mercy is being shown.

"Oh shit. Oh shit. Oh shit," she pants, as he tries to fuck the obedience out of her.

I grab her by the back of her hair and lift her head up. "If this dick is in your face, why isn't it down your throat?" She grabs a hold of my cock and stuffs it back in her mouth. "It better stay in there until I tell you to pull it out," I tell her. I grab the sides of her face and hold her tight while I try and push my dick through the back of her skull. Awk. Awk. Awk. She's choking. Tears well in her eyes, as we beat her body senseless.

Between Blade punishing her pussy and me murdering her mouth, Amber could do nothing but take it like the slut she is. I hear Blade grunt and I know he's about to blow his load.

I release Amber's face. She begins to choke on the fresh air in her lungs.

"Fuck. I'm finna cum in this pussy," Blade howls.

"Shit. Cum in this pussy. Fuck, you're killing meeeee," Amber cries out.

Blade pushes once more, forcing Amber's face into the mattress. He unloads his balls into her belly. Him nutting inside of her must have triggered something because she began cumming immediately. Just as I'm bout to tell Blade to scoot over, I notice the lil homies, Gator and T-Stripes, standing in the room watching. *Fuck it.* Ain't no fun, if the homies can't have none. I look at Blade and nod my head towards the homies.

Blade understands and smiles. He slips out of her pussy. Gator immediately begins to get undressed and crawls in the bed. Amber's face is still glued to the mattress. Once she feels the lil homie slide up in her, she looks back at him, then she looks at me.

"What the fuck, DC? So now y'all bout to gang bang a bitch?" she asks, as the lil homie begins to pick up the pace.

"I already told you, this how I get down. If you wanna get that gangsta dick, you got to play how the gangsta play." She shakes her head in shame. "Say, T-Stripes, come put something in this bitch mouth," I tell him. The homie does just that.

Stripes pulls out his limp dick and begins to wag it in front of Amber, but she acts like she doesn't want to open up. I reach back and slap her on the ass, while Gator is standing up in it.

"Bitch, open your motherfucking mouth up." She obeys and Stripes fills it with dick.

The rest of the afternoon is spent with us tossing her around like a bean bag. By the time she leaves the spot, each of us has fucked her in each of her holes. She can barely walk down the stairs. When she does finally get in the car, she texts me.

Amber: Man, dats wrong how y'all always tryna slut a bitch out.
Me: A nigga ain't doing nuttin 2 u dat u don't want done.
Amber: I fuck wit u. I'm not tripping bout Blade. Dats u're right hand, but damn, all dem lil niggas fucking me all types of ways. How old dem dudes n e way?
Me: Old enuff. Dey out here thuggin. Check it. If u wanna fall back, u can. No pressure. If u want dis G shit, den a nigga gone do what I want to dat pussy, when I want.

She didn't respond. I guess she's finally had enough. After about sixty seconds, she finally hits back.

Amber: So when can I c u again?

I had to smile. No matter how much shit a bitch be talking, if you slanging that dope dick like no other, and you carry the G shit on your chest, they gone always come back for more.

Me: I'm busy 2morrow but we can meet up Sunday.
Amber: I might need a few days. Y'all tore my shit to shreds. I'm hurting rite now.
Me: Lol. We told yo ass. Well let me know when u're ready.
Amber: I will.

I put the phone down and discussed the play with Blade. We elected to utilize a few of the homies, since they needed to earn some stripes anyway. We figure, we can give them a half a brick and ten bands apiece and they should be good with that.

I take the car to the spot Ja'Quell's supposed to be laying his head at. I stay out there about an hour, just checking out everything, just in case we have to end up hitting him up there.

Later on, I head home, anxious about the lick of a lifetime. This the type of move that niggas wait their whole lives to hit. Ain't no more falling off after this.

I'm surprised to see my dad sitting in the living room, since his truck is gone. At first glance, I can tell he seems upset about something. I think that maybe he's found out that I fucked his wife. I'm on high alert.

"Pops. What's going on?" He picks his head up and I notice the left side of his face is purple and swollen. "What the fuck?"

He shakes his head in shame. "I got robbed, son. I was in Copper Tree, dropping a friend of mines off, when a group of niggas drew down on me. They took my wallet, my watch, my truck, even my shoes."

Now I'm pissed. "Do you know any of their names, or what they looked like?"

He thinks about something and looks over to the bedroom to make sure the door is closed.

"The lil bitch I was dropping off is named Meesha," he whispers.

Hearing that, I already know what the business is. The bitch set him up. I made sure he gave me all the info he had on the grimy bitch. I hit some of the homies in Acres Homes to see if they knew a chick named Meesha, who matches the description. They told me to give them a few days and they'll have something for me.

"Pops, I'll take care of it," I assure him, as I make my way to my room.

One thing I'm not about to let you do, is play with my family. Yeah, I just fucked his wife, but that's just pussy. I love my pops. He was the only one that made sure I had what I needed when I was on lock. Once I find out where this Meesha bitch is located, best believe her and everyone else that was involved, will regret they ever seen my old man.

***

Chelsea Johnson
"Oohh Weeee. This motherfucka is lit," I scream from the backseat, as we pull into the mansion in River Oaks. The scene looks like a block party at an exotic car lot. I'm seeing Phantoms, Bentley's, Benzes and some cars I can't even pronounce. My pussy's already getting wet, seeing all this money parked outside. We found a place to park, then we approached the gate.

Brittany texted her cousin to let him know that we had arrived, while Tammy did the same with Wacco. We waited about two minutes, until Wacco arrived dressed in Givenchy. I always had a thing for him. He really wasn't all that cute, but his gangsta made my pussy drip every time I came near him.

"What's up, Cuz," he hugs Tammy as they greet each other. "What's craccin Chelsea?" he greets me with a smile.

"Hey, Wacco, I appreciate you for inviting us to this party. This bitch is off the chain," I admit.

"Ain't shit, you family. Look. Do y'all ladies want something to drink?"

"Sure," we say in unison. Wacco leaves, but before long, he returns with three cups filled with liquor.

"Say, girl. I need to find my sister real quick. I'll hit you up as soon as I do," Brittany tells Tammy as she leaves the three of us standing there.

Wacco looks at me. "So. Would you like to meet the man of the house?"

My jaw drops. "What? You mean Lo-Life? Of course, I want to meet him." Even though he was an up and coming artist, Lo-Life was already a legend on the East and the music industry was taking note. He'd just signed a mega deal and was projected to go triple platinum on his debut album. If a bitch can lock him in now, she might be able to ride the gravy train. I don't even have to be his main. A side bitch position would be just as good, in my book. Wacco and I take off to go meet him.

I look at Tammy. "Bitch, you ain't coming?"

"Naw, I'm good girl? I know how much you want to meet bro, so."

"Suit yourself," I tell her. As Wacco and I maneuver through the party, I take notice of the decor. It seems as if Lo-Life has big screen Plasmas on every wall in the house, even in the kitchen. I see hood celebrities from all over the city, as well as some prominent local artists. My body is hot and tingling.

The Molly has my pussy bubbling, like a cauldron. Add that to the liquor I'm sipping, and my hormones are on raging bull. The way I'm feeling, I want to snatch Wacco into one of these rooms, just so I can eat his dick and balls.

After surfing through the hallways, we end up at a closed door. Wacco knocks a few times and a sixfoot six inch, two hundred eighty pound, dark skin, mammoth of a man opens it. He sees Wacco, nods his head, and steps to the side.

As we walk in, I'm amazed at the scenery. The room has been remodeled to look like an office, with a bed placed in the corner. Sitting behind a great big Mahogany desk, is none other than Lo-Life "The General" himself.

He appears to be talking business with someone, so I take a seat on the couch across from his desk. Wacco stands next to the couch, while we wait. Someone knocks on the door. The bodyguard, who I later learn is named Big Tron, goes to answer it.

I watch Lo-Life's lips move and I cross my legs, hoping to ease my kitty from purring. Images of him using those lips to suck on my pussy, flash through my mind, and my body begins to heat up.

"Aye, what it is, Flame?" he asks our new visitor.

Flame is kind of cute. He's about six feet, two hundred pounds, with light brown skin, light brown eyes and a body full of ink. Flame approaches the desk, and he and Lo shake hands.

Lo takes notice of us and makes the introductions. "Flame, this my nigga, Wacco. And this his people, Chelsea." I was taken back that he already knew my name.

"What's the deal?" Wacco says, as he shakes Flame's hand.

"Nice to meet you, Ms. Chelsea," Flame says, as he takes my hand. I smell his cologne and it's intoxicating. Wacco has stepped to the side with Flame, as they discuss some business.

I use this free time to try and put my bid down with Lo. "So. Congratulations on your record deal," I say. I cross my legs, giving him a good view of my silky smooth thighs.

"Oh yeah. I appreciate that. It's been a long time coming, but you know I'ma put on for the city, especially the East."

I bite my bottom lip and smile. "No doubt. They say, you bout to go on tour soon," I hint.

"Yeah. We got forty cities in sixty days. It's gone be hell on the road. Matter of fact, I'm putting together a crew of people to take with me."

"Oh really," I say, just a bit too enthusiastically. "I wish I was lucky enough to go on tour with a big name celebrity," I offer.

"Really, luck has nothing to do with it. Sometimes, it's all about dedication, loyalty, commitment, and sacrifices. What are you willing to do for the team?"

I'm not sure but I feel I catch the underlying meaning in what he's saying. I need him to know that I'm down for whatever, however, whenever, in order to get on that tour.

I look him straight in the eyes and buss my legs open, so he can see how saturated he was making me. "I promise you, if you give me the chance, I will show you why you have to have me on that tour with you.

He takes a second gaze at my camel toe, wetting his lips in the process. "Well, hopefully, soon you'll be able to convince me."

Just as the conversation is getting good, Wacco tells me that he has to take care of something, but I'm welcomed to chill.

"Well, that's up to Lo-Life," I say, hoping I get an extended invitation.

"Of course, you can chill," he says, as Wacco makes his exit. Once I, he and Flame are alone, he offers me a drink, but I'm still nursing on the one I came in the room with. "Go ahead and slam that down, so I can give you some of this Rosé."

I turn the cup up, and within seconds, I swallow all of the liquor. Lo pours me a glass of Rosé.

"So, what were you saying earlier about having a chance to convince me?"

I take a sip from my cup, put it down, and then stand up. I remove the straps from my dress, allowing it to fall to the floor. There I stand. Nothing on but a pair of red laced Victoria Secret thongs.

Lo looks at me with hunger in his eyes. "You know red's my color, right?"

I smile, bite my bottom lip and say, "Yeah, I know. That's why I wore it."

I feel a hand caressing my titties. My nipples are hard as marbles, as he tweaks them between his fingers. Flame sits down on the couch, in nothing but his socks. I never saw him get undressed. His dick is at least eight to nine inches and hard as granite.

My mouth waters as I drop to my knees. I tie my hair in a ponytail and breathe in his scent. He smells fresh and clean. I open wide and slowly feed myself his cock, inch by Inch. I rake my teeth against his shaft, as I bob my head to an imaginary beat.

"Ssshhhit. Ohh yeah, baby. Suck that dick," Flame urges, as I suck on the head, while jacking him off.

I can taste his pre cum, glazing my tongue, and my pussy is crying for attention. I stand up, turn around and slip my thong off. With my back towards Flame, I stare Lo in his eyes. I bend over at the waist and reach back to pull my ass cheeks apart. I look back at Flame. "Put your face in it."

Without hesitation, Flame licks up and down the crack of my ass. I moan, as I feel his long tongue slither into my anal ring, as he sucks on it gently.

"Ohhh yeah. Eat that ass up, nigga."

Flame tosses my salad expertly. His warm tongue drives me crazy, as he licks all between my crevices.

With my hands on his desk and his homeboys' face in my ass, Lo looks at me and asks, "Can you handle more dick?"

"I can handle as much dick as you can give me."

With a smirk on his face, he texts someone on his phone. Seconds later, the room's filled with six more niggas. I honestly thought that when he said "more dick," he was referring to himself. Now, I'm in a fucked up predicament.

If I back out, then he will surely feel as though I was a waste of time, and my ticket on the bus would be null and void. On the other hand, six more dicks is a whole lot to handle. I have no choice but to put my big girl panties on.

I turn around and push Flame down onto the couch. With my back towards him, I reach down, grab his dick and guide him into my cunt, as I impaled myself. "Ohh shit .You got a fat ass dick," I groan, as I force his whole length between my folds. My pussy's so wet. I have to check myself to make sure I'm not bleeding. Slowly, I begin to work my hips up and down, while Flame reaches around and squeezes my tits.

Without warning, not one, but two nice size dicks appear in front of me, poking at my face. I reach up and with each hand, grab ahold of them. I suck in each one like it's my last.

The whole time, Lo-Life just sits at his desk, watching, observing me work. Knowing this, has made me insatiable.

I fuck in many different combinations. One in my ass, one in my mouth, and one in my pussy is the norm. Each time I nut, I scream out, "I want more". I ate someone's ass, while I got my ass ate. I had two sets of balls in my mouth at the same time. I let one eat my pussy, while his homeboys fucked my ass hole to pieces. I sucked dick fresh out my shit box. I even let a nigga piss in my mouth because I didn't want to let his dick go. I did any and everything they wanted.

By the time we are done, I smell like cum, piss and a light scent of shit. Lo-Life shows me into the shower. I make sure I wash up real good, confident that I made the cut. I still don't understand why he didn't join. Maybe, he wants to save the best for last. I would love to see what he's working with.

Maybe he has a small dick, and he's embarrassed. Or maybe he's one of those niggas that gets his rocks off by watching. I hope next time I get to put this pussy and throat on him. One thing I can say, tonight has been very memorable. I dried off and put my dress back on, but kept my panties off. I left them on his towel rack as a gift.

I go back in the office and everyone is gone but Wacco. He must see the look of disappointment on my face.

"He had to go handle some business, but he told me to tell you that he was thoroughly convinced, whatever that means." I instantly brightened up. "Here." He hands me another drink.

I'm already lit like a skyscraper, but I gulp down the liquid. My insides are on fire, but I'm soon floating on cloud nine. I look back at Wacco with longing. *Why not?*

"Wacco. Can I suck your dick?"

He nearly spits his drink up. "Say what? You wanna suck my dick?"

"It won't take long. I promise."

He thinks about it for a few seconds, then starts to unbuckle his belt. He pulls his beautiful black cock out, and lets it hang. I grab him and pull him by his dick, towards the couch. I sit down and have him stand before me, while I suck his dick the way I intended to do Lo-Life.

With plenty of spit and grip, I pull the cum out his nut sack in less than five minutes.

"Aww shit. Aww shit. Here it cums. Fuuuccckkk," he growls, as he fills my mouth with his tasty treat. I pop his dick out.

"Mmmm, I knew you had a delicious tasting dick."

He chuckles. "Girl. You hell," he says, as he tucks his rifle back in its holster. I pull my makeup kit out, wipe the cum from the corners of my mouth, and we head to go find Tammy. We make our way around the house, and I'm starting to feel extremely nauseous and disoriented. My eyes feel heavy and my knees become weak. I put my hand on the wall for support.

"What's wrong?" Wacco asks.

"I don't feel so good. Something's wrong?" I start to notice people start staring and pointing at me. I didn't understand until I looked at the TV's on the wall. I'm on every screen in the house. There I was, surrounded by six dudes, taking dick, eating ass and getting pissed on.

Women walked by with their noses up and looks of disgust on their faces. Dudes were laughing and pointing, pretending to pull their dicks out to piss on me, while I laid there throwing my guts up. My heart is beating so fast, I think I'm going to have a heart attack. I feel as though I'm about to die. Then, I black out. I begin to hear people talking around me. I try to make out the voices, but I don't recognize them.

"Yeah. We need a hundred thousand dollars delivered to 137 Black Rock. It's a wooden plank that's broken on the side of the store. Put the money behind the fence, and once we see everything is accounted for, we'll let her go. You have twenty-four hours. If it isn't there, then she dies."

I open my eyes, but still can't see a thing. I realize that whoever has me tied to this chair, also has a black pillow case over my head. I can tell there is more than one person involved. I stay still and listen. I try to amass any clues that I can. All types of questions flood my mind. Who are they? How do they know me? Why me? Who were they speaking to? Then to make matters worse, I had to pee like a racehorse.

***

Rev. Lucas Johnson
I can't wait to get Dennis out of my truck. I love the nigga like a brother, but I have some Grade A pussy to get to and his ass is cock blocking.

"Yolanda must be gone," he says as I pull up to his house.

"Why you say that?" I question.

Dennis looks at me as if I'm remedial. "Because her car's gone."

"How you know she's not parked in the garage?" I legitimately ask.

"She never parks in the garage. Let's go in."

We both get out the truck and make our way into the house. As soon as we enter, Dennis makes his way into the kitchen to grab some ice cubes for his swollen face. I head into the living room.

As I take a seat, I glance over to the bedroom and notice that the door is wide open. Yolanda is laid out on the bed naked, pretty pussy on display. Her sex lips look bruised and swollen. Her pussy hole, dilated.

I get up quickly, shutting the bedroom door so Dennis won't catch her in this compromising position. He comes back to the living room, just as I'm sitting down.

"I wonder where Derrick ran off to," he asks out loud, while placing the ice pack over his eye.

"Maybe he took Yolanda's car and she's asleep in the room," I offer up lamely.

"Let me use your phone."

I hand him my phone and watch as he calls his son.

"Hey, son. Yeah. Aye, you got Yolanda's car? Ok. Yeah, I just came home. Naw, I'm good. I'll see you when you get here. A'ight." He hands me the phone back. "You're right. He's got Yolanda's car. She must be in the room sleep. He's on the way back now."

I start to raise up. "Well, now that your ass is safe at home, I got some cat to go catch," I joke, as I make my way to the front door. I look back at my best friend and the ice pack over his face, bloody shirt and bruised ego. "Bro, you have to leave the young hoes alone. Next time, you might not get to leave with your life," I say, as I close the door behind me.

Now I'm at the hotel suite, laid back with Sister Pam's lips wrapped around my dick, while her hair is wrapped around my fist.

"Eat. That. Dick. Bitch. Eat. That. Dick," I punctuate with each stroke. Spit flies from her mouth as she struggles for air. With her hands on my thighs, I feel her squeeze and claw, but I show her no mercy. "You love eating this dick up, don't you?" I ask.

She mumbles, "Uh huh," nodding her head.

I pull her head back. My dick flops out of her mouth. Spit hangs from her chin to my dick head.

"Awww. Yessss. I love eating this dick up, daddy," she says, gasping for air. I yank her head down and guide her straight to my nuts.

Without instructions, Pam begins to kiss, lick and suck on my balls. "Aww yess. That's it. Get them nuts clean."

Pam is the wife of Brother Clayton. At fifty-five, she is a little older than what I'm used to, but she makes up for it with sexual exuberance. She lets me fuck her in any hole I feel like. And no matter how hard or how rough I am with her, she never complains. Not only that, but she never minds paying for it. She's a little overweight, but her pussy still gets wet as a lake, especially when I fuck her in her ass.

As she nibbles on my nut sack, my phone rings. Of course I ignore it, but the person calls, not once, but twice. Finally, irritated, I answer. "Hello?"

"Is this the Reverend Johnson?"

"Yes, this is him. Who's this?"

Pam stuffs my dick back in her mouth and I have to fight not to moan into the phone.

"We have your daughter, Chelsea, and we want a hundred thousand dollars delivered to 137 Black Rock. There's a loose plank behind the store. Put the money behind the fence. You have twenty-four hours. If it's not there, she's dead." Then the caller hangs up. My heart's pounding in my chest. I look at my phone. Of course, the call was blocked.

"What's wrong, daddy?" Pam asks.

I just noticed she's still here. Apparently, my dick has lost its luster. She holds my limp noodle in her hand.

"Nothing. I got to go."

"Got to go? But we just got here," she complains.

Ignoring her, I get up and retrieve my clothes. "Something important came up. I'll call you later," I say, as I rush out the door.

I get in my truck and head straight home, hoping this is some sick joke. I call my wife. Her phone goes straight to voicemail. I call Chelsea. Her phone rings, but no one answers.

"What the fuck?" I yell in frustration, as I wait on the traffic light to turn green.

I decided to call my daughter's boyfriend, Bobby. "Hello?" he answers calmly.

"Is Chelsea with you? Please tell me Chelsea's with you," I ask frantically.

"No. She went to a party with Tammy earlier. What's wrong?" I hang up in his face and call Tammy's phone.

"Hello?," she answers. I can hear people talking, like she's at a party or something.

"Tammy. I need to speak to Chelsea real quick. Put her on the phone," I spilled out.

"Mr. Johnson, I'm looking for her right now. Last time anyone saw her, they said she was leaving the party with some dude."

"Some dude? What the hell did he look like? What kind of car was he driving?" I fire off questions, trying desperately to get the right answers.

"Mr. J, I'm trying to find all that out, right now."

"Where's the party at? I'm on the way." She texts me the address.

Even though I'm a preacher, I'm from the streets, so I know calling the cops is out of the question. Luckily, I have some money coming in from the play with Lucky. I decided to call him.

"Speak," he answers.

"Say, Lucky, something's come up, so I'ma need that bread from you as soon as possible."

"Ok. That's cool. Look, call me at around like noon tomorrow and we can meet up," he tells me.

Thank God. "A'ight. That's a bet then. See you tomorrow." I disconnected the call. Once I get that money, I can pay the ransom and I'll have enough to pay off Benny, I reason.

I pull up to the address Tammy has given me, and the place is packed. I text her to let her know where to meet me. Minutes later, she arrives. I debate on telling her about the phone call, but decide to go ahead and share info.

"Damn, that's messed up," she states. "Are you going to pay it off?"

"Of course, I am. I don't have a choice," I say. I think I detect a slight smirk, but I must be mistaken.

"Well, I'ma keep asking around here, and hopefully I can come up with some info we can use," she says, as she leaves to go rejoin the party.

I call my wife again, still no answer. This is very unlike her. I can't do anything but go home and wait on tomorrow to get here, so I can collect that money from Lucky.

When I get home, I see Charllessa's car is gone, and the whole house is empty. I take a shower and call my wife one more time. Same result. Fully exhausted and emotionally drained, I pass out on the living room couch. Just when everything seems to be going right, out of nowhere, disaster strikes.

***

Lucas Jr.

I've been sitting in the dark for the last few hours, drinking liquor and toying with my gun. My heart is shattered. I know I'll never be the same. My tears have long since dried up. Now, all that's left for me to spill is hate and bloodshed.

It's close to midnight and Amber still isn't home. I call her phone multiple times. She chooses to ignore me. I wonder what lie she's going to try and come up with.

I hear keys jingle, as she tries to unlock the door. I take a deep breath to try and settle my nerves and suppress my anger. She walks in exuberantly, but I can tell she's also walking gingerly, as if she's gotten injured somehow.

For the first few seconds, she doesn't notice me sitting in the dark, not until she flicks the light on.

"Oh shit," she yelps, clearly startled. "Damn, babe, why you sitting in the dark?" she has the nerve to ask.

Instead of dignifying her with a response, I ask, "Why you ain't answer your phone?"

"Huh? Oh, I went to my parents' house and messed around and misplaced my phone. I've been looking for it all day." She gives me the lamest excuse she can think of.

"Oh yeah? So you been at your parents' house all day, huh?" My anger is boiling just beneath the surface. My hands are trembling. The tears begin to form, and I'm afraid I can't hold them back any longer.

"Yeah, babe. What's wrong with you? Wait. Is that a gun, Lucas?"

Instead of answering, I push the clip in and cock it, putting one in the chamber. With menace dripping from each word, I stand up and respond. "Just tell me why, Amber. Huh? Why would you sleep with the enemy? Why would you allow them to slut you out, like you ain't shit?" Fresh tears begin to well.

Amber starts to back up, her hands up in surrender. Her voice shaking, she pleads. "Baby. Please calm down. I don't know what you're talking bout. Can you please just put the gun down?"

I point the gun at her chest and ask again. This time with a menacing growl. "Just. Tell. Me. Whyyyy."

She begins to cry, shaking violently. "Please, baby, don't kill me. I'm so sorry. I don't know why, I swear I don't." She backs all the way up to the kitchen counter and begins to slide down to the floor. She holds her hands up, palms facing me, begging for forgiveness.

I stand over her. My vision's blurry from constant tears. "Amber, I loved you so much. You were my world. I pray to God you forgive me."

She reaches for my feet, frantically begging me not to kill her, and at the same time, professing her love.

I feel nothing but hatred and disgust. I aim the gun at the back of her head. I whisper, "I love you," and squeeze twice.

Her body goes rigid as her cranium opens up. Pieces of her skull slide across the kitchen tile as her life's blood begins to pool beneath her still corpse.

I look at her body and something snaps inside of me. "Oh my God. What have I done?." I begin to sob uncontrollably. I sit down next to her lifeless body. I start to reminisce about all the good times we shared, from our high school days, when I used to convince her to skip class, so we could make out in the stairwell. "I love you so much, baby," I whisper to her. My one true love is no more. I put the barrel in my mouth, inhale, and then *bocka*.

Chapter 7
Saturday

Tammy Taylor
What's done is done. It's not like the bitch didn't have it coming. *Fuck her.* I make a right on Normandy, headed to the rendezvous spot. My burner phone vibrates. I see it's Mako calling.

"Hello? Yeah, I talked to him. He says he's going to pay it. Naw, he didn't say exactly when, but he knows he has until tonight. Naw, I don't think he'll call the laws. Her dad's from the streets. Yeah, I'm almost there. A'ight."

My blood is pumping with adrenaline. I need to see this bitch tied up, vulnerable and terrified. I damn near came on myself last night, seeing the look of embarrassment and shame on her face, when she realized her little orgy had gone viral. It took a lot of convincing from Wacco to get Lo-Life to agree with the plan, but at the end of the day, it was well worth it. Now, I'm bout to hit her where it really hurts, her dad's pockets.

Ever since her family came into that lil money, she's been acting like she's better than everybody else. She would fuck her friends' men without regards for their feelings. Yeah, she's getting everything she deserves.

I park in front of an abandoned house in Riviera East. I walk in and see Mako and a couple of his homeboys in the kitchen talking. "Where's she at?" I ask.

Mako excuses himself and leads me to a room at the back of the house. There, alone in the room, strapped to a chair, with a pillowcase over her head, is my former best friend. I'm careful not to say anything. I don't need her to be able to recognize my voice.

She must have heard our footsteps because she speaks. "Whoever you are, please, I need to pee really, really bad. Can I please use the restroom?" Mako looks at me, shrugs his shoulders, and makes a move as if he's about to assist her. I stop him, shake my head, and whisper in his ear. He looks at me for a few seconds to try and determine if I'm serious or not.

When he sees that I am. "Ain't no restroom breaks. If you wanna piss, piss in that chair." Chelsea is obviously struggling to hold in her liquid. Her right leg is bouncing up and down as she fidgets in her seat. "Pleeaasse. You can keep my hands tied. Don't make me piss on myself," she begs.

Mako looks at me again but I shake my head "no." I lean over and whisper in his ear again. This time he smiles, as he shakes his head in disbelief. I stand three feet away from Chelsea, watching her suffer, trying her best not to debase herself.

I pull my tights down to my knees as Mako gets behind me, jacking his dick off slowly. Once he's fully erect, he pushes me forward until I'm bent over at the waists, pussy dripping in anticipation. I feel the heat from his monstrous cock as he lets it sit on the crease between my cheeks.

I reach back and spread my ass apart. He grabs his dick, inserts the head into my opening. I know what's coming. I close my eyes and bite down on my fist as I prepare. Once he feels I'm ready, he lunges forward. I jerk and howl silently as Mako bores into my essence. His egg shaped balls tap against my clit as he stretches me out to my limits.

Honey dew drips down the backs of my legs, as our bodies make sweet music. Clap. Clap. Clap. Clap. My ass reverberates off his midsection. I feel my nut begin to build.

I open my eyes and see the bitch Chelsea sitting there. Tied up, helpless, scared, and pissing on herself. I explode like never before.

"Awwwww gaawwwdd dammmn fuuuccccckkk," I can't hold back my screams as the biggest nut I ever had in my life takes place in that room. My eyes become crossed. I see different colored spots dance before my eyes. My knees become weak and give out on me.

Mako continues to pipe me down on the floor. With my knees in the carpet and my face looking up at my former best friend, he fucks me hard, until he unloads his cum all into my belly. Even after he withdrew, dick falling out of my pussy, wet and creamy, I still shake from the spectacular orgasm.

Mako wipes his dick clean on my ass cheeks, before putting it up. I pull my tights up, pussy still overflowing with our cream, saturating the crotch. I motion for him to follow me out of the room. Once we get out of earshot of Chelsea, I tell what I've learned.

"I will keep a close eye on the situation. Like I said over the phone, her dad told me that he's going to pay the money, so wait around until five before you call him," I instruct.

"A'ight, Tammy. Make sure he pays the bread, and let me know if the cops get involved."

"That's a bet. I got you on both fronts," I assure him, as I make my way to the front door. I catch one of Mako's homeboys eyeing my camel toe, which I know is soaking wet. "Y'all haven't had any fun with her yet?"

Before they can answer, Mako interjects. "We don't get down like that. Only thing we take is money and lives."

I shrug. "Suit yourself. I know for a fact, her head game is ferocious."

I walk out the house and get back in my car. I must admit, today is starting out lovely.

Chelsea Johnson
My bladder feels like it's about to bust. I ask for a lil mercy. To be allowed to piss, but whoever's holding me hostage, tells me to piss on myself. My head is spinning, tryna figure out who would do this to me. Having a pillowcase over my head, renders me virtually blind. I struggle to hold my piss in, but I can feel tiny droplets begin to leak out.

I can smell a familiar fragrance, but I can't put my finger on it. I pray I make it out of this situation alive. I think about my family, my dad, my mom, and my annoying ass brother. I start to miss the little things they do that always seem to get on my nerves. I think about Bobby, and I regret the way that I've been treating him. I tell myself, when I make it out of this situation, I will treat him better.

I feel their presence a mere few feet away from me. Tears begin to well in my eyes, as I begin to lose the struggle to hold my urine. I smell the familiar scent of pussy, as I hear the unmistakable sounds of sex occurring. Clap. Squish. Clap. Squish. Skins are slapping and someone's pussy is extremely wet. My clit begins to tingle and throb.

Despite myself, my coochie gets hot with need. With a sigh, I release, and hot piss shoots forth and saturates the chair, as it cascades down to the floor. Relief and shame consume me, as I smell a strong whiff of Ammonia.

I struggle, trying not to throw up on myself as my visitors continue their sex session a few feet away from my soiled self. The female climaxes. I can tell that she is struggling, trying to contain her screams, but the nut is too good. She can't help herself. I hear sounds of her cunt swallowing his dick like a starved nun.

I want so bad to finger my clit but my hands are tied behind my back. I have no choice but to rub my thighs together, in hopes that it's enough friction to give me the relief I desperately need. Before I realized it, my visitors seemed to have stopped and left me alone. I want so bad to be fucked viciously. The way I'm feeling right now, I would welcome someone coming in and having their way with me, forcing me to take their dicks in whichever hole they felt needed occupying.

Not too long after, I hear the faint sound of the door being opened. My heart skips a beat. Slight panic takes a hold of me. Up to now, no one has told me my purpose for bondage. I try to invoke some sympathy.

"Excuse me. I don't know what's going on, but my dad has money, and I'm sure he'll give you some, if you let me go," I offer. No response.

I decided to try another approach. "Can you please get me something to drink? I'm thirsty as hell," I pleaded. I wait a few seconds.

"A'ight. I'll be right back," my new visitor says. I take notice that he's not the same one as before.

A short time later, he returns. "Damn," I hear him say. "I'ma have to cut a hole through the pillow case, so you can drink from this cup."

"Ok," I acknowledge, as he cuts through the fabric, allowing my mouth to fit through the makeshift hole.

"Here." He grabs under my chin and puts the cup to my lips.

I drink greedily, water pouring from the corners of my mouth. After my thirst is quenched, my visitor removes the cup.

"Look. Ole girl said you're a monster on the head. You don't have to if you don't want to, but um, I'm trying to see if it's true," he admits.

Ole girl? So the female knows me. My mind flips and turns, trying to figure out the pieces to the puzzle. Then, it hits me like a ton of bricks. The familiar scent. I can't believe it. My shame and despair turn into anger and rage. How could she? I have to figure out a way out of this situation, and fast. The way I was abducted. Where I was abducted. I almost forget about my visitor, until he speaks up.

"So, what's up? The big homie's gone right now, but a nigga ain't got that much time. If you gone bless me, then we need to get it poppin."

A thought hits me. If I can get this nigga on my side, then maybe I can get out of this mess. "Are you gonna let me use my hands?" I gamble.

"Naw, I can't do that, baby girl. Shit, the way your girl was talking, if you're bad like that, you don't need no hands," he counters. I can't argue with that point.

"What you waiting on?" I challenge.

Seconds later, I feel the tip of his dick head pressed against my pillowy lips. I open up wide to receive him. He has a nice, thick cock, that stretches my jaw to the max. My clit begins to thump. He grabs the back of my head with his right hand, and guides his tool with the left. His skin feels velvety soft, as his cock slides across the top of my tongue.

I suck hard, trapping his dick head at the back of my throat, while I allow enough air to seep through the sides of his shaft. This causes my mouth to get even wetter. Once my mouth is fully saturated, I start to bob my head back and forth.

He fucks my throat with hard, powerful strokes. His balls swing wildly, drumming against my chin, through the pillow case, as I gobble him up, like the bad bitch I am. Ghlop. Ghlop. Ghlop. My throat opens up and allows him access.

"Oh. Oh. Oh. Sssshit. I'm bout to cummm," he cries out, as he pulls my head forward.

With his dick head pressed against the back of my throat, I feel warm jets of sperm coating where my tonsils should have been. His cock twitches and jerks, as he unloads the contents of his heavy balls.

"Aww shit. Awww shit. Damn girl," he chants as his dick deflates.

I continue to suck gently, extracting the last remnants. I feel him trembling in my mouth before he finds the strength to step away. I refuse to let him go, and his flaccid dick stretches, before it pops out of my mouth.

"Whoa. Mannn, you the truth," he proclaims, as he struggles to catch his bearings. I lick around my mouth, hoping to catch the extra "crumbs" from my meal. "I ain't gone lie. A nigga need some more of that, before you leave," he lets slip.

"When am I going to leave?"

I can almost hear the gears shifting in his head, as he's deciding on something. "A'ight look. As soon as your pops pays the ransom, then we'll drop you off."

Now I know for a fact, Tammy has something to do with this. These dudes don't know me and they don't know that my dad has a lil money. As soon as my dad pays them off, I'ma be all in that bitch shit. I can't believe she would do me like this. Then it hits me. She knows about Scott.

If so, I don't see why she's even tripping. As many niggas as we've fucked and sucked, she shouldn't be tripping on one nigga that she doesn't even fuck with anymore. "Why don't you let me use your phone, so I can call my dad. I'm pretty sure when he hears my voice, he'll pay the ransom even quicker.

"I can't. The big homie said not to let you out of this room, on the phone, or even to use the restroom. If he knew we uh, you know, he would kill me."

I don't want to push too much, so I let it go, but not before stroking my ego. "So, you don't think that head was to die for?"

He chuckles and smiles sheepishly. "Hell yeah," he says, as he leaves the room.

I hear the door softly close behind him. So, now I know exactly why I'm here and what needs to be done to set me free. Now I just have to wait patiently for daddy to pay the ransom. My dad has done a lot of fucked up shit, but he would never leave his family on stuck. I just have to keep faith and wait.

Rev. Lucas Johnson

I dial my wife's number once again. Straight to voicemail. Fuck. I slam my hand against the kitchen counter. This shit can't be happening. My daughter has been kidnapped and neither my wife nor my son's answering the phone. I'm pacing, wearing a hole into the kitchen tile. I've never felt so helpless. I look at the time, 12:45 pm. I said I was going to wait until after 3 to hit up Lucky, but desperate times call for desperate measures.

I dial his number. "The number you've dialed is no longer in service." *I had to have dialed the wrong number.* I look at the screen. His name and number are plastered on the screen. My heart begins to race. I dial the number again. "The number you've dialed is no longer in service." I drop the phone. The screen instantly cracks. My body temperature skyrockets. My whole left side has gone numb, and I can't breathe.

"No. No. No. No. No," is the only thing I can utter, as the realization hits me. Lucky 400 has conned me. I flash back to our conversation, to see if I notice any clues of deception. I haven't cried in years, but as I sit on my kitchen floor broke, with my daughter being held for ransom, I cry like a newborn baby. I feel so helpless as a father, as a man, and as a husband. I really don't know what to do.

I pick up the cracked phone and dial the only other person I can count on. "Hello? Dennis. What's up man? I need your help." I go on to explain everything to Dennis. I cry my eyes out, as I tell him about Chelsea being kidnapped. He listens attentively.

Damn, Lucas. A hundred thousand dollars? Damn, dawg, that's damn near everything I have saved up," he admits.

"I know I'm asking a lot, but I wouldn't ask if I didn't actually need it. This is literally between life and death."

Dennis takes a deep breath and gets silent. "A'ight, dawg, I got you. I'll have to go to the bank right now, before it closes," he offers. I can't believe my luck.

"Man, bro, thank you so much. Man, I love you, dawg. I'ma get you back every penny," I say and I mean that shit.

I disconnect the call, feeling like the Lord is finally smiling down on me. Dennis and I have been through hell and back together. I can honestly say, he's always been there for me, even though I don't deserve it. I pick myself up off the floor and head to the shower. I have nothing else to do but wait on my best friend to come through for me, once again.

***

Charllessa Johnson

"Look out new boot." I turn my head and see a woman who can easily pass for my cousin, Rodger, standing next to the shower area. I spent the first night trying to learn everyone's names before I spoke to any of them. This one's name is Trilo, pronounced Trill-Oh.

Trilo is five feet six inches, a hundred forty pounds, light skin, with tattoos and a taper fade. She looks to be in her late twenties or early thirties. If I didn't know she was a woman, she would have had me fooled in a club, on a drunk night. I look at her for a second before I decide to get up and go see what she wants.

"What's up, new boot?" she greets me.

I meekly acknowledge her greeting with a "what's up" of my own.

"I can tell you've never been to jail before, but I'ma tell you how this works. You need to choose a man. If not, these bitches will try and take advantage of you, stealing your bags, while you're in the shower, eating your trays, while you're sleep."

She's right about one thing, I am new to jail, but she has me confused when she says "choose a man." Of course, I would love to do that, but where all the men at? Instead of risking sounding dumb, I simply say, "Ok. Who all do I have to choose from?"

This brought a smile to her face. "Well, the good thing is, I've already chose you."

I'm taken back. Now I understand what's going on. There are no men in here, just manly women. Besides letting that conniving bitch, Jessica, munch on my box, I've never had any other experiences with women. I honestly don't know what I should say or do.

Luckily, the D.O. calls my name. "Johnson 548. Attorney visit."

"Right here," I eagerly answer, as I walk through the sea of people in the day room. I approach the officer and can't help but to notice how cute he is. He has to be over six feet, with a solid build and hazel eyes. He is definitely my type. I know I'm not at my best hygienically, so I keep it short and simple. "Where do I need to go, officer?"

"Head out the double doors and make the left. When you get to the central picket, give them your name and tell them you have an attorney visit," he directs me.

I follow his directions and find myself at the window of the central picket. I give the officer my name and she hands me a slip and says, "Interrogation room five."

"For what?" I ask.

"Lady, I don't know. That's your business, not mine," she states matter factly. I enter the small room and see, what looks like, two plain clothes detectives, a man of Hispanic descent, and an African American woman.

The woman is the first to speak. "How are you doing, Mrs. Johnson? I'm Detective Lane and this is Special Agent Siez. Go ahead and have a seat."

"Uhh. What's this all about?" I ask, now thoroughly worried.

She begins, "Well, it's a complicated matter dealing with a ten year old murder case and an ongoing FBI investigation."

"I'm still not understanding."

Detective Lane pulls out a folder and lays it out on the desk. "Do you recognize this woman?" I take a look and almost faint. Staring me in the eyes, is none other than Jackie Taylor.

"Yeah, I know her. She used to be my neighbor."

"That's right. Ms. Jacqueline Taylor was shot and killed on March 29, 2013. At first, detectives thought it was a random act of violence, but later on, they discovered a key piece of evidence." She then flips the page and shows me a picture of a tube of cherry red lipstick. "Do you know what this is?"

"Uhh. Lipstick?" I counter.

"No. That's *your* lipstick. It was left about ten feet away from the scene. After DNA and forensics, we determined that the lipstick had to have been dropped as someone, namely you, was in a hurry to get away." I try not to show any nervousness or concern on my face, but I know that they know my secret.

"Look, Mrs. Johnson, I'm not going to sit here and bullshit you? We know you had something to do with Ms. Taylors' death, but we're willing to forget about it, plus drop these new charges, if you're willing to help out Mr. Siez here."

I guess that was Siez's turn to begin his spiel. "Mrs. Johnson, I'm Special Agent Siez, with the FBI. We have been investigating your husband for the last few years, dealing with money laundering, tax evasion, and fraud. Due to the fact the the church is under Federal jurisdiction, his crimes can get him twenty-five to life."

I can't believe what I'm hearing. The Federal government is looking to arrest Lucas for crimes dealing with cheating the church. "Uh. Mr. Siez, is it? I'm not sure I know what it is you want me to do."

"Well, according to Ms. Lane, you have some very serious state chargers. As a Federal Agent, I have authority to guarantee those charges be dropped, if you agree to testify against your husband."

I can't believe what I'm hearing. This can't be real. Never in all these years of marriage, have I ever thought about turning on Lucas. Yeah, he cheated, like it's a sport and he's trying to get MVP, but Lucas has always taken care of house and home. Our kids have everything they need and I've lived a comfortable life, as a preachers' wife. On the flip side, I don't think I can go to jail for a murder, not to mention, all the other charges they have stacked against me. If convicted, I could easily spend the rest of my life in jail.

I'm consumed with helplessness. I honestly don't know what to do. It seems like either way, my kids are going to be without one, if not both, of their parents. If I help the Feds, then Lucas is for sure gone. If I don't, it's still a great possibility he'll go down, and my sacrifice will have been in vain, because we'll both be gone.

"Mr. Siez, this is not a small task you're asking of me. Is it possible for me to get some time to think about it?"

"Well, of course. I understand. This is your husband we're talking about here. I'll be back soon. Just remember this Mrs. Johnson, if we're on to him, that means that he's most likely already done for. Don't leave your kids out here by themselves. Don't throw your life away with his."

We end the meeting, and I head back to the tank heavy hearted. I have to figure out who I can trust to go get that money out of my secret bank account.

I had set up a security measure, where all I have to do is call my bank, give them my security codes, along with the name, D.O.B. and Social of the person coming to pick up the money, and they will release it. I just didn't want Lucas to find out, and if I used either one of my kids, he would surely know.

***

Yolanda Cooper

I pack my bags with my necessities. Even though Ja'Quell insists that I don't need anything, and that he will make sure we go shopping for a whole new wardrobe, I still feel the need to pack.

I accidentally knocked over a wedding picture. I pick it up and stare at it. My heart hurts for the pain I'm about to cause a good man, a man who saw the good in me, enough so, to take a chance on a bonafide hoe. I inhale, put the picture down, and decide the least I can do is write him a letter. I sit and write down my thoughts and regrets, apologizing for betraying his trust, and letting him know that I will always love him. I leave the letter on the dresser.

As I walk through the house that I called home, I can't help but wonder if I'm making a mistake. So many fond memories. I lock up for the last time, place the key under the mat, and then drive away. I intend on leaving the car in a parking garage, and texting Dennis to let him know where to come get it. I don't ever want him to think that I viewed him as a trick. I truly do love him, but it's a part of me that he cannot conquer, a part of me that needs a special type of man to control it. Until that part of me is subdued, I will always be restless.

I call Ja'Quell. "Hey," I answered solemnly.

"Yum. Are you alright?" he asks, concerned.

I breathe heavily. "Yeah, I'm good. Where you at?"

"I'm at the Omni, suite 137. Just tell them your name downstairs, and they will give you a key card."

"Alright. I'm almost there," I say, as I exit the freeway. We talk for a few more minutes, then we hang up. My heart is heavy, but I need to suck it up. This is my decision, and I must live with it.

As I enter the hotel suite, I notice rose petals littered everywhere. Tyrese is going on about a "sweet lady," while the unmistakable scent of " I Am King" by Sean John, fills the air. Ja'Quell appears from the back with a glass, and a bottle of Ace of Spade champagne. I smile at the display of affection. It makes me feel better about my decision. Maybe Ja'Quell is finally the man to tame every side of me.

"Here beautiful. Take this." He hands me the empty glass, then fills it up.

"Thank you, baby," I tell him, while he kisses me softly on the lips. He grabs my hand and leads me into the bathroom, candles lit and incense burning.

Ja'Quell draws me a bubble bath and undresses me, while placing kisses all down my body. I want so badly to feel him inside of me. I know he can tell how wet he has me, but he doesn't capitalize.

"Get in the tub, baby," he insists. I lower myself in the bath and let the warm water soothe my muscles. I continue to sip on the champagne, drifting off, as Tyrese continues to serenade me.

Ja'Quell washes my body tenderly, making sure to pay close attention to my most sacred parts. Once I'm thoroughly clean, he escorts me out the tub and dries me off. I stand naked, completely vulnerable, while Ja'Quell kneels before me. I look down at him with pleading eyes, desperate for the release, only he can give. He senses my distress.

"Later, babe. I'll take care of that ass tonight. Right now, I just want to take you shopping and fill your stomach up. You'll need all your energy and strength, when I get a hold of your ass."

Exasperated, I allow him to lead me to the closet. He already has a few outfits he felt I might like. I slip on a creme colored, low cut, spaghetti strap dress, with some white and gold heels.

Ja'Quell and I spend most of our day shopping in the Galleria. We dine at "The Melting Pot". Once the sun begins to go down, he takes me back to the suite with close to twenty thousand dollars worth of clothes, shoes and handbags. If a bitch like me can't be satisfied with a man like him, I can never be satisfied.

He's a certified street nigga that looks even better in corporate clothing. I offer to give him some quick head, so I can ease the pressures and stress of the streets, but he insists we wait until later. I reluctantly submit. I kiss him goodbye and go get ready for his return.

While I'm in the bathroom, waxing my legs and my kitty cat, my phone vibrates. I see Dennis's face pop up on the screen. I know he's probably found the letter and isn't too happy about it. I can't bare to talk to him right now, but I know he'll continue to call until he gets through. I decide to just turn my phone off. When the time is right, I'll give him closure. Right now, all I want is to enjoy the night with Ja'Quell.

***

Deacon Dennis Cooper

I slam my hand on the dashboard. "Fuck. I know this bitch ain't just play me for all my shit," I yell. I'm in the bank parking lot and I'm pissed ass hell. Furious enough to kill the no good, slimy ass hoe. Everything's gone. My whole account has been drained. The manager showed me the transactions. This bitch withdrew a hundred thirty-two thousand five hundred fifteen dollars and thirty-two cent. All my hard work, down the drain.

Once again, I dial the bitch's number. Now it's going straight to voicemail. I damn near threw my phone out the window in frustration. I can't believe I trusted that dirty ass, slut bucket. I can't even call the cops if I wanted to, because my dumb ass put her on the account.

Technically, there's nothing I can do about it, but wring her motherfucking neck. I have to find her, and fast. I have an idea. I call the cops and tell them my wife's car's been stolen from our driveway. With an APB on her license plate, I know it won't be long before they catch up to her ass. I head home and wait for the cops to pull up, so I can fill out the police report. After they leave, I search the house for anything that might give me a clue as to where she might be. I find a note addressed to me on the dresser.

Dear Dennis,
I know this letter will confuse you. To be honest, you might can make the case that it's me who is confused, or maybe I used to be, but not anymore. You have been a wonderful husband, more than I deserve. I want you to know that me deciding to leave is purely selfish and I will understand if you're never able to forgive me. You gave me a chance, when everyone else looked at me as trash. You showed me that I am not worthless and I deserved to be loved. I didn't take anything from you. I'll let you know where to pick up the car. The keys will be taped under the bumper. I know it's hard to believe me now, but I truly do love you. God Bless You, Yolanda.

I ball up the letter and toss it on the floor. How the hell can she fix her lips to say she didn't take shit, when she literally took everything? I know she's smart enough to know that the bank was going to show me all the transactions. Well, the jokes on her, because now the laws were out looking for her car.

My phone vibrates. I look down and see Lucas's number pop up. *Damn.* I totally forgot about him needing the money for Chelsea. "Shit." I answer the phone and tell Lucas the bad news. He can't believe it. He's rambling on about needing to figure something out. I want to console my brother, but I'm going through hell myself.

We agree to meet up later to try and see if we can come up with something. I hang the phone up and begin to remove every item that reminds me of Yolanda's disloyal ass. Piece by piece, I break, shatter and destroy her memory. I pour myself a glass of cognac and take in the mess I've created, not only in this room, but my life. I head to my room, grab my .40 and make sure it's fully loaded. I'll be damn if I let this hoe steal everything from me. With my heart heavy, my liver full, and my pistol loaded, I go on the hunt for a scandalous hoe.

***

Derrick Cooper aka DC

"So look, we were the only ones in the spot besides old man Curtis and a couple of strippers. Once we tighten these niggas up, the strippers will get ghost, and we smoke Curtis before we leave," Blade informs me, as we head to the hole in the wall strip joint, called Gold Diggers.

I load up the Mini 14, wiping down each shell, as I load up the clip. "I thought Curtis was the one who put old man Smitty up on the info for the play," I say.

"Yeah, but Curtis had snitched on Perry J and them, on that Jewelry store lick that went sour five years ago. You know them old niggas don't forget shit," Blade explains, as he turns into the parking lot.

"OG, what you want us to do?" the lil homie, Gator, asks from the back seat.

"Gator, you gone come in with us. Lil T, we need you stay out here in the parking lot, so none of them niggas make it to their cars. You the last line of defense, so be on note," I tell them, as they load up their assault rifles.

"Bet. Overstood," They both say in unison.

The parking lot is scarce. Only a few cars are parked. We hide the dope fiend rental, a navy blue Explorer, next to the dumpster behind the shopping center.

We make our way to the club's back door entrance, so that the strippers never see us enter. After knocking eight times, old man Curtis opens up. The three of us head in, while T Stripes heads back to the front.

Curtis gives us the layout. Apparently, the meeting will take place in the VIP section of the club. Curtis wants us to hide out in the restroom and behind the bar. The plan sounds sketchy, so I ask. "You mean to tell me, they about to make a million dollar drug transaction, and they not about to check the restrooms to make sure everything is straight?"

"Naw, young blood. This ain't the first time they've done business here. Plus, his plug, G, has a baby with my lil cousin, Lauren. So it's all trust."

Man, this old nigga is basically bout to set up his own family. I wonder what Smitty promised him to do this, but decide not to ask. After all, what he didn't know is, he won't get to enjoy none of it.

Curtis's phone rings. He holds up one finger, while he answers, to let us know to keep quiet. I take the time to scan the room for all exits and or entries.

"That's G. He says they're on the way. I'm about to call Ja'Quell and see what his ETA is."

My heart starts to pick up pace. My adrenaline starts pumping. I don't care how many times you go in on one of these, each one is like the first, 'cause each one could be your last. I tell Blade and Gator they can camp out in the bathroom, I'ma take the spot behind the bar. We all get in position.

My phone rings. I see it's my pops. I try to ignore it, but he keeps on blowing my shit up.

"Yo?" I answer.

"Son. Son, where you at?" he asks, clearly drunk.

"Pops, I'm busy right now. I got to call you back," I say, trying to rush him off the phone.

"If you see that hoe, Yolanda, let me know. I'ma kill that bitch," he slurs into the phone.

"Say what? What you got going on. You drunk?"
"Son. The bitch took everything from us. Everything."
Now he has my attention.
"What you mean she took everything?"
Pops went on to tell me the whole scoop, how he went to the bank, and found out the account had been wiped out. He told me about the note she left him. I'll be the first to admit, I didn't trust her, but even after we fucked around, I felt like maybe she and my pops belonged together. I honestly didn't see this coming. Now this lick meant that much more. I assure my pops that everything will be alright, and I disconnect the call.

"They're here," Curtis announces, as we scramble to get in position. Curtis heads to the front of the club to allow them in. That way the strippers could identify the bodies, as the ones that came in the club, once the smoke settled. That was the whole point. When the laws start asking questions, we want the strippers to say that they only saw the victims enter the club, no one else.

I crouch behind the bar, with the Mini 14 cocked and ready. I steady my breathing, waiting on the catch phrase from Curtis, letting me know he was leaving the room, so we could conduct business.

Once he leaves the room, he'll text Blade to let him know it's showtime. I hear a door open up. I tighten the grip on the stick. I can hear a man with a heavy Spanish accent along with another man, who has to be Ja'Quell. I hear Curtis ask Ja'Quell and G if they want something to drink. They both decline.

"What about you two gentlemen? Would y'all like something to drink?" They both decline also, but now I know the magic number is four. After some more small talk, Curtis excuses himself, so they can get on with the transaction.

I'm about to pop up and handle bidness, when I hear a phone begin to ring. I have to make sure it isn't mines. After my pops had called, I turned mine off. Still, a nigga had to make sure. Ja'Quell excuses himself, so he can take the call. He maneuvers right next to the bar, to hold his conversation.

"What's up, babe? I'm in my meeting right now. Oh yeah? Man, that's fucked up. I know you gone make it up. I'll grab some on the way back. A'ight, bye."

I wait ten seconds for Ja'Quell to rejoin the group. I let them start talking, then I pop out from behind the bar. The Mini 14 has a green infrared beam on it, which I immediately tag on to one of the other two men. Pap. Pap. Two quick shots leave contestant #1 with his chest blown out.

Before he can hit the ground, I swing the strap around, double tap and give contestant #2 a new haircut. His skull opens up and caves in on itself. He drops like a sack of potatoes.

Now that the element of surprise is over, both Ja'Quell and G have their bangers out, but Blade and Gator appear out of the restroom with their red beams aiming at each of their tops.

Realizing their chances are slim to none for surviving a shootout, Ja'Quell lowers his gun and tries a more diplomatic approach.

"Look, homie, I don't know you, fam, but if it's money you looking for, go ahead and run with it. I ain't seen shit, I don't know shit," he reasons.

I walk from behind the counter. "I can respect that, Blood. But we want the dope, too. If y'all just open up the lock boxes, then we gone be out this bitch, and y'all can keep y'all's lives."

Ja'Quell takes a second to assess the situation. He looks into my eyes and sees nothing. He knows he's dead regardless. He's been on the other side of the gun, many a time. Sometimes, Karma will wait years to come pay you a visit. Ja'Quell tightens the grip on his pistol. I tighten my grip on the stick. I know he's bout that action.

"Just give us the shit, nigga. Don't try and be no hero," I warn him.

Suddenly, Ja'Quell ups his strap, and all three of us light into him. Every bit of thirty rounds plus, chew through his skin and bones. Pieces of flesh litter the carpet, as the high powered rounds decimate his body.

Before he gets the chance to, I turn the Mini 14 onto G and put him out of his misery. Now that he's seen us kill Ja'Quell, he knows he's a dead man, and that's the last thing we need. A nigga with a gun, who has no hope of living.

Once the smoke settles, we collect the lock boxes, as well as the suitcases. I send Blade and Gator to the car, while I wait on Curtis. It doesn't take him long to poke his head into the room.

After seeing Ja'Quell and his buddies dead, he struts in, as if he just put the work in himself. He looks around for the lock boxes. "Where's the dope and money at?"

"It's in the car."

"What you mean it's in the car? Smitty said I would get a quarter mill and ten birds for setting the play up," he argues.

I begin to chuckle. "How the hell you gone get all that, if you're a rat? Where I'm from, snitches don't get shit, but a hole in their head," I state matter factly.

Curtis throws his hands up in surrender. "Look, DC, I don't know what they told you, but I ain't on nobody's paperwork. Man, just ask."

Pap. Pap. Pap. Pap. Shells rip through his head and neck before he can finish his lie. His head snaps back, as his cranium slides across the tabletop.

I stand over him and hit him two more times. Pap. Pap. After I do the same to Ja'Quell and G, I escape out the backdoor. The guys are waiting for me, with the engine running. I jump in and we mash onto the freeway.

The whole ride home, I have an eerie feeling. Something is wrong. I go over every detail of the play in my mind, and it appears flawless. I can't figure out the source of my worries, but I can't shake it off.

We pile up in Blades spot in Coke Apartments, so we can buss down the dope and money. We end up giving the lil homes fifty thousand dollars and five birds apiece. After putting Smitty's to the side, Blade and I walk away with thirty-five keys and nine hundred thousand dollars to split. I decide to take less work, and more money. I end up with sixteen birds and five hundred thousand dollars.

Instead of doing like most do, I don't take the stash to my house. I buy a vacuum sealer to seal the money and dope up. Then, I go bury it in a secret location. I figure, I'll wait about four to six months, before I pull it out, just in case a nigga receives some type of blow back from the lick.

I go home to my pop's house and see his brand new truck there. It's a good thing he has A-1 credit, and was able to grab him a brand new blood red, Yukon Denali. I guess he got tired of looking for Yolanda, so he came home. I walk by the truck and see him sleep in the driver's seat. I go in, grab some clothes, and head to the hotel room I've reserved. I call the dopefiend to come pick up their car. Then I call Ms. Battle to come scoop me up. She'll be my Alibi for the night. I spend the rest of the night taking out my frustration and worries on her.

Yolanda Cooper
Oh my God. Please Lord, let this be a mistake. I stare at the phone in disbelief. I just overheard something terrible happen. I called Ja'Quell to ask if he could pick me up some tampons because my period has started. I guess he thought the phone had hung up, but I could still hear him clearly. What I heard broke my heart.

My stepson, DC, was apparently at the same business meeting, and it sounded as if he wasn't invited. I heard DC tell him to give him the money and the dope. Then I heard gunshots, lots of them. I waited patiently for Ja'Quell to get back on the phone, once the gunshots ceased. After twenty minutes, with no word, I knew he was dead. Still, I stayed on the phone until Ja'Quell's battery died.

How could DC do this? Is this retaliation for leaving his father? How did he even know Ja'Quell?

All these questions flooded my mind at once. I feel like I'ma, "Ughhhhh." I throw up all over the floor. I reach for my purse, the pain is killing me. I reach into the side pocket and pull out a small pill bottle. I pour the contents in my hand. Four yellow pills fall out. I look at them intensely. I've never popped more than two at a time. Then again, I've never felt pain like this. I reach for the champagne and toss all four pills into my mouth. With a swig, I gulp all four of them down. I sit back and wait for them to take effect. I think about Ja'Quell and my tears erupt.

I pick up my phone and go through my voicemails. I hear that I have voice messages from Dennis. I play one of them. The first thing I hear is his slurred speech. He rarely drinks, so I know he must be hurting, also.

"Yolanda. How? How could you do this toooo mee. After erything I done fo you. You clean me out, left me wit nuttin. How can you fix yo lips to say you love me at same time steal from me?" he cries.

Steal? What the hell is he talking bout? I haven't stolen shit from him. Damn. My heart feels funny. I feel as if something heavy is sitting on my chest. I reach for my phone to call him, but I don't have the strength to pick it up. Something's wrong. I'm feeling cold all of a sudden. I want so bad to let Dennis know, I haven't taken anything from him. His son is the one who stole everything from me. My eyelids are so heavy, I can't keep them open. I'll just get some sleep real quick. When I wake up, I'll call him.

***

Chelsea Johnson

My legs are numb from sitting in this chair for all these hours. I haven't been fed anything. I've pissed on myself, but thank God, I haven't needed to take a shit. I've been hoping my lil friend gets an opportunity to come back and kick it with me. Whoever's in charge, seems like they don't ever want to leave.

I don't know how long it's been, but it feels as if twenty-four hours have gone by since I've arrived here. They're probably trying to figure out another spot to meet up and exchange the money. What if they've already been paid, but just didn't want to let me go? What if they start demanding more money? I promise you, Tammy will pay for this.

The door opens up. "Excuse me. Can someone please tell me what's going on? I know my dad's already paid y'all. Y'all said y'all will let me go, once y'all got the money." No response.

This must be the one in charge, he barely talks. I feel his presence creeping on me slowly. His voice is low and menacing. "Actually, your dad never paid the money."

"Huh? Say what? No. No. No. That's got to be a mistake. Can I please talk to him? He'll do it for me. Please." I don't know what's going on. It has to be a mistake. My dad would never leave me on stuck like this.

I hear a gun cock. My body begins to tremble. My teeth are chattering like crazy. I beg for my life. "Please, man, I don't want to die? I promise I can get the money. Just let's talk to my dad. Oh my God. Oh my God. Daddy, whhhyyyy?" Bocka.

Rev. Lucas Johnson

I'm sitting outside of the HPD station. What I'm about to do goes against everything I've been taught. What else can I do? My daughter's been kidnapped. I haven't heard from my wife, or son, for that matter. I had until earlier tonight to pay the ransom, but of course, I didn't have the money. Then, on top of that, I would have had it, if I wouldn't have given Yolanda's info to Lucky, so he could run the scam. Karma's definitely a bitch.

Lucky wiped out her and Dennis' whole bank account. The money Dennis would have used to help me, is all gone, and it's my fault. Yeah, I know it's fucked up, but Yolanda and I have been fucking for months now.

The first time it happened, we were at a church function. Dennis had left to take Sister Carla's daughter, Candice, home. Apparently, her car wouldn't start, so he volunteered. Yolanda had come up there with Dennis, and instead of waiting for him, she wanted to go home. I could tell she was under the influence of something more than liquor. I put some Luther on low, and we cruised, talking about her stripping days and how she turned her life around.

"You ever miss the club?" I asked.

She thought about it before she answered. "Sometimes I do. I really do."

Of course, the next question I asked was, "What do you miss?"

Her answer was almost instantaneous. "The hustle and bustle. I appreciate Dennis taking care of me, but I'm a natural born hustler, and I like going out there and getting mines."

"I can dig that," I answered.

I watched her wind and grind in her seat, as Luther serenaded her. Yolanda's silky smooth thighs and legs were on full display. I know I shouldn't have had those thoughts, but I started to fantasize about those thighs wrapped around my waste, as I dropped this heavy ass dick up in her snatch.

As she sung with Luther, I imagined her succulent lips wrapped around my cock, as I fuck her face, nice and slow. When we pulled up to the house, I had it on my mind, I was going to get up in that pussy before I left.

She invited me in. I watched her fixing our drinks and my dick began to rise. Her ass cheeks were peeking from up under her skirt, and I could see them jiggle with each step she took.

"When was the last time you gave a lap dance?" I asked, slyly.

Her face lit up? "Mannnn. It's been some years."

I reached in my pocket and pulled out a hundred dollars.

"How bout a few lap dances?"

She smiled and walked towards me. She bit her bottom lip and snatched the money up. Then she sashayed over to the entertainment system, put some Trina on, and walked back over to where I was sitting.

I sat there and took it all in. She began with a slow wind, then turned around and flipped her denim skirt up. Now, her ass cheeks were out and fully exposed, separated only by a yellow and black bumble bee thong. Her cheeks began to clap as I unzipped my slacks, to give my cock more room to breath. She sat down and felt my dick poking at her. She reached back, laid my cock flat and nestled it between her cheeks. She rocked back and forth, twerking in my lap.

I sat amazed at how beautiful and sexy her body was. I used my finger to curl and pull her thong to the side. Her chunky sex lips popped out. Her pretty, tight, round brown asshole winked my way.

Yolanda leaned forward and put her hands on the floor. My dick popped out of place, but instead of laying back flat, I grabbed the base and slid it into her cunt as she sat back on it. She froze, then looked back at me, but didn't get up.

I grabbed her hips and began to work mine slowly, stirring my stick in her honey pot. She moaned, and I knew I had her.

That night, I fucked her right there on my best friends couch. Each time I nutted, she hopped off the dick and swallowed the load entirely. I even called Dennis to see where he was at, while his wife had my balls between her lips, cleaning them with her tongue.

Yolanda and I had agreed that it could never happen again, but two weeks later, I was balls deep in her asshole, while she screamed and played with her clit. We'd been fucking ever since.

I hate the fact that I did that to her and Dennis. I honestly didn't know Lucky was going to use that information to drain their account. The fucked up part is, Dennis thinks Yolanda jacked him. Even though she likes to get her rocks off, she would never steal from him. He's gotta know that.

I hope that blocked number that has my baby girl will call once again. When I told them I didn't have the money, they just hung up in my face. That's the only reason I'm down here at the police station. I ran out of options.

I walk in the police station to report my daughter has been kidnapped. I instantly become sick. Growing up, I was taught to loathe and detest the cops. Who would have thought that I would turn to them for help?

I approach the desk. A middle aged white woman, with brownish red hair and green eyes, is typing away at the computer. I notice her wedding ring, and it does something to me. I suppress the urge.

"Excuse me." She acts like she doesn't hear me. I clear my throat and try again. "Ahem. Excuse me."

Finally, she lifts her head up, as if she's being annoyed. "How may I help you?"

"I want to report a kidnapping." Hearing the words kidnapping, brings a change in her demeanor. She gives me her undivided attention.

"Who is the person and how did you come to the conclusion they were kidnapped?"

"It's my daughter, Chelsea Johnson, and I received a call for a ransom yesterday." Even though I know this is what I'm supposed to do, telling them still feels like snitching.

"Ok. And you are?"

"Lucas Johnson, Sr." At the mention of my name, she cocks her head to the side, as if trying to figure out where she heard that name before. I notice a young Hispanic officer, nearby eavesdropping. I pay him no mind. After I give her all the information, they have me meet with a detective. I tell him everything I know, and he tells me to go home and wait. They will send a team to my house to help with the negotiations and recovery. I walk out of the precinct, feeling less of a man. I resorted to asking the dirty ass cops for help to take care of my family.

As I'm about to hop in my truck, I hear someone calling my name. "Mr. Johnson. Mr. Johnson." I turn around and come face to face, with the same young Hispanic officer that was eavesdropping. He sticks his hand out. "Mr. Johnson, I'm Detective Martinez." I reluctantly take his hand and shake it. "I overheard you saying that your daughter was kidnapped? Is that correct?"

"Yeah that's right, but I done told your coworkers everything I know." I turn to get in the truck, not trying to hold any type of conversation with him, but he doesn't take the hint.

"Damn, man, I know that's gotta be super hard for you? First, your wife gets arrested, then your daughter gets kidnapped."

"Wait. Wait. What?" I know this pig in a blanket ain't say what I think he said. "What you mean, my wife got arrested? My wife doesn't even have traffic tickets."

He looks at me, as if he feels sorry for me being such a fool. "Your wife's Charllessa Johnson correct?"

"Yeah. That's her name."

"Yeah, I know her. I'm the one that took her in Friday. I'm surprised you don't know. You mean to tell me, she hasn't called you," he has the nerve to point out. Just when I thought things couldn't get any worse.

"What's she locked up for?" I ask. Now that he's realized I'm actually clueless about what my wife has done, he attempts to backpedal.

"Look, Mr. Johnson, I'm sorry to have been the one to tell you that, but due to the fact that it's an ongoing investigation, I can't divulge any more information at this time." *Ain't that a bitch.*

"Mannn. You know what, nigga? Fuck you," I say, as I hop in the truck. I turn on some Keith Sweat, and head to 1200 Baker Street. When I get there, they inform me that it's too late to visit, so I make plans to pull back up, first thing after church. A part of me is relieved that she hasn't left me, but then another part of me can only imagine what she has done to get herself locked up. One thing I do know, I need answers, and she's going to have to give them to me.

Now, I'm driving around aimlessly. Frustrated and feeling helpless. My world is collapsing, and I'm powerless to do anything but watch it occur. I make a silent prayer to God, to please spare my daughter. With nowhere else to go, I head home.

Chapter 8
Sunday

Tammy Taylor

I check the time. It's almost 1:00am. Reverend Johnson should have already paid the ransom by now. I'm waiting on Mako to let me know where to meet up to get my cut of the hundred thousand. I hope this nigga don't try and fuck over me. If he does, I'ma make sure I get Paccy and his homeboys to pull up.

My phone rings. It's a number I don't recognize, but I answer. "Hello?"

I hear Mako's baritone voice come through my bluetooth. "Where you at?" he asks.

"I'm at the house right now. Why? What's good?"

"Meet me at Greenwood Park," he says coolly.

I pick up a strange tone, so I ask. "Is everything good?"

"Yeah, everything went according to plan," he says evenly. "Meet me at Greenwood, behind the pool house, so I can give you your cut."

I perk up at the mention of my cut. "I'm on the way."

It only takes me ten minutes to arrive. When I turn into the parking lot, I notice it's completely empty. I park my car, and make my way to the pool house, to wait on Mako. I text him and let him know I'm here.

Two minutes later, he arrives. Dressed in all black, with a pair of black leather gloves, he doesn't look happy to see me.

Chills crawl up my spine. I stare in his eyes and see only sadistic anger.

"Wh-what's going on?" I ask nervously.

"The nigga never paid, Tammy."

"What? What you mean? He said, he just needed time to the get the money together." My body begins to tremble. "Look, Mako, please just give me a chance to call him. I'm pretty sure this is all a terrible mistake."

Mako cocks his head to the side and stares at me for a few seconds. He reaches into his pocket. I flinch, then realize it's just a cell phone. He tosses it to me. As I catch it, I notice he's clutching a small black pistol in his right hand.

My hands are trembling so much, I can barely hold the phone in my hand. My teeth are chattering. It feels as if I'm freezing, but I know it's a warm and muggy night. I call the only number in the call register.

Reverend Johnson picks up. "Hello? Hello? Look, man, I need more time."

"Mr. Johnson," I interrupt.

"Say what? Tammy? Is that you?"

I know he's shocked to hear my voice on the same line the kidnappers use. "Yes, it's me, Mr. Johnson. Please. You have to pay the money. If you don't, they'll kill Chelsea." I look up at Mako. He has the gun to his side, but I can tell he's itching to use it. "And they'll kill me, too," I cry in panic.

"Tammy, please. Just tell them to wait. I don't have the money right now. Tell them to give me bout a week," he begs.

My heart drops. Mr Johnson doesn't have the money? I watch as Mako ups his pistol. I throw my hands up and start to back up. "I told you, if he didn't pay, your ass would," he growls.

I instantly turn and run. My heart's leaping out of my chest, my feet feel like I'm running through quicksand. I travel maybe ten feet before I hear a loud bang, and suddenly

I'm on the ground crawling. My legs refuse to work. My body feels as if it's on fire. The pain I feel is so intense, I can't do anything but pant.

Liquid floods my throat. I taste the unmistakable flavor of copper. My stomach spasms, and I feel like I'm about to throw up. Mako stands over me, then kicks me in the ass.

"Turn your stank ass over," he commands. I struggle to lay on my back. I try to plead for my life, but blood bubbles in my throat. I cough, and it pours out of my mouth. I look up at Mako standing over me, pistol pointed at my head. I think I see my mom, and I smile. A flash goes off and…

Rev. Lucus Johnson

"Tammy. Tammy. Tammy, you a'ight?" Did I just hear what I think I heard? Damn.

Deacon Dennis Cooper

Ring. Ring. Ring. Ring. My phone continuously rings nonstop. I reach over to the nightstand and grab it. "Hello?" I say groggily.

"Is this Dennis Cooper?" some woman asks.

"Yeah, this him. What's going on?"

"Mr. Cooper, this is Nurse Jones from East Houston Medical Center. We have Mrs. Yolanda Cooper in ICU right now."

I shoot out of bed, as she goes on to explain that Yolanda has had an overdose. Apparently, she has taken a bad batch of pressed pills, and a hotel maid found her unconscious, and hanging on for dear life. I jot down the address and struggle to get dressed, not even taking time to brush my teeth.

DC is on the couch sleeping as I pass him by. I wake him up to let him know that Yolanda has overdosed, and I will be at the hospital with her. He grunts his acknowledgement, as I rush out the door.

I arrive at the hospital in record time. The nurse has me wait in the waiting room for four hours, until they release Yolanda from the ICU.

I go up to her room. My heart breaks and my eyes flood, as I watch my wife, laid up in the hospital bed, with IVs and machines hooked up to her. They tell me she's sedated, and will probably be out of it for a few hours. I don't care. I'll sit here and wait until she awakes. I don't care about the money, the note, or the fact she was leaving. Her near death experience made me realize what's really important. I place her soft hand in mine, and I pray for mercy and forgiveness.

I haven't been the husband God intended me to be. I put my head down. I promise to do better. Her hand begins to twitch. My head lifts up, and I see my beautiful wife staring at me, with tears in her eyes. "Dennis?" she croaks.

"Ssshhh. Don't talk, baby. Let me get you some water."

She nods, as I get up to go fetch her some Dasani. She looks so fragile and vulnerable. My heart breaks at the thought of possibly losing her.

She takes a few sips before she gulps the rest down, smacking her lips.

"You want another one?" I ask.

She nods her head, and I grab another bottle. She drinks only half. I sit patiently, watching her. I honestly don't know how this conversation should begin. I wish I could forget all about it, but I know that's impossible now. I also know that, no matter what, we have to eventually discuss it. She reaches for my hand, and I give it to her.

"Dennis, I'm so sorry, baby," she begins. "I don't know what I was thinking. You have been a great man and husband to me, and I honestly don't deserve your forgiveness, but..."

"Don't worry about it, babe," I cut her off, but she insists that she needs to continue.

"Look, baby. I need your love, especially now, more than ever, but before I can ask for it, I have to be completely honest with you about everything."

My heart begins to palpitate. As men, we always ask our women to be completely honest with us, but the truth is, many of us can't handle the truth. "What is it, baby?"

She takes a deep breath, squeezes my hand, and begins to confess. "As you now know, I've been back taking pills. I've been taking them for a while now, ever since I had that accident, and um. I haven't been faithful either."

I close my eyes. I suspected it, but to hear her verbalize it, hurt like hell.

I rub the back of her hand. "It's cool, baby. We've both made mistakes," I tell her, hoping she doesn't have more to say.

"No. It's not. You've been way too good to me, for me to be fucking your best friend."

My head jerks back, as if she just literally slapped me. I let go of her hand, not believing what I just heard.

"Say what? No. No. No. I know you ain't just say that shit, Yolanda. Lucas?"

"I'm sooo sorry, Dennis. It just happened."

"When?"

She looks like she's debating telling me the rest of the truth. As if, maybe she's realized her mistake in telling me.

"We've been fucking for some months now."

"Some months?" I yell. I stand up and begin to pace around the room, talking to myself. I can't believe what the fuck I'm hearing. My best friend and my wife? How could they? Then I realize, I'm no better. While Lucas was having sex with my wife, I was having my way with his daughter. One sin isn't greater than the other. I look into my wife's eyes and I see her sincerity. I see her need to be forgiven. I sit back down, grab her hand and kiss it softly.

"It's all good, baby. All that doesn't matter anymore. From this day forth, it's a new day. A new slate. I love you, and I don't want to live without you," she squeezes my hand and a tear rolls down her cheek. I lean forward and kiss her tear away. Then, I kiss her on her chapped lips, sucking on them gently, while lubricating them in the process.

She moans into my mouth.

I whisper, "I love you, Yolanda."

She emits a soft whine. "I love you, too, Dennis. I love you so, so much."

I sit there and hold her hand until she falls asleep. I know she feels better about cleansing her soul. I wonder to myself, should I do the same? *Probably not.* As I watch her sleep peacefully, I make that promise to myself again. No matter what, I'm going to do better.

***

Derrick Cooper aka DC

Pops just left, talking bout he's going to the hospital to go see Yolanda. I try to go back to sleep, but I can't. I turn on the TV, and decide to check out the news. Mainly, to see if the move we made last night made the six o'clock news.

Sure enough, a reporter is standing in front of the club. I turn up the volume.

"We're standing in front of the strip club, Gold Diggers, on South Main, where five people have been found shot to death, by what looks like a gangland execution. The witnesses report, they saw the victims enter the establishment and go straight into the VIP section with the owner, who apparently is a victim as well. They state, after they heard multiple gunshots, they exited the establishment and reported that they never saw any other suspects leaving the building. If anyone has information, they are urged to call 222-TIPS.

That's what I like to hear. The next story on the news left me speechless.

"Today, police were called to a residence on the Southwest side of Houston, due to a wellness check. Upon arrival, police discovered what appears to be a murder/suicide. Both victims were found with one fatal gunshot wound to the head. Police say they are still investigating the matter, but are confident, the male shot the female, then shot himself."

The picture on the screen is the apartment Amber and Junior shared. I wonder if he found out, we were slutting his bitch out, and he couldn't handle it. Damn. That's some crazy shit. I shake my head in disbelief. That was some good ass pussy that he wasted.

I decided to go ahead and get up, take my morning piss, wash my hands, and head to the kitchen to fix me something to eat. I open the fridge, grab a carton of eggs. Boom. The front door collapses.

"US Marshalls. Get on the ground now. Get on the ground."

In nothing but gym shorts, I get on the ground, as what seems like thirty officers storm my dad's crib. At first, I think that maybe it has something to do with Yolanda, but then I realize, there wouldn't be this many officers for an overdose.

One of the officers approaches me, while slapping on cuffs. "Derrick Cooper. You're under arrest for the murders of Floyd Haynes, Ja'Quell Peters, Germano Gomez, Curtis Smith and Patrick Glass. You have the right to remain silent. Anything…"

I hear nothing but white noise as the realization kicks in. I'm in Texas, so the death penalty will surely be on the table. My mind is racing. I don't understand what could have gone wrong.

We just ran the play, less than twelve hours ago. How did they get on my trail so fast? Once I get to homicide, I discover the truth.

Apparently, Curtis has a hidden camera in the VIP. When he left the room, he must have activated the cameras. Who would have guessed the nigga would want to record a major drug deal. Then again, he was a snitch, so I guess that makes perfect sense.

There I was, on camera, smoking, not one, but five individuals. It didn't matter that we all hit up G's ass. They still hit me for his body, also. I hit the lick of a lifetime and I don't even get to enjoy it. I'm booked in Harris County Jail, 7th floor, double door locked down. Officially charged with five counts of capital murder. The homicide detectives claim they were on the way to get Blade and the lil homie, Gator. Lil T was never on camera, so unless one of those two tell on him, he'll walk away scot free. I'm cool with that. As soon as I get a phone call, I'll call pops and let him know what's going on. When he comes up here to see me, I'll tell him where the dope and money is, because I'm about to definitely need it.

***

Rev. Lucas Johnson

I stand in front of my congregation, heart filled with sorrow, doubtful I can deliver the sermon I need to uplift my flock.

"How are y'all doing this morning?" I ask.

They all respond, "God is good."

"I know many of you might not be aware of what's going on, so let me be the first to let you know. Early this morning, I received a phone call from a homicide detective." Tears begin to flow down my cheeks. Now, everyone has given me their undivided attention. I continue. "My daughter was murdered sometime last night, and my son committed suicide late Friday evening."

I hear many gasp from the congregation, as well as "Lord, have mercy."

"I had contemplated not getting up here today. I'm pretty sure a lot of you would have understood. Then, I realized. This is the time the Lord needs me the most. This is the time I need Him the most. I haven't been an entirely just man, nor have I been the husband and father the Lord intended me to be. I know none of us is perfect, but we should always strive to be like the Lord. My message this morning is about cherishing the blessings the Lord bestows onto us, whether those blessings are a good family, a great job, or even good health."

My tears blanket my whole face, as I struggle to continue. "It took for me to lose my blessings to realize that. I pray that none of you make that same mistake. Cherish your family. Cherish what you have because, no matter how safe and comfortable you may believe you are, those blessings can be taken away, in the blink of an eye."

I delivered my first "real" sermon since I became pastor at Last Hope Missionary Baptist Church. I've realized, all these years, I've taken my blessing as pastor and squandered it. It took me to lose everything, to realize I had everything.

Church lets out and, for the first time, I don't take any money from the coffers. I close up and head to my truck. I put on my wife's favorite album, "Confessions" by Usher. I can't wait to head up to the jail, so I can make sense of what's going on. I turn down Normandy, headed to I-10. I stop at the red light, lost in my thoughts. I scroll through my phone to see if I have any missed calls from the jail. I still can't believe she hasn't called me yet.

I see movement in my peripheral. A black truck pulls up on my driver side and parks diagonally, right in front of my Escalade. Before I realize what's going on, I see the passenger door open up. Next thing I know, two AR-15s are pointed in my direction. I instinctively duck, as shots ring out. I feel them coming through the truck's frame. My body jerks. I notice my shoulder and arm are no longer attached. Before the pain sets in, another shell rips through my stomach. My body spasms. I curl up on the floor board, my insides soaking up the mat, as I bleed out. As I lay there, I think about my family. I smile. I'm on the way to meet my junior and my baby girl.

Chapter 9
Three Sundays Later

Reverend Dennis Cooper
I look out at my congregation. Today is my first sermon as the new pastor of Last Hope. I look at a picture of Lucas on the wall, and my hatred begins to boil. Yolanda ended up having a full recovery. We had a long talk. She confessed to her affairs, including the one with my supposed best friend. We came to the conclusion, Lucas was responsible for the draining of our account. Rumor has it, Benny finally cashed in on Lucas' debt.

The loss of Chelsea, Junior, Amber and Tammy is tragic for sure. They were all so young, and had a full life ahead of them. Our congregation has suffered a tremendous loss, and need to heal.

Come to find out, Charllessa is locked up for an assortment of charges. Yolanda has been to see her, but she hasn't specified exactly what those chargers are. She did say, Charllessa is facing a lot of time. I'ma pray for her.

My son, DC, has been charged with five counts of capital murder, and the state indicates, they'll be pushing for the death penalty. He gave me the location of his money and drugs, along with a list of names, that would liquidate said drugs for him.

I purchased DC two of the best lawyers in the state, put ten thousand dollars on his books, and with the rest, I opened up a few more businesses. Right now, things are picking up.

Yolanda and I have reconciled, but have decided to open up our marriage a little bit. She assures me that if I allow her the occasional fling, she won't ever attempt to leave me again. In return, I get to do my little tricking on the side. As I look towards my congregation and prepare myself for my first ever sermon, I make a vow to myself. Never be the topic of Sunday gossip.

***

First Lady Yolanda Cooper

I'm watching Dennis up there on the podium and I don't know what to feel. A part of me loves him dearly, and I'm thankful that he forgave and welcomed me back with open arms. Then, there's a part of me that resents him. A part of me wishes Ja'Quell was alive, instead of him. Then, to add insult to injury, he's spending all the money DC took from Ja'Quell on DC's legal defense.

Two days ago, he dragged me up to the jail to go visit DC. I wanted to spit at him through the glass, but I couldn't let Dennis know how I truly felt. I wonder, how he would feel if he found out his precious son had his dick stuffed down his wife's throat, or how he fucked me with his big ole dick in our marriage bed.

If I was a fuck bitch, I would have told him. I know Dennis would have forgiven me anyway. I held my composure, as DC made small talk with me. We looked into each others eyes, and I knew that he knew that Ja'Quell and I had been seeing each other. How he knew, I have no idea, but he knew.

Now, I'm watching my husband, the newly crowned pastor of our church, preaching, and I'm sick to my stomach. Sometimes, I feel like I wish I would have just died in the hospital. My emotions are all over the place.

SEX, MURDER AND GOD | LO-LIFE

I look at my watch, 12:15pm. Church will be over at 1:00. I can't wait. I catch the eye of Brother Bryson. A five foot eleven inch, two hundred pound specimen of a man. I bumped into him on social media four days ago. I noticed his post about attending our church, so I got at him in his DM. After twenty minutes of chatting, I met up with him at JB's. Thirty minutes after that, I had his beef link stuffed down my throat, until he power washed my face with his cum. I kept on sucking him up, until he was stiff again, and then rode him long and hard, until I rained down on his cock.

We had made plans to meet up again after church, but I can't wait. I give him a signal, as I get up and head outside. I sent him a quick text to let him know to meet me in the parking lot.

Moments later, he's coming out of church, headed over to my husbands' truck. I let him in the passenger seat.

"We have to hurry. We only have a lil over half an hour before church lets out," I say, as I reach for his buckle. I yank out his eight inch dick and immediately gulped it down. Lawrd. This boy's dick taste so scrumptious. My pussy lubricates. I reach under my skirt and push my panties to the side, so I can play with my hardened nub.

Bryson grabs ahold of my weave, gripping it tightly in his fist. His cock hardens in my mouth. I roll his balls around in my hand. I suck him in deep, pre-cum dancing over my taste buds. I think about my husband, preaching on that podium, while I got a fat cock deep in my throat, and my pussy creams.

"Ohh shit. Ohh Shit. I'm bout to nut," Bryson chants, as his balls twitch and jump in my hand.

I bob my head even faster, eager, fiending for that delicious nut he has stored away. Then he blesses me with the first spurt of it.

"Awww shit," he yells, as I swallow his load with ease, hungry for the next.

Another shot fills my mouth. I let it swim around and pool on my tongue, using it to lubricate the head of his cock as I jack him off, squeezing whatever I can to the top.

Once I feel assured nothing is left, I swallow the entire load. My whole body's tingling from the electric current of eating a man's dick in the church parking lot, while my husband is inside preaching.

With his cock still in my mouth, I check the time on my watch. Maybe I have enough time to get one more nut out of him, 12:55. Damn. I let it fall from my mouth, "We can pick this back up later tonight," I say, rushing him out of the truck.

Moments later, church is over, and all the patrons are rushing out, eager to get back to their sinful ways. I watch from the shadows at different men, who I wouldn't mind fucking. Women, that I would make unsuspectingly eat out my twat filled with their husbands cum. I reach down and tap my clit, as I fantasize about different sex acts I will commit. It doesn't take long for me to cum all over my fingers.

Once the parking lot is cleared, I see my husband coming out, strutting, and looking regal with each step he takes. He opens the truck and hops in. He immediately gives me a great big kiss. I know my mouth is still filled with residue from Byron's nut sac. Just knowing he has another man's essence on his tongue, makes me have a small, tiny orgasm.

"I want to go see DC today," he states.

When he says "I," what he really means is "we." Of course, I don't want to set off any alarms, so I just simply say "sure." As we ride, I feel my phone vibrate. I text the number and confirm some things. I have to be very careful from this point on. Every detail has to go off smoothly. Yeah, I love Dennis, but if he thinks he and his son will get away with taking away my chance at true happiness, they have another thing coming.

***

Charllessa Johnson

I lean back in my bunk, with this cheap ass blanket covering my lower life. My coochie is on fire. My clit's about to explode. Trilo has her long, thick tongue slithering within my creases. I feel her fat fingers penetrate my box and tap at my g-spot. I bite my bottom lip, trying my best not to scream out her name.

"Fuck. Dammnnn, baby. Eat that coochie," I whisper.

Other inmates walk by, acting as if they don't know what's going on. I catch one eyeing me from her bunk. I lock eyes with her, while Trilo's head is underneath the covers. I feel the tip of her tongue swipe against my clit and my muscles jerk.

My juices trickle down the crack of my ass. As if reading my thoughts, Trilo spreads my cheeks apart, using her tongue to mop up every drop that spillled. I spread my legs wide, grinding my ass into the cheap plastic mat. I feel it coming and I want it more than anything else in the world.

I clench my fists, and press them hard into the bunk, as my orgasm shatters all over her lips. I stick my fist in my mouth and bite down as I cum everywhere. The whole time, I never take my eyes off the chick in the bunk. I lay back, panting, trying to catch my breath.

Trilo brings her head from up under the covers. Her mouth is greasy and her head is covered in sweat, hair sticking to her forehead. She crawls up my body and kisses me on the lips. I taste myself and I must admit, I taste delicious."

"Good morning, baby," she tells me. That has been our ritual. Every morning, Trilo tries her best to wake me up with some early morning head. It didn't take me long to get with the program. Four days after I had gotten there, I had chose her to be "my man." We celebrated by her eating my coochie and my booty for two hours straight, after rack time.

I finally found the strength to get up and head to the showers. While allowing the water to caress my curvaceous frame, I think about my predicament. I close my eyes as sadness takes over me. My whole family's gone. I still can't believe I've lost everyone in a forty-eight hour period. My baby boy committed suicide. My daughter was kidnapped and murdered. According to Yolanda, Dennis said the kidnappers wanted a hundred thousand dollar ransom.

My heart aches, knowing I had the money stored away, but due to my reluctance to trust anybody, my daughter died thinking nobody cared enough to come get her. I can't hold my tears back.

My mind goes to Lucas and how they say he was gunned down in the middle of the street, like a common gang banger. He wasn't perfect, but I know he loved his family. Now that he's dead, it looks like I'll be facing these multiple charges, head on.

I finish showering, dry off, and prepare to put on my cosmetics.

"Johnson 548. You have a visit," the officer announces over the intercom. Since I've been in jail, the only person that has come to visit me, has been Yolanda.

She confided that she had almost died a couple weeks back and she wanted to come ask me for forgiveness. Naturally, I asked, "For what?"

Imagine my surprise, when she told me that she had been fucking my husband for months before he was killed. When I chuckled, she seemed surprised

"What's so funny?" she asked.

"So, Lucas finally found someone to fuck that looks better than me."

"Girl, please. You're forty plus and look better than most bitches my age," she complimented.

"I hear you. I'm just surprised you would even fuck with him. I mean, Dennis is a really good man."

I see my statement must have hit a sore spot, because she puts her head down in shame. Seeing as she's my only visitor, I don't want to run her off.

"Look Yolanda, we all make mistakes. The thing is, we have to learn from them. Lucas and I didn't have a perfect marriage. Shit. No one does. But I understood who he was and I came to respect and accept it. You and Dennis have a chance to start over. Cherish that. Have some kids, live life."

Yolanda smiled for the first time since she had arrived.

When she prepared to leave I asked, "When will you be coming back?"

She explained, her and Dennis had came to visit DC. "Yeah, girl. What's going on with that? I saw it all over the news."

Her face fell into a frown. I attributed it to the fact that DC was her stepson, and like family. "I'll be back Charley," *she promised, as I watched her walk away. Her ass vibrating with each step in her heels..*

Now that they're calling me to visit, I wonder if it's her. I get dressed and head down to the visitation windows. When I round the corner of the last row of windows, I can't contain my smile.

There, sitting with a pair of vanilla tights on, a pink Donna Karen top, no bra, so her nipples were protruding, was none other than Yolanda Cooper. The first lady of our church.

Her lips were glossed with a light pink color. I licked my own, wondering if hers tasted like bubble gum. I don't know what had gotten into me, but I began to wonder if she knew her way around a nice wet coochie.

"Heyyy, girl," she greets me cheerfully.

"What's up? How was church?"

She shrugs her shoulders. "Dennis got up there and did his thing. He's at 701 visiting DC right now."

"Oh ok. Well, tell him I said hi."

"I got you, but look. What if I told you, I have a way you can beat all your charges?"

My ears instantly perk up. I look her square in her eyes. "I would say I'm down, and I don't give a damn what I have to do, I'ma do it."

That seems to be what she wants to hear. Yolanda leans in close, as if someone could overhear us. She spends the next twenty minutes lacing me up on her master plan for my release, and for her revenge.

To be continued...

Lock Down Publications and Ca$h Presents Assisted Publishing Packages

BASIC PACKAGE $499 Editing Cover Design Formatting	UPGRADED PACKAGE $800 Typing Editing Cover Design Formatting
ADVANCE PACKAGE $1,200 Typing Editing Cover Design Formatting Copyright registration Proofreading Upload book to Amazon	LDP SUPREME PACKAGE $1,500 Typing Editing Cover Design Formatting Copyright registration Proofreading Set up Amazon account Upload book to Amazon Advertise on LDP, Amazon and Facebook Page

***Other services available upon request. Additional charges may apply

Lock Down Publications
P.O. Box 944
Stockbridge, GA 30281-9998
Phone: 470 303-9761

Submission Guideline

Submit the first three chapters of your completed manuscript to ldpsubmissions@gmail.com. In the subject line add **Your Book's Title**. The manuscript must be in a Word Doc file and sent as an attachment. Document should be in Times New Roman, double spaced, and in size 12 font. Also, provide your synopsis and full contact information. If sending multiple submissions, they must each be in a separate email.

Have a story but no way to send it electronically? You can still submit to LDP/Ca$h Presents. Send in the first three chapters, written or typed, of your completed manuscript to:

LDP: Submissions Dept
P.O. Box 944
Stockbridge, GA 30281-9998

DO NOT send original manuscript. Must be a duplicate.
Provide your synopsis and a cover letter containing your full contact information.

Thanks for considering LDP and Ca$h Presents.

NEW RELEASES

BLOODLINE OF A SAVAGE 1&2
THESE VICIOUS STREETS 1&2
RELENTLESS GOON
RELENTLESS GOON 2
BY PRINCE A. TAUHID

THE BUTTERFLY MAFIA 1-3
BY FUMIYA PAYNE

A THUG'S STREET PRINCESS 1&2
BY MEESHA

CITY OF SMOKE 2
BY MOLOTTI

STEPPERS 1,2&3
THE REAL BADDIES OF CHI-RAQ
BY KING RIO

THE LANE 1&2
BY KEN-KEN SPENCE

THUG OF SPADES 1&2
LOVE IN THE TRENCHES 2
CORNER BOYS
BY COREY ROBINSON

TIL DEATH 3
BY ARYANNA

THE BIRTH OF A GANGSTER 4
BY DELMONT PLAYER

PRODUCT OF THE STREETS 1&2
BY DEMOND "MONEY" ANDERSON

SEX, MURDER AND GOD | LO-LIFE

NO TIME FOR ERROR
BY KEESE

MONEY HUNGRY DEMONS
BY TRANAY ADAMS

Coming Soon from Lock Down Publications/Ca$h Presents

IF YOU CROSS ME ONCE 6
ANGEL V
By Anthony Fields

IMMA DIE BOUT MINE 5
By Aryanna

A THUGS STREET PRINCESS 3
By Meesha

PRODUCT OF THE STREETS 3
By Demond Money Anderson

CORNER BOYS 2
By Corey Robinson

THE MURDER QUEENS 6&7
By Michael Gallon

CITY OF SMOKE 3
By Molotti

CONFESSIONS OF A DOPE BOY
By Nicholas Lock

THA TAKEOVER
By Keith Chandler

BETRAYAL OF A G 2
By Ray Vinci

CRIME BOSS
By Playa Ray

Available Now

RESTRAINING ORDER 1 & 2
By **CA$H & Coffee**

LOVE KNOWS NO BOUNDARIES 1-3
By **Coffee**

RAISED AS A GOON I, II, III & IV
BRED BY THE SLUMS I, II, III
BLAST FOR ME I & II
ROTTEN TO THE CORE I II III
A BRONX TALE I, II, III
DUFFLE BAG CARTEL I II III IV V VI
HEARTLESS GOON I II III IV V
A SAVAGE DOPEBOY I II
DRUG LORDS I II III
CUTTHROAT MAFIA I II
KING OF THE TRENCHES
By **Ghost**

LAY IT DOWN I & II
LAST OF A DYING BREED I II
BLOOD STAINS OF A SHOTTA I & II III
By **Jamaica**

LOYAL TO THE GAME I II III
LIFE OF SIN I, II III
By **TJ & Jelissa**

IF LOVING HIM IS WRONG…I & II
LOVE ME EVEN WHEN IT HURTS I II III
By **Jelissa**

PUSH IT TO THE LIMIT
By **Bre' Hayes**

SEX, MURDER AND GOD | LO-LIFE

BLOODY COMMAS I & II
SKI MASK CARTEL I, II & III
KING OF NEW YORK I II, III IV V
RISE TO POWER I II III
COKE KINGS I II III IV V
BORN HEARTLESS I II III IV
KING OF THE TRAP I II
By **T.J. Edwards**

WHEN THE STREETS CLAP BACK I & II III
THE HEART OF A SAVAGE I II III IV
MONEY MAFIA I II
LOYAL TO THE SOIL I II III
By **Jibril Williams**

A DISTINGUISHED THUG STOLE MY HEART I II & III
LOVE SHOULDN'T HURT I II III IV
RENEGADE BOYS 1-4
PAID IN KARMA 1-3
SAVAGE STORMS 1-3
AN UNFORESEEN LOVE 1-3
BABY, I'M WINTERTIME COLD 1-3
A THUG'S STREET PRINCESS 1&2
By **Meesha**

A GANGSTER'S CODE 1-3
A GANGSTER'S SYN 1-3
THE SAVAGE LIFE 1-3
CHAINED TO THE STREETS 1-3
BLOOD ON THE MONEY 1-3
A GANGSTA'S PAIN 1-3
BEAUTIFUL LIES AND UGLY TRUTHS
CHURCH IN THESE STREETS
By **J-Blunt**

CUM FOR ME 1-8
An LDP Erotica Collaboration

SEX, MURDER AND GOD | LO-LIFE

BLOOD OF A BOSS 1-5
SHADOWS OF THE GAME
TRAP BASTARD
By **Askari**

THE STREETS BLEED MURDER 1-3
THE HEART OF A GANGSTA 1-3
By **Jerry Jackson**

WHEN A GOOD GIRL GOES BAD
By **Adrienne**

THE COST OF LOYALTY 1-3
By **Kweli**

BRIDE OF A HUSTLA 1-3
THE FETTI GIRLS 1-3
CORRUPTED BY A GANGSTA 1-4
BLINDED BY HIS LOVE
THE PRICE YOU PAY FOR LOVE 1-3
DOPE GIRL MAGIC 1-3
By **Destiny Skai**

A KINGPIN'S AMBITION
A KINGPIN'S AMBITION II
I MURDER FOR THE DOUGH
By **Ambitious**

TRUE SAVAGE 1-7
DOPE BOY MAGIC 1-3
MIDNIGHT CARTEL 1-3
CITY OF KINGZ 1&2
NIGHTMARE ON SILENT AVE
THE PLUG OF LIL MEXICO 1&2
CLASSIC CITY
By **Chris Green**

SEX, MURDER AND GOD | LO-LIFE

A GANGSTER'S REVENGE 1-4
THE BOSS MAN'S DAUGHTERS 1-5
A SAVAGE LOVE 1&2
BAE BELONGS TO ME 1&2
A HUSTLER'S DECEIT 1-3
WHAT BAD BITCHES DO 1-3
SOUL OF A MONSTER 1-3
KILL ZONE
A DOPE BOY'S QUEEN 1-3
TIL DEATH 1-3
IMMA DIE BOUT MINE 1-4
By **Aryanna**

A DOPEBOY'S PRAYER
By **Eddie "Wolf" Lee**

THE KING CARTEL 1-3
By **Frank Gresham**

THESE NIGGAS AIN'T LOYAL 1-3
By **Nikki Tee**

GANGSTA SHYT 1-3
By **CATO**

THE ULTIMATE BETRAYAL
By **Phoenix**

BOSS'N UP 1-3
By **Royal Nicole**

I LOVE YOU TO DEATH
By **Destiny J**

I RIDE FOR MY HITTA
I STILL RIDE FOR MY HITTA
By **Misty Holt**

SEX, MURDER AND GOD | LO-LIFE

LOVE & CHASIN' PAPER
By **Qay Crockett**

TO DIE IN VAIN
SINS OF A HUSTLA
By **ASAD**

BROOKLYN HUSTLAZ
By **Boogsy Morina**

BROOKLYN ON LOCK 1 & 2
By **Sonovia**

GANGSTA CITY
By **Teddy Duke**

A DRUG KING AND HIS DIAMOND 1-3
A DOPEMAN'S RICHES
HER MAN, MINE'S TOO 1&2
CASH MONEY HO'S
THE WIFEY I USED TO BE 1&2
PRETTY GIRLS DO NASTY THINGS
By **Nicole Goosby**

LIPSTICK KILLAH 1-3
CRIME OF PASSION 1-3
FRIEND OR FOE 1-3
By **Mimi**

TRAPHOUSE KING 1-3
KINGPIN KILLAZ 1-3
STREET KINGS 1&2
PAID IN BLOOD 1&2
CARTEL KILLAZ 1-3
DOPE GODS 1&2
By **Hood Rich**

THE STREETS ARE CALLING
By **Duquie Wilson**

SEX, MURDER AND GOD | LO-LIFE

STEADY MOBBN' 1-3
THE STREETS STAINED MY SOUL 1-3
By **Marcellus Allen**

WHO SHOT YA 1-3
SON OF A DOPE FIEND 1-4
HEAVEN GOT A GHETTO 1&2
SKI MASK MONEY 1&2
By **Renta**

GORILLAZ IN THE BAY 1-4
TEARS OF A GANGSTA 1/&2
3X KRAZY 1&2
STRAIGHT BEAST MODE 1&2
By **DE'KARI**

TRIGGADALE 1-3
MURDA WAS THE CASE 1-3
By **Elijah R. Freeman**

SLAUGHTER GANG 1-3
RUTHLESS HEART 1-3
By **Willie Slaughter**

GOD BLESS THE TRAPPERS 1-3
THESE SCANDALOUS STREETS 1-3
FEAR MY GANGSTA 1-5
THESE STREETS DON'T LOVE NOBODY 1-2
BURY ME A G 1-5
A GANGSTA'S EMPIRE 1-4
THE DOPEMAN'S BODYGAURD 1&2
THE REALEST KILLAZ 1-3
THE LAST OF THE OGS 1-3
By **Tranay Adams**

MARRIED TO A BOSS 1-3
By **Destiny Skai & Chris Green**

SEX, MURDER AND GOD | LO-LIFE

KINGZ OF THE GAME 1-7
CRIME BOSS 1-3
By **Playa Ray**

FUK SHYT
By **Blakk Diamond**

DON'T F#CK WITH MY HEART 1&2
By **Linnea**

ADDICTED TO THE DRAMA 1-3
IN THE ARM OF HIS BOSS
By **Jamila**

LOYALTY AIN'T PROMISED 1&2
By **Keith Williams**

YAYO 1-4
A SHOOTER'S AMBITION 1&2
BRED IN THE GAME
By **S. Allen**

TRAP GOD 1-3
RICH $AVAGE 1-3
MONEY IN THE GRAVE 1-3
CARTEL MONEY
By **Martell Troublesome Bolden**

FOREVER GANGSTA 1&2
GLOCKS ON SATIN SHEETS 1&2
By **Adrian Dulan**

TOE TAGZ 1-4
LEVELS TO THIS SHYT 1&2
IT'S JUST ME AND YOU
By **Ah'Million**

SEX, MURDER AND GOD | LO-LIFE

KINGPIN DREAMS 1-3
RAN OFF ON DA PLUG
By **Paper Boi Rari**

THE STREETS MADE ME 1-3
By **Larry D. Wright**

CONFESSIONS OF A GANGSTA 1-4
CONFESSIONS OF A JACKBOY 1-3
CONFESSIONS OF A HITMAN
By **Nicholas Lock**

I'M NOTHING WITHOUT HIS LOVE
SINS OF A THUG
TO THE THUG I LOVED BEFORE
A GANGSTA SAVED XMAS
IN A HUSTLER I TRUST
By **Monet Dragun**

QUIET MONEY 1-3
THUG LIFE 1-3
EXTENDED CLIP 1&2
A GANGSTA'S PARADISE
By **Trai'Quan**

CAUGHT UP IN THE LIFE 1-3
THE STREETS NEVER LET GO 1-3
By **Robert Baptiste**

NEW TO THE GAME 1-3
MONEY, MURDER & MEMORIES 1-3
By **Malik D. Rice**

CREAM 2-3
THE STREETS WILL TALK
By **Yolanda Moore**

THE STREETS WILL NEVER CLOSE 1-3
By **K'ajji**

SEX, MURDER AND GOD | LO-LIFE

LIFE OF A SAVAGE 1-4
A GANGSTA'S QUR'AN 1-4
MURDA SEASON 1-3
GANGLAND CARTEL 1-3
CHI'RAQ GANGSTAS 1-4
KILLERS ON ELM STREET 1-3
JACK BOYZ N DA BRONX 1-3
A DOPEBOY'S DREAM 1-3
JACK BOYS VS DOPE BOYS 1-3
COKE GIRLZ
COKE BOYS
SOSA GANG 1&2
BRONX SAVAGES
BODYMORE KINGPINS
BLOOD OF A GOON
By **Romell Tukes**

CONCRETE KILLA 1-3
VICIOUS LOYALTY 1-3
By **Kingpen**

THE ULTIMATE SACRIFICE 1-6
KHADIFI
IF YOU CROSS ME ONCE 1-3
ANGEL 1-4
IN THE BLINK OF AN EYE
By **Anthony Fields**

THE LIFE OF A HOOD STAR
By **Ca$h & Rashia Wilson**

NIGHTMARES OF A HUSTLA 1-3
BLOOD AND GAMES 1&2
By **King Dream**

GHOST MOB
By **Stilloan Robinson**

SEX, MURDER AND GOD | LO-LIFE

HARD AND RUTHLESS 1&2
MOB TOWN 251
THE BILLIONAIRE BENTLEYS 1-3
REAL G'S MOVE IN SILENCE
By **Von Diesel**

MOB TIES 1-7
SOUL OF A HUSTLER, HEART OF A KILLER 1-3
GORILLAZ IN THE TRENCHES
By **SayNoMore**

BODYMORE MURDERLAND 1-3
THE BIRTH OF A GANGSTER 1-4
By **Delmont Player**

FOR THE LOVE OF A BOSS 1&2
By **C. D. Blue**

KILLA KOUNTY 1-5
By **Khufu**

MOBBED UP 1-4
THE BRICK MAN 1-5
THE COCAINE PRINCESS 1-10
STEPPERS 1-3
SUPER GREMLIN 1-4
By **King Rio**

MONEY GAME 1&2
By **Smoove Dolla**

A GANGSTA'S KARMA 1-4
By **FLAME**

KING OF THE TRENCHES 1-3
By **GHOST & TRANAY ADAMS**

SEX, MURDER AND GOD | LO-LIFE

QUEEN OF THE ZOO 1&2
By **Black Migo**

GRIMEY WAYS 1-3
BETRAYAL OF A G
By **Ray Vinci**

XMAS WITH AN ATL SHOOTER
By **Ca$h & Destiny Skai**

KING KILLA 1&2
By **Vincent "Vitto" Holloway**

BETRAYAL OF A THUG 1&2
By **Fre$h**

THE MURDER QUEENS 1-5
By **Michael Gallon**

FOR THE LOVE OF BLOOD 1-4
By **Jamel Mitchell**

HOOD CONSIGLIERE 1&2
NO TIME FOR ERROR
By **Keese**

PROTÉGÉ OF A LEGEND 1&2
LOVE IN THE TRENCHES 1&2
By **Corey Robinson**

THE PLUG'S RUTHLESS DAUGHTER
By **Tony Daniels**

BORN IN THE GRAVE 1-3
CRIME PAYS
By **Self Made Tay**

MOAN IN MY MOUTH
By **XTASY**

SEX, MURDER AND GOD | LO-LIFE

TORN BETWEEN A GANGSTER AND A GENTLEMAN
By **J-BLUNT & Miss Kim**

LOYALTY IS EVERYTHING 1-3
CITY OF SMOKE 1&2
By **Molotti**

HERE TODAY GONE TOMORROW 1&2
By **Fly Rock**

WOMEN LIE MEN LIE 1-4
FIFTY SHADES OF SNOW 1-3
STACK BEFORE YOU SPLURGE
GIRLS FALL LIKE DOMINOES
NAÏVE TO THE STREETS
By **ROY MILLIGAN**

PILLOW PRINCESS
By **S. Hawkins**

THE BUTTERFLY MAFIA 1-3
SALUTE MY SAVAGERY 1&2
By **Fumiya Payne**

THE LANE 1&2
By Ken-Ken Spence

THE PUSSY TRAP 1-5
By **Nene Capri**

DIRTY DNA
By **Blaque**

SANCTIFIED AND HORNY
by **XTASY**

BOOKS BY LDP'S CEO, CA$H

TRUST IN NO MAN
TRUST IN NO MAN 2
TRUST IN NO MAN 3
BONDED BY BLOOD
SHORTY GOT A THUG
THUGS CRY
THUGS CRY 2
THUGS CRY 3
TRUST NO BITCH
TRUST NO BITCH 2
TRUST NO BITCH 3
TIL MY CASKET DROPS
RESTRAINING ORDER
RESTRAINING ORDER 2
IN LOVE WITH A CONVICT
LIFE OF A HOOD STAR
XMAS WITH AN ATL SHOOTER

Made in the USA
Monee, IL
08 April 2025